Past My Time

THE WITCH'S CULT

Willow Hewett

Past My Time – The Witch's Cult/ Willow Hewett. -- 1st ed.
ISBN 978-1-66640-934-5

Dedication

I dedicate this book to my sons, Miles, and Charlie. I also dedicate this book to my editor, Sarah. Without her, I would probably be stranded on an island somewhere, still crying at my laptop....

This is for my mum. Thank you, mum, for all the times we made up weird stories together when I was younger. It's finally paid off.

And, to Adam, this is for you. Forever and always.

CONTENTS

Prologue

When Destiny Unfolds

My name is Mary Carver and I never imagined that my world would be surrounded by a crew of burly males whom I called family. Yet there I was, standing on the deck of 'The Drifter', savouring the ocean breeze while observing the waves crash against the sturdy ship. 'The Drifter' was my home, sailing through the blue blanket of ocean with my two loves, John and Miles. The two men were polar opposites. Where John was harsh and stern, yet with a softness to him, Miles was soft and nurturing. Both had helped me find my parents in my greatest time of need. They were different, but if put together to form one man, they'd be perfect.

The horrible events that had come to pass had left me without a family of my own. My parents had been cruelly murdered by the witch Elizabeth before I took her life by turning her own magic against her.

A life for a life John had said, and it was true.

It was fated that I would discover Miles's father's invention and be transported back in time to face the witch, just as my parents had done many years earlier but failed to stop her. It was me who had torn her apart in front of her loyal followers, including my grandfather, Captain Carver. Trying to convince Captain Carver that I was his granddaughter who had travelled back in time to save him and end the evil magic that ensnared him and his crew, strained every fibre of my being. The witch had had him under her control and had been using him as a puppet to carry out her horrific intentions. But I'd stopped that, and after much convincing, Carver had eventually given in to my reasoning.

The twists and turns of fate had brought me to where I was now, and I had the scars to show it. After the battles, fighting against Elizabeth's dark magic, and many heartaches of losing my fellow men, it had only made me stronger. As I stood on the deck of 'The Drifter', relieved to have survived the battle against Elizabeth, I had no way of knowing just how wrong I was in the belief that it was all over now. Fate had more twists in store for me, and there was nothing I could do to stop it.

CHAPTER ONE

Miles's Return

The horizon stretched out in front of me, with the setting sun slowly disappearing behind the ocean. A vast expanse of turquoise-blue water spread out from the ship, lapping up its sides and gently swaying it. The gentle embrace of the sea breeze caressed my skin, keeping me warm. It swung the sails gently, causing them to flap loudly. It all moved in unison, creating a soothing rhythm.

Even though the scenery was lovely, I couldn't take my gaze away from Miles. He was standing there in front of me, alive and well, with a huge grin on his face. The last rays of sunlight caught the light gold streaks in his hair. His shirt was still stained with blood from the fight, and a rip ran up the side of his leather pants. I didn't mind that he was scruffy. He was standing in front of me, even though I had seen him die a few hours before. I was taken aback and couldn't believe he was there. I thought I had lost him to Elizabeth forever. Since the day I met Miles, my life has been turned upside down. He helped me find my parents, though we had no idea that Elizabeth had murdered them long before I ever found Miles.

Images of the previous battle flashed through my mind, with Miles' death at the forefront, replaying over and over. I still smelled like gunpowder and had blood on my clothes. We all did. We all looked terrible and were in great need of a wash. We'd been through hell trying to stop a deranged witch from destroying the world. We had prevailed, and I felt relieved yet still terrified.

My emotions were all over the place, and John, whom I also loved and admired, stood beside Miles, smiling, only with a different look in his eyes. Sadness. John was the older and wiser man, but he was so ignorant and demanding. Miles was the youngest and bravest captain I had ever met, but he always acted so childishly whenever another man approached me. I adored them both, and now that Miles has returned from the dead, I'm back in the position of having to choose which man to love.

There was one thing that Elizabeth was right about, and that was that I couldn't choose either of them for fear of upsetting the other one. I wanted them both. I shook my head from my thoughts, realising I was just standing there staring at them both, not saying anything.

My gaze returned to Miles, who was sheepishly smiling at me, the dimple on his cheek making my heart swoon gently, as it had before. I approached him slowly, wide-eyed, and poked him in the chest to make sure he wasn't just another cruel joke from Elizabeth. He took my hand in his and drew me into an embrace, smothering me with his chest.

Miles squeezed me close to him, and John took a step back, looking uneasy. When he noticed me looking at him, he instantly changed his expression from hurt and sadness to a smile.

"You're alive?" My voice stammered as I moved away from his embrace, not wanting to upset John.

"Well, obviously, Mary. I'm not imaginary," he chuckled.

"It worked, Mary. It took longer than we thought. But it worked. He is alive and well and is still our captain, all because of you," John spoke up, smiling at me while holding out the locket for me to take.

"So, what say you? Are you ready to embark on another adventure with us?" Miles beamed.

"Miles, I wouldn't call defeating Elizabeth an adventure. We were all on the verge of death, and you were the one who died. Don't forget that," I warned.

"Unfortunately, this adventure isn't over yet. We're still looking for Elizabeth's followers. They have the ability to bring her back to life, which we do not want," John stated.

"Do you know where her cult is?" I asked.

"Some yes, others no. This will be a mission, but if we don't hunt them down, then we better get ready for Elizabeth to come back and wreak more havoc," John explained.

"We need a plan," I said.

"We are already on course back to Stone Hill Bay. That's where we will start," Miles clapped his hands together. "But first, we shall get some food when we arrive and drop Carver and his crew off safely."

"How long until we dock?" I asked.

"It won't be long. However, we must remain vigilant. So, what do you think? Do you want to go on another adventure?" Miles asked again, still grinning.

"There's nothing else for me to go back to. You're now my family. We've been through so much together that I don't think I'll ever be able to return to my old life." I confessed.

John gave me a friendly smile. "Mary, I'm glad you're staying. It wouldn't be the same without you."

"But, John, you once told me that having a woman on board a ship is bad luck," I grinned, teasing him.

He averted his gaze, his face full of guilt. "I used to be a very arrogant man, Mary, but you've transformed my life. I'm not like what I used to be; I promise."

"Good to hear, John. Now I need you and Mary to come to my cabin with me so we can devise a strategy. Get back to your stations, everyone!" Miles ordered, looking envious.

Without looking back, he turned away from us and entered through the door that led below deck. His jealousy was all over the place. John shook his head and followed his captain disappearing through the doorway. I paused for a moment to admire my new home, with its white sails flapping in the breeze, the mast creaked loudly.

The salty sea could be tasted in the air, spraying up the ship's sides and hitting the deck. The rigging shook in the breeze, reminding me of the rope burns on my hands. Tom was lounging around in the crow's nest looking bored, his bright red hair standing out brightly against the blue sky. Several crew members were climbing the ratlines attached to the main mast.

The ship's wheel was left unattended, spinning freely until someone arrived to take over and correct the course. I smiled to myself, knowing that while I had some terrible memories of this ship, I also had some amazing ones, particularly of defeating the witch. But something was niggling at me from the pit of my stomach, making me feel uneasy.

Was the witch truly dead?

I still had that dreadful feeling, as if she were out there somewhere, waiting to come back and finish me off. She had been ripped to shreds by the earth's elements before me, but I still couldn't quite believe she was dead. The dagger I'd used to kill her was still on the floor, drenched in her black blood. I picked it up and examined the engravings on Miles' father's knife.

Where had Miles' father gone?

Elizabeth's ghostly crew vanished immediately after she died. They must have been set free. I can't think of any other place they could be. Questions swirled around inside my head, causing my mind to whirl; my mind was weary from everything that had happened. So many questions, so few answers but I knew I'd find out sooner or later.

"Mary, come on!" John shouted at me from the doorway, pulling me back to the present.

"Coming," I yelled back, placing the dagger into my belt.

As I walked towards John, I noticed a blur of a red dress moving towards the ship's wheel out of the corner of my eye. My heart pounced forward, and I turned to face the enigmatic red blur, only to find nothing.

Were my eyes deceiving me, or was that Elizabeth?

CHAPTER TWO

The Plan

As we entered Miles' cabin, he fixed his gaze on both of us. John moved to the corner and remained there, avoiding Miles' stare. I sat down in the chair across from Miles's desk.

Miles exhaled a sigh. "Before we port, I'd like you to change back into your dress, Mary."

"Of course. I'd like to feel like a woman again," I laughed softly.

Miles gave me a lopsided grin. "It makes no difference what you wear, Mary. You will always appear to me as a woman."

John muttered something under his breath and shook his head. "Captain, what are your plans?"

"So, we'll have Mathew show us Elizabeth's followers. He must know a few people. He betrayed us for a reason, and we must discover what that reason is," Miles explained.

"I had forgotten about him. Where is he now?" I asked.

"He's imprisoned in the hull. Right now, Mark is watching over him. Despite his deformity, he is our most powerful crew member, and he will ensure Mathew's safety," Miles stated.

"So, you're saying we should interrogate Mathew until he tells us why he betrayed us after we helped him escape the witch?" I asked.

Miles nodded, stroking his chin in thought. "Yes, he's our only hope of finding Elizabeth's followers."

"Well, then, what are we waiting for? Come on, let's get it moving." John said, pushing himself away from the wall and heading towards the door.

"I'm the one who gives the orders around here, John.

Not you," Miles grunted as he rose from his chair.

"I understand, Captain. But we need to act quickly before the cult brings her back from the dead. I don't know about you, but I don't want to go through that ordeal again. I'm still healing from my injuries," John stated.

Miles let out a yawn and stretched his arms. "I suppose you're right. My muscles are still slightly stiff. Let's go interrogate our prisoner, shall we?"

We both followed Miles out of the cabin and down the dimly lit corridor to the stairs leading down into the hull. The crew were busy cleaning the stains from the floor and the wall, scrubbing as hard as their aching muscles would allow. The ship was in tatters, but it wouldn't take long for it to be put back together.

As Miles and John walked side by side, an awkward atmosphere surrounded them. I had a feeling it had something to do with me. I just wish they'd stop acting like children about it. Choosing between them could mean I would have to leave the ship, or one of them would have to. I couldn't let myself love either of them fully for that reason, although it would hurt me greatly to hold back. I also knew it was the best way to keep the peace and hoped for happiness for all of us.

"Mary, keep up," John yelled over his shoulder as they descended the stairs.

I dashed after them down the creaky, wooden stairs. Mathew was yelling to be let out, his voice echoing eerily around the hull.

"I suggest you keep quiet, or you'll lose your tongue," Miles cautioned him.

Mathew glared at him but remained silent while Mark paced up and down the hull, his deformed foot scraping loudly across the wood. He smiled warmly when he noticed us.

"It's nice to see everyone looking well," he slurred, his cleft lip preventing him from properly pronouncing his words.

"Has Mathew said anything yet?" Miles asked, oblivious to Mark's greeting.

Mark shook his head, his dark mop of hair swaying. "No, Captain; he's not telling me anything."

"John," Miles motioned for John to approach Mathew.

John nodded and grabbed Mathew's arms, kicking him to the ground. Mathew screamed, his chains rattling as he clutched his shin in agony.

"Are you going to tell us the location of Elizabeth's cult?" Miles questioned, his raging eyes blazing.

Mathew shook his head. "They'll kill me if I do. They know everything, and they are well aware that you are on to them."

"Once again, John. I don't think Mathew realises what we're about to do to him if he doesn't speak up."

John grabbed Mathew's shoulders and kneed him in the back, causing him to howl like an injured dog.

"Just tell us, Mathew," I said, not wanting to watch any more of the violence unfolding before me.

"They'll kill me if I do!" he screamed.

"And if you don't, we'll kill you!" John yelled at him.

Miles nodded once more, motioning for John to continue. Mathew was thrown against the wall after John grabbed him by the shoulders. I heard a loud crack coming from his back as Mathew slumped to the ground, whimpering.

"That's enough, John," I stated.

John didn't listen and carried on beating Mathew. The violent spark in his eyes terrified me to the core. I hadn't seen John like that before, and it sent a cluster of shivers down my spine.

"I said that's enough, John! He won't be able to tell us anything if he can't talk! He's just a boy!" I growled, shocked to see John's violent side.

John stopped, realising that I was watching. He dropped Mathew to the ground with a guilty look in his eyes.

"Mary, if you don't like what you see, I recommend you return to the main deck," Miles warned.

I locked my gaze on him. "Let me remind you, Miles,

that Mathew is still a young man. You will have young blood on your hands if you kill him."

"And let me remind you, Miss Carver, that we need all of the information we can get about this cult of his. We must stay one step ahead of them, or Elizabeth will return, and you may not be able to defeat her this time," Miles stated, folding his arms with an irritated look on his face.

I turned away from Miles and faced Mathew, ignoring his remark.

"Mathew, if you want to be free of the witch, I recommend that you tell us everything you know. We can keep you safe from them," I offered.

He looked at me with pleading eyes. "I don't believe you can, Mary. They are extremely powerful individuals. Some of them are even noblemen."

"Noblemen? How many do you think there are?" Miles cocked his brow, intrigued.

"There's a swarm of them. They are mostly scattered across the country, but they all gather at Stone Manor House once a month. The rest of them are regular workers. They can blend in without being noticed for who they truly are," Mathew explained.

"This has just gotten a lot tougher, Miles," John said, his brows knitted together in thought.

Miles paused, scratching his chin. "I understand, John. Elizabeth has a larger following than we initially thought. This is not good. More men are required if we are going to take them all down."

"Why don't you do what you did last time? Recruit more men?" I asked.

"That's the idea, Mary. Once we get back to Stone Hill Bay, we shall recruit more men for the crew," Miles exclaimed, his eyes gleaming with excitement.

"What about Carver?" John asked.

"No way! He must locate my grandmother for my mother to be born; otherwise, I will not exist." I said through clenched teeth, peeved with John's idea.

"We're going to need all the support we can get," John said firmly, standing his ground.

I glared at him fiercely. "You can use any man you want, John, but you are not having Carver. He needs to meet my grandmother."

He thought for a moment before giving me a hesitant nod. "That's fine, Mary. Have your way with it. We're not going to use Carver."

"Good. We're not going to bring it up again, John," I then turned to face Mathew, bringing the conversation with John to a close. "Mathew, we need to know everything there is to know about this cult in order to have a fighting chance against them."

"I've only met a few of them, but I'm sure there are many more. There could also be a few members of royalty there. Elizabeth has a huge following. If you are determined not to have her return, I recommend that you get a move on. I can point you in the direction of a few of them. The rest of them will show up at the next meeting, making things easier for you," Mathew suggested.

"If there's royalty involved, we might have a war on our hands, Miles. We must tread carefully and make this appear to be an accident," John forewarned.

"How are you going to make it appear as if it were an accident? What you're about to do is mass murder," Mathew remarked, his face tense.

"We shall think about that on the way. It's not mass murder, Mathew. This is justice. We cannot allow Elizabeth to return, and if that means destroying her cult, so be it. You must show us the ones you are familiar with," Miles ordered, his expression full of determination.

Mathew nodded. "I'll show you when we arrive, but I'll warn you now. They are dangerous, and they know who I am."

"Then you will have to hide," John commented, unfazed.

"How will we know if they are members of the cult?" Miles asked.

"Depending on your rank within the cult, they all have the same marking on the back of their necks, just below the hairline, in the shape of elements. Fire, wind, earth, and water are the four elements. Fire has the highest ranking, particularly among nobles, while wind has the lowest ranking," Mathew explained, as he lifted his hair on the back of his neck to reveal a marking in the shape of a water drop.

I gave him a disappointed look. "What made you betray us, Mathew? Why did you join her? She's evil, and you know it."

Mathew turned away from me; his face solemn. "Mary, I'm sorry. I was terrified. It is preferable to be on the bad side and win than to be on the good side and lose. My father taught me that."

I could tell that Mathew felt guilty by the way he avoided my gaze. "But we won, Mathew. We are the good side."

He glanced up from the ground, giving me a weak smile. "You haven't won just yet."

Everything fell into an awkward silence. Mathew was correct; it wasn't over yet, as we all knew. We stood there staring at each other, unable to say anything else. John moved slowly towards the exit, his face full of worry. He took my hand in his and drew me towards the door.

"I'll return you to the main deck," John muttered as he pulled me out of the hull, leaving Miles with Mark and Mathew. As John ushered me up the corridor and out of Miles' sight, I could hear Miles telling Mark to stay with Mathew.

"Now that Miles is alive, are you going to be with him?" John whispered.

I stopped dead in my tracks and looked at him. "No, John. I cannot be with him."

He smiled as he took my hand in his. "Why?" he asked eagerly.

His brown eyes pierced mine. His tanned skin creased as he smiled at me, eager to know my response. His dark brown hair glistened in the candlelight, held up at the back by a piece of filthy-looking string. His lips were pursed, as if he were about to kiss me. I gently pushed him away with my finger on his lips, watching the smile fall from his face. My heart ached as I wanted to know how his lips felt against mine, but I knew I shouldn't push my luck. Even though I wanted them both, I didn't want to overstay my welcome on this ship.

"Because I can't be with him and have feelings for you at the same time. Don't get too excited. I am unable to be with you, too."

He looked upset as he dropped my hand. "You must choose one of us, Mary."

"No, I don't have to make a decision. You simply want me to decide. Now let's get moving. We have things to do," I walked off to the main deck, leaving him stunned in the corridor.

With salt-tinged air, the breeze whipped against my snowy white skin, delving into my already-sore lips and making them sting. My brown hair resembled a bird's nest rather than a bob. I was in desperate need of a wash and a change of clothes. I could smell my armpits whenever the breeze blew through them.

"Mary!" yelled a voice from behind.

I turned to see Captain Carver approaching me with a huge grin on his face.

"I wanted to say my final goodbyes before I left. We've arrived at port, and your captain is about to toss me overboard," he laughed.

"Keep yourself out of trouble, Carver. Please stay safe. You must find my grandmother in order for my mother to be born," I said, hoping that my words would stick in his mind.

He chuckled as he took my hand in his. "I have no idea what she looks like."

"She's a fiery woman with brown hair that resembles mine. I recall her telling me once that she first met you at the Caverns Inn. I'm not sure where that is, but you should start there."

He nodded. "Okay, Mary. I understand. You don't have to tell me twice; The Caverns Inn is my favourite place to visit."

"Then that's the place where you must go. It's been strange and rather eventful knowing my grandfather, even though you are not yet my grandfather," I laughed.

He cracked another grin. "It's been an honour, Mary. I'll stay out of trouble, but before I go, do you know how I die?"

"My grandmother never said anything. Apart from calling you evil, she never said much about you," I stated, feeling a tinge of guilt from my grandmother's words.

"It's not exactly romantic," he said, letting go of my hand. "It appears that I am living up to my reputation."

"I don't think I'm going to see you again, Carver. Have a good life and treat my grandmother well. Stay good," I took a step back, allowing him to leave.

He gave me one last look over his shoulder before disappearing down the plank leading to the mainland. He was dressed in his finest flamboyant waistcoat, his long brown hair mostly hidden by the colourful fabric pieces entwined in his hair. His dark blue doublet flapped in the breeze, revealing his black knee-high boots. He was a captain, just without a ship, which I was sure he'd get soon enough. I was going to miss him, even though he tried to kill me multiple times because of Elizabeth's cruel ways. I watched him walk away with his crew following close behind, disappearing into the crowd of people.

"Stay safe, Carver," I whispered as he disappeared into the crowd.

I returned to my cabin and took my blue dress from the chest. It was slightly wrinkled but still wearable.

Someone had left a bowl of fresh water on the table for me, along with a neatly folded towel. I removed Tom's clothes and stuffed them into the chest.

I shivered as the cold water touched my skin. I splashed

it over my face and wiped away the dried blood that had become encrusted in my hair. I still had my bandages on, covering up the many wounds Elizabeth had inflicted on me. I was sore and achy, but at least I was clean and respectable. I put on my dress and slid my arms through the sleeves.

I heard a small knock from behind the door and heard John asking to come in.

"Enter!" I yelled.

John walked into the cabin with a shy smile on his face. "Are you ready?"

I nodded. "Nearly, can you do me up?"

John's face flushed. "Of course, Mary." He came over and yanked on my bodice, tightening it with the laces.

"Is that alright, or is it too tight?" he asked.

"Tighten it up a little more and then tie it," I confirmed. "Are we leaving right now? I'm hungry."

"Yes, we are going to The Crow's Nest for food and to make a plan," he said while tying my laces. "All done; now let's go." He hesitated a little, holding onto my waist a little longer than was necessary before guiding me to the door.

"Is this going to be risky, John?" I asked, nervously.

He smiled warmly as he looked at me. "It's always going to be risky, Mary. There will always be something in our path, no matter where we go."

He took my hand in his and led me back to the main deck. Everyone was waiting for us to go. Miles stood next to Mathew while pulling a cloak over his head to disguise him.

I let go of John's hand and went to stand at the front of the group, waiting to leave.

Miles noticed my dress and came over to me, grinning. "You look nice."

"Thanks. I feel like me again," I replied, my cheeks blushing a crimson red.

"I prefer you in Tom's old clothes," John laughed, winking at me.

Miles rolled his eyes at John and pulled me away from

him, not wanting John near me. "Has Carver gone?" Miles asked, his arms intertwined with mine as he drew me closer to him.

"He has, indeed. I'm hoping he'll be okay," I muttered.

"He'll be just fine. Come on, we're going to get some food now. Then we'll devise a strategy," Miles said as he took my hand in his and led me away from the side.

I caught sight of John out of the corner of my eye, staring at Miles' hand on mine, looking envious. He didn't say anything as he followed Miles to the plank where Mark was walking with Mathew in his chains.

"Shouldn't we take Mathew's chains off so we don't draw attention to ourselves?" I asked.

"Good point, Mary. We need to stay inconspicuous," Miles replied. "If you make any sudden movements or you betray us again, I will kill you Mathew, and I won't think twice about it," he growled in Mathew's ear.

Mathew shuddered and nodded slowly. "I will never betray you again."

Miles pushed him forward, satisfied with his answer. The plank creaked beneath my feet as I followed the others onto the dock, surrounded by other large ships ready to set sail with cargo. The seagulls squawked high above us, looking for scraps of food.

The large sign welcoming us to Stone Hill Bay loomed ahead of us. That was the first thing I noticed when I had first arrived. It seemed like a lifetime ago now. I was once a weak and timid woman with no prospect of a future, but Elizabeth had changed my life for the better, and for that, I was grateful.

The bay had remained unchanged. Everyone was still going about their daily routine. The chimneys from the buildings belched large amounts of black smoke, making the bay appear foggy. The stench of sewage could be smelled for miles. People were rushing back and forth between the stall holders, purchasing food. As we pushed our way through the crowds, the smell of food made my stomach rumble.

One woman stared at me from a distance, wearing a blonde wig large enough to contain an entire bird's nest. Her flamboyant bodice stood out from the crowd, and her pristine white stockings disappeared into her gleaming black shoes. She appeared to be an important figure of noble blood by the way she looked, but I couldn't understand why she was staring at me.

Or was she staring at Miles?

As I walked through the crowd, I noticed her out of the corner of my eye. She kept staring while holding her light blue parasol above her head, shielding her face from the sun.

Miles was oblivious to the beautiful woman staring at us and continued on his way to The Crow's Nest alehouse. A man in a long black doublet and a large matching hat approached her from behind and whispered something into her ear. She nodded and stepped back, disappearing into the crowd. I looked through the throng of people for her, but she was nowhere to be seen.

"Mary, what's the matter?" John asked, approaching me with Tom in tow.

"I'm not entirely sure. A woman was staring at us, but she's disappeared now," I responded. I walked along the cobbled stone floor, following the others through the crowd, thinking about the woman.

"She's probably staring at you, Mary, because you're walking with a group of men," he laughed.

"I suppose you're right. There was just something about her that bothered me," I muttered more to myself than to John.

"Come on, keep up the pace. We don't want you to get lost in the crowd," John grabbed my arm and drew me along with him to The Crow's Nest.

I noticed a blue parasol coming our way through the crowd. It was heading straight for us, and I knew immediately that it had to be her. Miles had gone ahead with Mathew and Mark, leaving me and the others to dither.

I pushed my way through the crowd to reach Miles before he was confronted by the woman holding the blue parasol. She walked past him just as I arrived, smiling at him gracefully but with a tinge of lust in her eyes. Miles stopped and stared at her, mesmerised by her beauty. She slowed down and walked past him, her gaze fixed on his. She then faded back into the crowd, leaving Miles perplexed but amused by her presence.

"Who was that?" Mark slurred, also admiring her beauty.

"I'm not sure," he stuttered, looking flustered.

He shook his head and continued walking, catching a glimpse of me out of the corner of his eye. As I watched him smile to himself, probably thinking about her, jealousy seethed through me.

Who was that woman, and why am I so bothered by her?

CHAPTER THREE

Darkness Hides Behind Beauty

We took a seat in The Crow's Nest and cleared the table of plates containing food scraps. The room was packed with men and women who were laughing and enjoying each other's company. The fire was lit, sending waves of heat our way. The sun streamed in through the windows, warmly embracing the room. The bar at the back of the room held barrels full of liquid to fill a drunk man's stomach. A woman dressed in scruffy clothing stood behind the bar, busy cleaning the cups, ready for the next arrivals.

A flashback to Elizabeth's presence in this room flashed through my mind. She had killed one of Miles' men the last time we visited the place. A shiver ran up my spine as I leaned back into my chair and observed the room.

"Here's some money, Tom. Go get us a feast!" Miles ordered, thrusting coins in Tom's hand and chuckling.

"You seem to be in a good mood." John noticed; his brow scrunched together in thought.

Miles's smile suddenly faded. "Am I not allowed to be cheerful, John?"

"I was just wondering what caused your mood to shift," John muttered, watching Miles carefully from across the table.

He had also noticed what I'd noticed between Miles and that woman. So, it wasn't just my paranoia. That woman was up to something, but I couldn't figure out what. I couldn't let my jealousy get the best of me and cloud my judgement. I needed to keep my cool if I was going to try and figure out what was yet to happen.

"Mary, what do you want?" Miles asked, his gaze shifting

away from John.

"Whatever you're eating, I'm not bothered," I responded, trying to keep the irritation from my face.

Miles nodded and motioned for Tom to leave with a wave of his hand. "Mathew will take us to the first member of the cult after dark. From there, we'll go after each and every one of them until they're all dead. We can also try to get any additional information from them before getting rid of them."

"We'll have to hide them, or we'll be hanged for murder, Miles," John forewarned.

"Nice thought," Miles murmured, his mind racing.

"You can't just go around killing people," Mathew grunted under his breath.

"So, what do you suppose we do, Mathew? They are too dangerous to keep alive. They have to be destroyed," John said.

Before he spoke again, Mathew looked around twitchingly. "We could use their magic to our advantage. I'm familiar with their enchantment. Whatever spells they cast against us; I can return it unto them."

"Why would you do that?" I asked, intrigued.

"Because I, like you, want this to be over and done with. So, I'll assist in any way I can," he confessed.

The table fell silent as we all processed Mathew's words. I couldn't blame him for being fed up with the situation. The mere mention of her name sent shivers up my spine.

Tom appeared, carrying a tray of goblets, and a woman stood behind him, carrying a tray of food. My stomach growled once more as I caught a whiff of food, signaling that it was time to eat. The men dug their hands into the food as soon as it was placed on the table, grabbing fistfuls and shoving them down their throats. I mimicked them without even thinking about it, allowing a slither of chicken to slide down my throat.

With a smirk on his face, John looked at me. "You've been hanging out with us for far too long, Mary."

I laughed and shoved another handful into my mouth, chewing it to mush. A man stumbled up to our table, disturbing our peace with his drunken pointing at Mark.

"What in the name of God is that?" he said, slurring his words.

Mark smiled politely as he looked up from his food. "Sir, my name is Mark."

The man burst out laughing and slapped his hands on the table. "You don't need a name. You don't even look human."

Another flashback appeared in front of me, transporting me back to the sinking ship where we had first discovered Mark. Elizabeth's men had both said the same thing.

Miles raised his eyes from his plate of food and stared directly at the drunk man. "I wouldn't anger him if I were you."

The man's gaze shifted away from Mark and toward Miles. "And why is that? He probably can't even talk properly, let alone walk properly."

Mark glared at him from across the table, his cleft lip dripping with chicken grease. He held a chicken leg out in front of him and crushed it with his enormous hands, demonstrating his strength to the man. The man took a step back but then burst out laughing again, drawing everyone's attention to us.

"Do you think you're scaring me by doing that?" he slapped his hands together and chuckled before turning his attention to me. "And who exactly is this lovely lady? You like the male attention, don't you?" he winked.

"I suggest you watch your tongue, boy," John growled at him, his hands balling into fists.

"You're drunk, sir. I suggest you go home and sleep it off. We don't want any trouble here," I said politely, ignoring the man's leering gaze.

He approached my chair and reached out his stubby fingers to stroke my hair.

"I'm afraid I'm going to cause you some trouble, pretty lady," he smirked, pulling my hair tightly around his fist.

Miles threw his chair back and grabbed the man by the neck, slamming his head onto the table and holding it there.

"You heard her. Go home," Miles snarled, pushing the man's head aggressively into the table, causing it to crack slightly from the pressure.

The man flailed around, attempting to break free from Miles' grip, but Miles firmly held his head in place.

"I think that's enough, don't you think?" a woman's voice called out from behind me.

Miles stopped what he was doing and looked behind him, his eyes widening in surprise. We all turned to see who the dainty voice belonged to, surprised to see it was the woman we had seen earlier. Two black-clad men stood behind her, their hands clasped behind their backs in an authoritative manner. Their beady eyes moved from one man to the next until they rested on me.

The woman stood there, smirking at the situation, holding her parasol in her hands. Miles let go of the drunken man, allowing him to fall to the floor. The man got to his feet and brushed himself off. He then looked at the woman, his eyes telling us he recognised her.

"I'm truly sorry, miss," he stuttered.

She pointed a laced gloved finger at him. "I suggest you leave."

The man bowed to her and then stumbled out of the alehouse into the crowd outside. She gave one of her men a glance and motioned for him to go after the man. He silently nodded and followed him outside.

She then turned to face Miles, smiling sweetly with a glint in her eyes. "Please accept my apologies for him bothering you. It won't happen again."

Miles stared at her awkwardly, not knowing what to say. His cheeks flushed red, and he began to fidget with his fingers, becoming uneasy in her presence.

"Who are you?" John blurted out, asking the question we all wanted to know.

She cast a glance over Miles' shoulder to John. "I'm Lady Felicity Amelia Shawl."

"What is your business here?" I asked her.

"I heard a commotion, so I came inside," she said, not bothering to look in my direction.

"Are you always on the lookout for trouble?" I fixed my gaze on her, scanning her for any sign of danger.

She turned to me with her piercing blue eyes, boring straight into mine without blinking. "Yes, if it pleases me."

Her eyes were cold. It was as if she could turn anything into ice with her piercing look. White powder trickled from her wig and landed on her shoulder. She was dressed in a flamboyant, blue-patterned petticoat lined with dark blue bows in the middle, revealing her dainty waist. Her dress matched her petticoat, all the way down to her black, gleaming, buckled shoes. She wore white-laced, delicate-looking gloves that accentuated her elegant hands. Her pursed lips were stained a brilliant red. Her skin was as white as a snowy day, giving her the appearance of a winter flower, small and fragile, but her eyes were fierce and dangerous. She was stunning. She was the most beautiful woman I'd ever seen, even more beautiful than Elizabeth when she was at her peak.

With my tacky looking dress and ruffled hair, she made me look like a servant girl. Her presence intimidated me, and I didn't like her cold, foreboding eyes staring at me.

"I could also ask you the same question because you're sitting here with a group of men," she smirked at me before moving her gaze to Miles, not waiting for my response. "May I take a seat?"

Miles could only nod at her; his gaze never left her for a second. Felicity sat down after two of Miles' men budged up. Their cheeks turned crimson as they sat back down, unable to keep their eyes off her. She smoothed down her dress to keep it from ruffling up, enjoying the attention. The man behind her, who I assumed was one of her bodyguards, stepped to the side and leant against the wall, surveying the scene. Her other guard reappeared through the door and joined the first one against the wall, slightly puffed out from whatever Felicity had gone and made him do.

Miles sat down in front of Felicity, who dazzled him with a smile, her gaze fixed on him and no one else.

"I've heard a lot about you, Miles," she said, her grin widening.

"Have you?" he asked nervously.

"The man who saves everyone," she laughed. "You sail around, bringing young ladies with you to help them fix their lives."

"Mary was a one-time occurrence. I don't usually bring women on my journeys," Miles stated.

Felicity giggled like a little girl. "Maybe you could take me one of these days. I'm sure I'll be a lot more entertaining."

He cracked a grin, revealing his dimple. "Perhaps I will."

As I watched them both flirt with each other from across the table, jealousy and anger welled up within me. I could see John looking at me, waiting to see my reaction.

Miles cleared his throat, becoming even more nervous within Felicity's presence as she never took her eyes off him. "What can I do for you, Miss?"

She smiled while observing his crew. "I would just like to introduce myself, Miles. I'm sure that we will see much more of each other in the coming months."

"Now that you've introduced yourself, what are you going to do now? Wow us some more?" I asked sarcastically.

"Miles, can you ask your lady to remain quiet?" Felicity asked sweetly, turning her attention back to Miles.

"She's not my lady," Miles said bluntly, ignoring my hurt reaction.

His words pierced me to the core. I stared at him open-mouthed, but he didn't even bother to turn around. John took my hand in his and pulled me to my feet, knowing that all I wanted to do was get out of there. As we walked quickly out of the alehouse, he turned and glared at Miles, disappointed with his behaviour. I cast a glance behind me, feeling her icy-blue eyes boring into the back of my skull.

Felicity leaned in closer to Miles, stroking his hand while smirking directly at me and John as we walked away. After we headed out the door she returned her attention to Miles, and they continued their flirtatious conversation, chuckling to one another as if they were newlyweds.

CHAPTER FOUR

The First

"Are you all right, Mary?" John asked.

I averted my eyes from him, wiping away the tears that streamed down my cheeks. "I'm fine. All I needed was some fresh air."

"I don't understand why Miles was acting like that," John shook his head, deep in thought. "Would you like to go somewhere else for a while, just until Felicity leaves?"

I nodded and followed him through the crowd of stallholders to a more secluded area. John looked left and right before eagerly pulling me toward the dock.

"Why are we returning to the ship?" I asked.

"We aren't," he said over his shoulder as we made our way towards the dock.

Hundreds of masts loomed above the crooked stone buildings. The roofs were slanted with wonky-looking slates covered in soot. The windows reflected the calm waves of the ocean as we got closer to wherever John was taking me. With the buildings towering over them and blocking out natural light as they walked past, the cobbled alleyways before them appeared dark and gloomy. Yet the dock looked warm and welcoming with flurries of seagulls encircling food scraps on the ground.

I could now see the entire dock as far as the eye could see. The creaks and groans emanating from the hulls of ships could be heard across the bay. Men hollowing from the ships echoed up and down the dock, scaring the seagulls away. As John turned left, heading towards the end of the dock that led to a small, secluded sandy beach, the sea breeze picked up suddenly, whipping me in the face. There were only the seagulls to keep us company as we strayed away from the crowd of people and the hollering of the crews from the ships.

He slowed to a walk, giving me a chance to catch my breath. His hand lingered around my waist, and he grinned broadly, his body relaxing into mine. His eyes twinkled in the light as he smiled lopsidedly, revealing slight wrinkles beneath his eyes. His white shirt flapped in the breeze, revealing his tanned skin underneath. As I looked at him, I realised my feelings for him had grown stronger as he stood there with the sun beating down on him. He was the only one who could tell I was upset by Miles' remark, and he had removed me from the situation. I stood next to him, smiling up at him, grateful for his presence.

"There aren't many people who come here," he said, taking my hand in his and leading me further down the sandy beach.

"It's beautiful here," I said, admiring the scenery.

John was right. There were no footprints apart from ours, leaving our imprint in the golden sand that glistened in the sun. Crispy-looking seaweed lined the shore in clusters, with patches of debris mixed in. John picked up a brightly coloured seashell and twirled it around in his palm, admiring its unique shape. He then slipped it into his pocket and lightly tapped it.

He noticed me staring at him and smiled. "I like to collect shells."

I laughed softly. "I had no idea you had such a soft side."

He nodded. "There's a lot about me that you don't know, Mary."

"Don't worry. It's only made me like you more," I beamed.

He took my hand in his and gently kissed it while looking me in the eyes. My heart soared, but I also felt guilty about Miles.

If Miles wanted to go out with Miss Prissy Pants, he could. He hurt me, and John was there to cheer me up, dismissing his own hurt feelings. He plopped himself onto the soft sand, yanking me down with him. I fell into his lap, but I didn't get up. Instead, I rested my head on his shoulder and gazed out to sea, watching the waves crash against the exposed rocks. He gently stroked my hair with his hand on my head. I could hear him breathing heavily as he observed the seagulls hovering over us in search of food.

"What's the plan of attack?" I muttered.

"I'm just going to go with it," he smiled as he looked down at me. "I don't mind, as long as you're safe."

"I have a feeling that Felicity is dangerous, and she's up to something. So, we may not be safe."

"What makes you say that?" He asked, intrigued.

"It's just a gut feeling," I murmured, not wanting to admit my jealousy about the situation.

"I believe she is only interested in Miles. After all, he is a handsome man," John admitted but with a slightly envious tone in his voice.

"There's a little more to it than that, John. Besides, you're just as attractive."

He laughed. "I'm just as handsome but older. Is that what you're saying?"

"Quartermaster!" a distant voice yelled.

We turned to see Tom rushing towards us, his red hair gleaming in the light. John didn't move, but he acknowledged Tom's presence by nodding in his direction.

"I thought I might find you here," he puffed as he approached us.

He spotted John stroking my hair and looked away awkwardly, staring out to sea instead. "The captain requires both of you to return to The Crow's Nest.'"

"The captain can wait. We're taking it easy here for a while before the bloodbath begins. I think we deserve it, don't you?" John asked.

Tom nodded. "Yes, Sir."

"Come and sit with us," John said, patting the sand beside him.

Tom took off his shoes and sat down beside John. He

dug his heels into the sand, enjoying the sensation on his skin. He sighed loudly as he gazed out to sea.

"Is Miss Prissy Pants still there?" I asked nervously, not wanting to upset John. I could feel John tensing beneath my cheek as I said her name, but he remained silent, waiting for Tom's response.

"No, she left shortly after you two," Tom replied. "Miles is probably looking for us right now."

"How did you know where we were?" I asked.

"Because this is John's favourite place to go when he's upset or angry. I assumed he brought you here. I saw your expression when Miles told you that you weren't his lady. It wasn't a kind thing to say."

"You got that right. I don't know why he acted like that," John grunted.

"She's a pretty woman, John. You know what he's like with pretty women," Tom replied.

Another wave of jealousy washed over me. "What exactly do you mean, Tom?"

"Well...er..." Tom averted his gaze, unsure what to say, suddenly aware that he had said too much.

"Just tell her, Tom," John suggested, keen for me to know.

"Well, he just goes all soft when there's a pretty woman around him, and he does all he can for her. He's done it before," Tom explained.

"Why wasn't I told about this before?" I asked.

"Because he genuinely liked you, Mary. Well, that was until I saw the way he acted with Lady Felicity. I'm sure he still has feelings for you. He would not have gone to all that trouble and risked losing some of his men if he didn't believe it was worthwhile. He only acts like this now and then when a pretty woman notices him. Felicity, on the other hand, I'm not sure what she was after," Tom exhaled a sigh.

"It was me who asked Miles if you could stay," John spoke up, cutting Tom off before he could continue.

I lifted my head from his shoulder and looked him dead

in the eyes. "It was you?"

He nodded. "Before Miles was killed, he was telling me that he wasn't sure whether he should keep you on board or not."

My heart sank upon hearing those words from John. "I thought he wanted me to stay."

"Well, he did, but he was unsure of what the future held. Hence, I urged him to let you stay," John said.

"John!" a voice called out.

We all turned to see Miles standing on the dock nearby with his arms crossed, waiting for us. He had an angry expression on his face as he stood there, tapping his foot impatiently. We jumped up and walked slowly across the sand.

"Where have you been? I've been waiting for ages," he shouted from the dock.

We climbed the wooden steps to where Miles was standing and awaited his next command.

"Well?" he yelled.

"We were taking in the scenery," I grumbled loud enough for him to hear.

"It's time to go. We have a lot of work to do," he growled and walked away, clutching my arm.

I yanked my arm away from him. "You can't do that to me."

He stopped and looked at me. "I am your captain, Mary. You wanted to stay, remember? You will do as you are told."

"I will go with you if you stop yanking my arm," I argued back.

He extended his hand to me and forced a smile. "Mary, don't make this difficult for me. We need to get going. Mathew has led us to the cult's first member."

When he noticed my hesitation, he lowered his hand to his side. "Fine, walk with John then."

He turned on his heel and stalked away, dragging Tom with him. John gave me a weak smile and followed his captain, leaving me behind.

I let out an exasperated sigh and went after the others, feeling annoyed with Miles for being so arrogant with me. Miles was clearly envious and upset with me, but he couldn't have his way all the time. He hurt me earlier, and John had been there to comfort me. After Tom spilled too much information about Miles' behaviour, I no longer felt as I used to, especially after the way he treated me with Felicity. He thought it was okay to come back to me and act as if nothing had happened now that she was gone.

"Mary, hurry up!" Miles shouted over his shoulder, jolting me out of my thoughts.

I hurried after them, not wanting to be left behind. The bay had become less crowded, with only a few people purchasing items from the stalls. The sun was beginning to set, leaving a murky clouded sky above us.

I could see the others waiting near the alleyway leading to The Crow's Nest. Mathew wore his hood up so no one would recognise him, and Mark stood next to him, holding his arm. The others stood around, looking bored, until they noticed us approaching.

"Lead the way," Miles said as I approached them, puffing loudly for air.

"It's this way," Mathew said, pointing up a dark and dingy street.

The shop signs swung back and forth in the wind, loudly crashing against the crumbling stone walls of the shops that lined the street. The street was littered with straw and horse manure, making the air smell foul. Candles were lit across the street, casting elongated shadows across the cobblestones. The bay was getting colder by the minute, sending shivers down our spines as we started to walk up the street.

"We must act quickly," Miles insisted. "Mathew, where are we going now?"

"In this direction," Mathew took us up another alleyway, which led into a small archway with small cottage-style houses at the end. He stopped and pointed to the left cottage with a shaky finger. "She's in there."

"She?" John and Miles both asked at the same time.

"Yes, don't underestimate her. She is one of the ring leaders," Mathew explained.

"Why are we going to her first if she's one of the ring leaders?" I asked.

"Because she is the most dangerous of them all. If we can eliminate her first, it will make it easier for us to complete this mission," Mathew gulped nervously and continued. "She will kill me if she sees me. We need to get this over and done with as soon as possible."

"Right, Mary, you need to knock on her door and ask for help or something. You need to keep her occupied while we sneak in, and then Mathew can use his magic against her," Miles ordered.

"Why me?" I protested.

"Because you're a lady. If she sees us all waiting for her outside, she'll suspect something is wrong. Mary, use your common sense," Miles shook his head, annoyed.

"Don't talk to her that way, Miles," John growled at him.

Miles shifted his gaze to John. "If you want to stay with this crew, I highly suggest you keep your mouth shut."

John maintained his gaze. "Miles, you're putting her in danger. We have no idea what's beyond this door, and you're letting her go in on her own."

"All right, we'll all go in, but don't blame me if things don't go as planned," Miles grumbled.

He took my hand in his and led me to the run-down cottage's front door. He drew his pistol and cocked it, ready to fire at whatever was behind the closed door. The others did the same and drew their weapons, looking slightly terrified of what was about to happen. My heart rate increased as I stared at the black iron knocker in the shape of a lion's head, unable to bear the thought of going inside.

"Captain, this is a ridiculous plan," John stated. "We have no idea who's in there, and you're ready to barge in, full gun blazing."

"Do you have a better suggestion, John? Let's hear it if that's the case," Miles snapped.

"I do, indeed. We can shimmy our way up the drainpipe and into that open window," he indicated the window, which was slightly ajar. "She won't expect us to come in that way."

Miles stared at the open window and nodded reluctantly. "I suppose you're right."

"I can't shimmy up that drainpipe in a dress," I stated.

Miles turned around and looked at what I was wearing. "Then I suggest you enter through the front door. I'll stay by your side and hide behind the door. We'll wait for the rest of them to pass through the window before we go. Are we all ready now?"

Everyone nodded, except for John, who looked at me with a worried expression. He gently squeezed my hand before releasing it and joining the others, ready to climb up the drainpipe.

"Captain, I don't think I'll be able to get up there," Mark confessed.

Miles nodded. "Then you remain outside and stand guard. If there is any danger, yell."

"Of course, Captain," Mark hobbled off into the alleyway's shadows, away from the light, to remain hidden.

John went first and began slowly climbing the pipe, taking care not to slip and make a noise. He reached the top and opened the window just enough to peek inside. He lowered his gaze and motioned for the others to begin following him. He then pushed open the window completely and drew himself up onto the window ledge, edging his way inside before jumping in. The crew followed John slowly, one by one, disappearing inside the room without making a noise, leaving me and Miles alone outside.

"Are you ready?" Miles asked.

I nodded. "Yes, but I don't like this."

He sighed and shrugged his shoulders. "This is something we must do, Mary."

He put his hand on the doorknob and slowly opened it,

peering around the door into a pitch-black room. I could see him trembling in fear, holding his pistol out in front of him in case anything attacked. Half of his shirt was tucked into his leather trousers, while the other half flapped in the breeze coming from inside the cottage. It was icy cold, and we could see our breath in wisps of mist in front of us. Inside the cottage, it was colder than outside, which was unusual, to say the least. He looked at me with fear in his eyes, unsure what to do.

He took my hand in his and led me inside the cottage. Vines hung from the ceiling, tangling and entwining with one another, growing down the sides of the walls, sprouting sharp thorns. Mouldy straw was scattered across the stone floor, along with a black-looking substance.

To my right, there was a small opening into another room with a half-melted candle on top of a small, uneven table. In the middle of the back wall was a large soot-ridden fireplace, with an oval-shaped mirror hanging above it, reflecting the candlelight into the dingy-looking room. There were stacks of books against the wall, as well as scrolls and ripped pieces of paper scattered across the floor. There was another door to my right, but it was locked.

A flight of stairs led up to the first floor, where more mirrors hung on the walls, reflecting various aspects of the cottage. Whoever this woman was, I could tell she was cautious by the number of mirrors on the walls, which reflected every detail of the cottage, allowing her to see everything without having to move an inch.

I could see the reflections of John and the others in the mirrors, descending the stairwell. He had a worried expression on his face as he noticed the number of mirrors hung on the walls. We couldn't sneak up on her. she would be able to see us from every corner of the room if she was in there. Apart from the locked door, there was nowhere else to go. Miles looked at John and then at me, trying to come up with another plan.

"She isn't here, and this place gives me the shivers. It's freezing in here!" John hissed angrily.

"Mathew, where is she?" Miles asked.

"She is here. I can feel her. She must be behind that door," he pointed a shaky finger at the locked door.

The air became even colder, and a fine mist began to encircle our legs, freezing our skin with its delicate, wispy touch.

"What's going on, Mathew?" John demanded, waving his hand through the mist in an attempt to disperse it.

"She's using the elements against us. We must act quickly if we are to survive," Mathew insisted.

Miles nodded and moved his gaze to the closed door. He kicked at the door with his leg, hoping to break it. It didn't move an inch, but the noise was loud enough to scare away a flock of ravens perched on one of the other cottage's roofs.

"Well, she must know we are here now. Tom, go and get Mark." Miles ordered.

Tom nodded and disappeared out the front door into the approaching night. A few seconds passed before we heard Mark scuffling towards us with Tom in tow.

"Mark, I need you to knock this door down," Miles said.

Mark agreed and looked at the padlock that was attached to the door handle. He grabbed it with his gigantic fist and yanked it off in one fell swoop. As we stood there in awe of him, he seemed pleased with himself. He crushed the padlock in his hand and tossed the now-metal ball to the floor.

"I don't believe I've ever seen anything like that before. Excellent work, Mark," Miles chuckled.

He then kicked the door open while holding his pistol out in front of him, ready to fire. He came to a halt at the doorway's entrance, peering into the pitch-black room to see if she was inside or not.

"Can you see anything?" John asked, peeking over his shoulder.

I stood back, waiting for something to happen or for her

to jump out and scare us, but there was nothing apart from an eerie hissing sound coming from inside the room.

Miles shook his head. "I can't see anything. What's that noise?"

John looked around to see where it was coming from and froze while staring at the wall behind Miles.

"What's wrong, John?" he asked, noticing the expression on John's face.

John pointed to the wall, where the vines were coming to life and breaking away, heading straight for Miles and the crew. I took a step closer to the front door, not wanting to be snagged by the vines as they began to protrude towards us.

It was too late for Miles. The vines encircled Miles' ankles and wrists, their thorns digging into his skin and slicing through it as if it were paper. Before the crew could react, they were snatched by the vines and pinned against the wall, unable to move. John slashed through the ones that had wrapped themselves around his wrist, oozing a black liquid that burned through his skin. He screamed in agony as he watched his skin peel away, revealing the flesh beneath.

Mark began to panic, swiping at the vines with his sword, cutting through them with all of his strength. They began to approach me, stretching out from the wall and making their way across the floor to my feet. I stomped on them as hard as I could, moving closer to the other room and away from their grip.

"Mathew, what do we do?" I screeched as I pulled the dagger from beneath my dress and started hacking at the vines.

Mathew looked terrified as he stood on the stairwell, watching the carnage unfold in front of him.

"I'm not sure!" he sobbed.

"Mary, go after her and stop her!" Miles ordered.

The vines began to make their way towards Miles' mouth, attempting to penetrate through his gums to prevent him from speaking. I stood there in horror as John was dragged to the wall and lifted by his neck, choking the air from his lungs.

"Mary, hurry!" Mathew screamed from the stairs.

I snatched the candle from the room and dragged Mark with me into the darkness, hoping to find and stop her before she killed the whole crew.

I could now see her through the light from the candle. She sat in a corner, rocking back and forth, whispering to herself. The only thing in the room was her and a small altar table next to the window with black candles and a bowl full of dead vines on it.

"What do we do?" Mark asked, panicking.

"Grab her, Mark!" I shouted.

He obeyed and grabbed the woman, holding her up like a rag doll. Her eyes had misted over into a murky white as she screeched and stared at me. She wore a brown dress that looked more like a sack with long, scraggly brown and grey hair. Her bare feet kicked Mark, exposing her filthy black toes.

"Stop right now!" I yelled at her.

"I can't. She is forcing me to do this," she snarled.

"Who is making you do this?" I asked.

"Her blood courses through my veins like Elizabeth's," she whimpered as her face contorted in pain. Her veins began to darken and protrude from her skin like vines. She struggled to break free from Mark's grip, but his strength held her down.

"It burns!" she screamed as she flailed around, attempting to kick Mark in the shin.

"Tell us what we must do to stop this!" I screeched at her.

"Kill me! Do it now!" she cried, screaming in agony as her veins began to pop, oozing out the same black substance from the vines.

I didn't think as I drew my dagger. All I could hear were her agonising screams piercing through me and Miles's crew's unendurable wailing. She yelled at me to kill her over and over as she writhed in pain. I raised the dagger above my head and stabbed her in the heart, feeling unsure if it was the right thing to do. She breathed a sigh of relief and flopped into Mark, her body becoming limp. Her eyes returned to her normal colour, and her veins vanished into her skin, making her appear normal looking. The wailing from Miles's crew stopped, and I saw the vines that had held them turn rotten black, allowing them to break free.

"You took your time!" Miles bellowed as he moved his jaw around with his hand.

A small hole had formed where a vine had pierced his skin and entered his mouth. In a rage, he yanked out the rotten vine and threw it to the ground.

John looked worse for wear as he hobbled in with cuts all across his arms and legs.

"I did the best I could," I muttered, replacing the dagger into my dress.

"Mathew, get in here!" Miles ordered.

Mathew peeked into the room and entered when he realised it was over. He looked petrified as he stared at the woman on the floor. We all stood around, puffing for air, trying to remain calm.

Miles turned to Mathew and grabbed him by the collar. "What was that all about?" He demanded.

Mathew shrugged, trying to release himself from Miles's grip. "I don't know what she meant by it."

"Who was she talking about?" I asked.

"I really don't know, Mary. I know as much as you do. To me, it looked as if she was being controlled by something or someone," he shifted his gaze to Miles. "I was scared, alright? I didn't know what to do."

"We nearly died, and you stood there like a flailing fish!" Miles snapped.

"I said I'm sorry!" Mathew shouted. "I will help next time."

Mathew took a step back as he saw the anger in Miles's eyes. Mark saw and grabbed Mathew by the neck, planting him firmly on the ground so he couldn't move.

"What ranking is she?" John croaked from the back as he held himself up by the wall.

I knelt and lifted the back of her hair to reveal a mark in the shape of a flame. She wasn't noble, but she still had the highest ranking.

So, what made her so special?

"She has the highest ranking according to you, Mathew, but she was still possessed by someone else. How can this be?" Miles asked.

Mathew stood there, staring at Miles, unable to respond. He shrugged his shoulders and knelt beside the woman, searching through her pockets for anything that could help us.

"We need answers, Matthew," John snapped. In pain, he clutched his stomach and leaned against the wall for support. He had blood running down his arms and scratches all over his legs, which were visible through his ripped trousers. He looked at me and smiled weakly as if he were trying to hide his pain.

"John needs attending to by the ship's medic," I said. "We need to get out of here, as this is now a murder scene. We cannot make this look like an accident."

"I don't think that's going to be a problem," Tom muttered, pointing to the woman's body, which was now turning to ash.

"Well, that solved the problem. Tom, hide that dress, and then we can get out of here," Miles ordered.

Tom nodded and threw the dress beneath the alter table to keep it hidden from anyone who came in looking for her. I looked around for any kind of clue that could help us, but I couldn't find anything. I took the candle and returned to the room full of books to search through her things. John scurried after me, still clutching his stomach. He was turning greener by the second as if he were about to throw up all over himself.

"John, you need to sit down before you fall," I said as I dragged a small wooden chair over to him.

He accepted and sat down slowly, wincing in pain. He snatched my hand and squeezed it tightly. "I'm feeling rough," he sighed. "The entire room is spinning."

"Miles! Get John back to the ship as soon as possible!" I yelled, startling John.

Miles burst through the doorway, took one look at John, and picked him up, tossing him over his shoulder as he stomped away.

"I will stay here and look for anything that could help us," I called after Miles.

"Stay with Mary, Tom," Miles grunted and then vanished into the darkness, leaving John flailing around on his shoulder and groaning loudly.

The rest of the crew followed their captain, leaving me, Tom, and Mark to clean up the shambles. We looked at each other, unsure of what to do. The others had gone, and we were left alone with a candle that looked as if it was about to die any second.

"Let's get this over with," I muttered and began rummaging through the woman's belongings.

"What are we supposed to be on the lookout for?" Mark slurred.

"Anything that can help us understand Elizabeth's cult," I replied, rummaging through some strewn-up scrolls on the floor. "It appears that this woman can write, so she may have written down information that can help us."

"Few people have the advantage of being able to read and write. I am uneducated in both reading and writing." Tom mumbled.

I gave him a friendly smile. "One day, Tom, I'll teach you."

His face was serious when he looked at me. "Would you?"

"Yes, Tom. I promise. Now let's get on with this, so we can leave," I said.

Mark hobbled over to the fire pit and inserted his hand into the chimney. He coughed loudly as black soot trickled down, making a small black cloud that dispersed into the air.

"What are you up to?" Tom asked.

"I recall my father hiding things in the chimney when I was younger. We can't afford to ignore anything that could potentially hide what we need," Mark explained as he rummaged through the chimney with his hand. "Ah!" As he drew something from the chimney, he smiled triumphantly. "Here."

It was caked in black soot, but it resembled a small, leather-bound black book with no title on the front. He wiped the soot away with his palm and handed it to me. I flipped through the pages and realised it was some kind of diary.

"Excellent work, Mark," I said, reading snippets of her writing.

A loud bang from outside the cottage jolted us, tearing our eyes away from the diary. We exchanged shocked looks as we strained our ears to hear who it could be. Outside, I could hear voices, but they were too muffled for me to understand. I motioned with my finger to Mark and Tom to come upstairs with me and not make a noise.

I tip-toed out, with Tom and Mark following quietly behind, leaving the candle lit on top of the small table. The voices grew louder as whoever it was approached the cottage door.

"I don't know. I was just told that we should check on her. That's all I know," a male voice spoke from outside.

I pushed Tom and Mark further up the stairs so we wouldn't be seen. Another loud bang came from downstairs as the door flew open, revealing two large male shadows.

"Do you think something's happened to her?" one of them asked.

"I'm not sure." the other one said, coming increasingly closer to our hiding spot.

He sniffed the air loudly. "Something's not right here. The elements have been used."

The other one then sniffed the air. "You're right. Anthea! Anthea!"

They barged into the room where the woman's ashes lay, undisturbed since her death.

There was a lot of scuffling around the room until one of them said, "She was right. Someone's killed her, but whom?"

"I don't know, but she needs to know. Set this place alight, and let's get out of here. We cannot leave any evidence behind."

One of them appeared back through the door and grabbed the candle from the other room.

"What do we do?" Tom hissed.

"Do we kill them or run?" I asked.

"They need to be taken out," Mark said bluntly. "I'll do it. I'm the strongest here. You two wait outside for me; I won't be long."

He stepped quietly down the steps, careful not to make a noise, and crept towards the darkened room. While Mark snuck up behind them with his pistol raised, the two men began to argue about who was going to set the place on fire. I pulled Tom up from the stairs while holding onto the diary and dashed out of the front door, leaving it ajar for Mark to come out. Someone screamed from inside the cottage, which echoed down the small alleyway, raising the hairs on the back of my neck. As we listened to the commotion inside the cottage, Tom clutched my hand and held it tightly.

"Do you think Mark is all right?" Tom hissed next to me.

I could feel him trembling beside me, but I couldn't tell if it was from the cold breeze outside or the screaming from inside. He was still a child. This was not the place for a boy his age.

"I'm hoping so, Tom," I muttered.

A loud gunshot rang out from within, terrifying us to our core as we stood frozen on the spot, unsure of what to do. Tom let go of my hand and crept slowly up to the front door, listening in on what was going on inside.

The door swung open unexpectedly, throwing Tom backward outside. Tom fell onto his back, letting out a loud oomph as Mark appeared in the doorway, huffing and puffing and looking sweaty.

"All right, let's go," Mark snatched Tom from the ground and scuttled through the alleyway. "Mary, please hurry!"

Before I chased after Mark, I looked back at the cottage and saw that he had already set it on fire, hoping to leave no trace behind.

"Mark! Why did you set fire to the place?" I asked, approaching him as he hobbled away.

"It's important to leave no trace," he exhaled a puff.

As we returned to the street, Mark stopped and placed Tom down. He was perspiring profusely, and he began to smell bad.

"Did they turn to ash too?" Tom asked.

Mark nodded. "Yes, but I wanted it to appear that they did their job of burning down the place, so whoever is in charge doesn't think something is wrong just yet."

My eyes widened in surprise. "I didn't think of that. Good one, Mark."

"Did you check their ranks?" Tom asked.

Mark stopped to catch his breath. "Yeah, they were both ranked. I also checked to see if there was anything on them that would help us, and one of them had this in their pocket."

Mark took a gleaming gold key from his pocket and held it out for us to inspect. The key was studded with a red ruby at the top and etchings swirled around the sides. It appeared to be big enough to be a master key for a large house or mansion.

"I think you're on to something," I murmured as I examined the key.

There were no words engraved on the key, just the beautiful swirling pattern. It also looked like it was made out of real gold. If that was the case, then the key had to be very important.

"We should talk to Mathew about this key," Tom said as he began walking toward the dock. "Let's get back to the ship!"

"Mary, I'm afraid I can't run. I'm too exhausted," Mark moaned, clutching his chest.

I gave him a friendly smile. "Take things at your own pace. I'll keep an eye out for you."

People stumbled out of the alehouses, laughing and swaying with each other, bringing the street back to life. I realised we'd been gone from the ship for far too long. Miles hadn't yet come looking for us, which surprised me. I followed Tom but kept Mark in sight, hoping he'd hurry up because the bay was getting colder by the second and I was only wearing a dress that barely covered my arms. There were also a lot of people coming out into the open, making the street even more crowded.

It felt good to know I was on my way to a nice, warm bunk. Today had been a strange mix of emotions and stress, and I didn't want to have to go through it again. I was happy on the ship when Miles returned from the dead, but the rest of the day went downhill from there, leaving me stuck in another quest that I didn't want to be in.

I couldn't decide which quest was the most difficult and dangerous. The one in which I had to destroy Elizabeth, the most powerful witch who haunted the bay, or bring down her powerful and discreet cult. We were walking right into a spider's web with our eyes closed. We had no idea what dangers were in store for us, and I didn't want to find out. But there was nothing else for me to go back to. My home had been destroyed, and my parents had been murdered by the witch. Miles and his crew were the only people I had left. They were now my family. Lady Felicity, on the other hand, had a strange aura about her.

Why would a stunning noble lady like her be drawn to a struggling captain like him? It doesn't make sense, and why would she be standing there in the middle of the crowd, staring at us? She wants something from him, but what? The others think there is nothing wrong with her, but they're wrong. As a woman, I notice things the men don't or can't, and she is one of those things.

I looked over my shoulder to make sure Mark was still following me as these thoughts flitted about in my head, and noticed a man in all black staring at us from the shadows. An uneasy feeling ran up my spine as I realised he had something to do with Lady Felicity. If he were there keeping an eye on us, she wouldn't be far behind.

He stood next to one of the now-closed stalls, hands clasped behind his back, staring at us. He didn't even blink as he watched Mark hobble his way through the crowd towards me.

"Mark, someone is watching us," I whispered to him as he approached me.

He turned his head and noticed the man. "Let's keep moving. We will be a lot safer when we are back on the ship."

I nodded and kept moving. Tom had vanished by this point because we were moving too slowly. We were getting close to the dock, and I could see The Drifter's masts swaying in the breeze. The lanterns had already been lit to help us on our way.

"Mary, wait. What's that?" Mark asked, pointing to the steps that led to the small beach where John had taken me earlier.

Something white was flapping in the wind, half hidden by the sand. I took Mark's hand and guided him down the steps to the beach. We came across a pair of wet black boots neatly placed side by side on one of the steps. As we got closer, a horrible, dense feeling began to develop in the pit of my stomach. I noticed a wet, debris-covered hand sticking out of the sand. I could see a tuft of brown hair escaping from a mound of seaweed through the white material, which was part of a shirt.

My first thought was of John as I left Mark to walk alone and ran towards the body, which someone had attempted to cover with sand. I kneeled beside it and drew it closer to me to see who it was. It was difficult to tell, but it wasn't John or Miles.

He did, however, appear familiar, and I knew I had seen him somewhere before. His face was green with algae, and his left arm was bent unimaginably, making my stomach turn.

"That's the same man who was being mean to me earlier at the alehouse," Mark paused for a moment, trying to catch his breath. "Why is he here?"

"I don't know, Mark. I think he's been murdered," I said as I lowered him back into the sand.

There were no marks on him, but I knew that he had been murdered. A memory from earlier of Lady Felicity gesturing for one of her men to follow him out sprang to mind.

Did she have him killed, and if she did, then why?

Listening to a strong urge from within, I lifted up the back of the body's hairline to reveal a rank.

"His ranking is Earth," I muttered more to myself than to Mark. "Something doesn't feel right here. Why would someone try and half-cover him in the sand, and why hasn't he turned to ash like the rest of them?"

Mark suddenly grabbed my arm. "Mary, we have to leave right now!"

I looked up to see what he was so scared of and saw a dark figure sprinting across the sand towards us from the other side of the beach.

CHAPTER FIVE

The Diary

My heart leapt into my throat as we both ran for our lives back to the ship. When I looked over my shoulder to see where the figure was, all I saw was the empty beach. There was no one else around, aside from the body still lying in the sand, half-covered by wet seaweed.

I stopped in my tracks and drew Mark back. "They've gone."

"We must keep moving," Mark huffed and dragged me forward to the sand-covered stairs where the boots remained untouched.

"They have to be his, but why are they here?" I asked, confused.

Mark shrugged his shoulders. "I don't know, and I don't want to know until we're safely back on the ship."

He snatched my hand and yanked me up the stairs, not looking back. I couldn't blame him for looking absolutely petrified. I was terrified, and my heart felt like it was about to jump out of my mouth at any moment. I turned again, and this time I regretted it. I could see him now, running up the stairs towards us in an all-black suit.

"Run!" I yelled and shoved Mark forward.

He didn't need to be told twice. He ran as fast as his deformed legs would allow, but I outpaced him. I dashed up the plank leading to the ship and collapsed onto the deck, trying to catch my breath. Mark nearly tripped over me as he reached the ship, collapsing onto the deck next to me.

"Has he gone?" I puffed, struggling to breathe.

"I believe so," Mark said, dribbling slightly as he leaned back on the deck and gazed up at the night sky.

"What on earth have you two been doing?" Miles

screamed from the upper deck.

I sat up, still trying to catch my breath and turned to face the source of his voice. He looked angry as he stood at the top of the stairs, looking down at me and Mark. Felicity stood next to him with a smirk on her face as she placed her hand on Miles' shoulder as if he were her puppet.

I was shocked at first to see Felicity with Miles, but once I was past the initial shock, anger took over.

Why was she here?

I couldn't be bothered with her games and her taunting smile anymore. There were bigger problems to attend to than having to deal with her.

I rolled my eyes at them, no longer caring. "We were very busy."

"You're going to tell me where you've been," he demanded.

Mark looked as if he were about to speak before seeing the stare that I was giving him to shut him up.

"I'm not going to say anything until she's gone," I said, jabbing my finger at Felicity.

Miles groaned and descended the stairs towards me. He motioned for me to join him below deck. Felicity stared at him, stunned, as he left her alone on the top deck. I couldn't help but smirk at her before following Miles below, leaving Mark to catch his breath.

"Where has John gone?" I wondered out loud.

Miles gave me a sidelong glance but remained silent. I could tell he was upset with me, but I couldn't figure out why. He didn't bother coming to find me; I could have been kidnapped or hurt, and he wouldn't have known.

He aggressively pushed open his cabin door and pointed to the chair he wanted me to sit in. I walked into the room and sat down, waiting for him to do the same. He slammed the door shut and stood in front of me, arms folded.

"Well?" he snarled.

I looked down at the floor, afraid to look into his eyes for fear of seeing something that would frighten me.

"TELL ME!" he yelled.

I set down the diary and the key on the table. "We discovered these."

He didn't even bother looking at our findings, instead glaring at me.

"What exactly are they?" he asked.

"I'm not sure what the key is for, but we'll ask Mathew. The diary is from the woman, and it may help us learn more about the cult," I explained.

He slowly nodded, calming down. "I'll read the diary to see if there's anything useful in there. You can keep the key until we figure out what it's for."

"There is one thing that I ask of you, Miles," I spoke quietly, carefully choosing my words.

He perched himself against his desk and leaned into me. "Go on."

I looked him in the eye. "Please do not inform Lady Felicity of our findings."

He stared at me, confused. "Why?"

"I don't trust her, Miles. Please, just do this for me," I urged.

He hesitated slightly before agreeing. "I won't say anything for now, but you need to stop being jealous."

I glared at him. "This isn't jealousy, Miles. I just have a gut instinct not to trust her."

He laughed. "I think you're mistaken. She is not like that."

"Miles, you hardly know her. You've only met her today. We cannot trust anyone at the moment. That man whom Felicity asked to leave, and made her man follow, is dead. "

A worried expression crossed his features. "How do you know that?"

"Because he's lying on the beach a few yards away from your ship. As I said, Miles, don't trust her," I warned.

"Alright, Mary. Have it your way," he muttered under his breath, clearly very annoyed about my remark.

"I'm trying to keep you safe, Miles," I insisted.

"I can look after myself." With that, he stomped away,

leaving me alone in his cabin.

I let out a long sigh and closed my eyes. He no longer made me feel welcome. She had a strong hold over him, but I wasn't sure why. My love for him was fading quickly, replaced by resentment. I didn't want to hate him, but his arrogance was making it very difficult.

I sat up slowly and dragged my aching feet out of the cabin towards the medic's room, hoping to find John resting there. I knocked loudly and was greeted by an order to enter.

Henry sat in the corner of the room, cleaning his medical equipment with a cloth. His bald head gleamed in the candlelight, with his spectacles drooping low, nearly falling off his nose. He raised his head and smiled, his blue eyes crinkling up. He still wore his leather apron, which was splattered with dried blood. His legs were crossed with his thigh-high black boots pointing in my direction.

He cracked a grin as I entered. "It's great to see you, Mary."

I returned his smile. "I was hoping to find John in here."

Henry pointed to the bunk with John's body slumped in it. "He's resting at the moment."

"Is he going to be alright?" I asked, worried.

"Don't be concerned, miss. He'll be just fine. I've extracted all the poison from his blood, but he'll need some time to recover. He'll have to stay here for a while," Henry explained.

"So, he isn't allowed to leave this room?" I asked.

He nodded. "Yes, if he wants to recover. You must persuade him to remain here. He will pay attention to what you have to say." He added with a knowing glint in his eye.

"I can try to persuade him, but he might not listen. There is something I'd like you to do for me," I stated.

He raised his brow as he looked up from cleaning his equipment. "Go ahead."

I took a seat next to him and set the diary on the desk. "I'd like you to read through this and then report back to me on what you discover. No one else, not even your captain, should know."

He picked it up and began flipping through the pages. "How come the captain isn't aware of this?"

"Lady Felicity, another woman, is lurking around him, so, for the time being, I'd like to keep this between us," I explained.

He leaned back in his chair and placed the diary on the table. "It's not a jealousy thing, is it?"

I sighed deeply. "No. This isn't a case of jealousy, Henry. I have a feeling she's planning something. I don't know what it is yet, but I'm sure I'll find out soon."

"Give me a few days to read it, and I'll come find you," he agreed.

"Thank you, Henry." I stood up and walked over to John, who was now snoring loudly in his bunk.

His lanky legs dangled from the sides of the bunk, and one of his arms rested across his face. He was covered in bandages on his arms and legs, and he appeared to be sweating profusely. I stroked his hair as he lay peacefully snoozing, a small smile spreading across his lips.

"He needs to rest, Mary. You also need to rest," Henry advised, watching me from across the room.

I nodded. "I know. You know where to find me when you've finished reading."

With that, I gave John one last longing look before leaving Henry alone to read the diary. Before going to my cabin, I went down to the hull, where Mark was keeping an eye on Mathew.

"We found this key, Matthew, and we need to know what it's for," I asked as I approached him.

He looked up, his eyes gloomy. "It's the key to the manor house, where they all meet once a month. The nobles are given one, but the rest of us are not. We must be on the list in order to gain entry."

I put it back in my pocket. "That's what I assumed. Where can I find this manor?"

"On the bay's outskirts. It's known as Stone Hill Manor.

The house on the hill, surrounded by trees. You can see it from the track," he stated.

I bent down to his level and looked him in the eye. "When is the next meeting?"

"In the next few days, I can take you there, but I cannot be seen," he insisted.

I nodded. "We need to make a plan. Who's next on the list?"

"There's a small lighthouse east of here. A few miles down the road. We will need horses to get to it, as it is marshland. There's a marketman who sells horses around here somewhere."

"Who lives there?" I asked.

"He's an elderly man, but don't underestimate him. He's extremely powerful. He's one of the cult's oldest members." Mathew averted his gaze and focused on a hole in his shoes. "Will you let me go when this is all over?"

I got to my feet and brushed myself off. "Mathew, it's not up to me. It is the captain's decision. When you see the captain again, tell him what you've told me, so he knows what the next step is in the plan. I need to get some rest now."

I turned away from him and walked back up the stairs, away from the hull. I made my way back to my cabin, relieved to finally be able to sleep. My legs dragged as I walked into my cabin. I couldn't even bring myself to take my dress off. Instead, I threw myself into my bunk and wrapped myself in it like a cocoon. My mind drifted off into a deep sleep, unaware that someone was watching me from the doorway.

CHAPTER SIX

Betrayal

The sun streamed in through the open window, sending a warm sea breeze into the room as I awoke. I smiled to myself, feeling more relaxed and less achy within my body.

As I jumped out of the bunk, my stomach rumbled loudly. Another bowl of water had been neatly placed on the table, along with a fresh cloth while I had been asleep. My eye caught a plate of fruit nearby as it released a sweet aroma into the room, making my stomach rumble even more.

I took a banana off the plate and peeled it open. The flavour hit me hard as I rammed it into my mouth. I then grabbed a bunch of grapes and shoved them in one by one, being careful not to choke. The juice burst through its skin, leaving a sweet taste in my mouth. The banana flavour mixed with the grapes left a sensation of wanting more. An apple was the final piece of fruit. As I picked up the apple to admire its smooth, deep red skin, it gleamed in the sunlight. I took a bite and immediately spat it out. It had a bitter and acidic taste, burning my mouth. I examined the apple bite in my hand and noticed a cluster of small black veins etched deep into its flesh.

I turned it around in my hand and examined it more closely. A small pinprick appeared on the apple's surface, with a small amount of black gunk oozing out as I pressed on it. It wouldn't have been noticeable if the taste hadn't been so bitter. Someone had poisoned this apple, and the first name that popped into my head was Felicity. Her taunting smirk clouded my mind as I imagined her standing over my dead body, imitating a look of sorrow to appear innocent in front of Miles. Anger welled inside as I replaced the apple on the plate, staring at the black pigmentation of its flesh, relieved that I hadn't swallowed the bite.

I splashed some water on my face to wake myself up even more, trying to devise a strategy for convincing everyone of Felicity's true callous nature, instead of the innocent, girly personality she had been projecting. I jumped as a knock at the door interrupted my thoughts.

"Come in," I yelled.

I heard shuffling outside the door, and the door creaked open behind me. When I turned to see who it was, all I saw was an empty doorway.

"Is anyone there?" I called out as a pang of anxiety whipped through me, realising that no one was there.

Nothing but the sound of waves greeted me as I poked my head out of the room, scanning the corridor for whoever had knocked on my door.

I shook my head, confused, thinking I must have imagined the knock. I shut the door behind me, leaving the apple on the plate and headed towards the medic room. My thoughts turned to John, hoping that he was awake and feeling a bit more refreshed than when I had last seen him.

I opened the door and walked in before Henry could say anything. John lay in his bunk, but this time he was awake. He appeared tired but healthy. Relief flooded through my body as I grinned at him.

"Hello, you," he smiled weakly.

I returned his smile. "I wanted to make sure you were okay. I stopped by yesterday, but you were sleeping."

He shifted in his bunk, attempting to find a comfortable position. "I'm fine, just a little tired."

I snatched his hand in mine and clutched it tightly. "Henry says you should rest here for a few days."

He nodded slowly and looked me in the eyes. "I can't protect you in this way, Mary. Please be cautious out there. Miles has already spoken with Mathew and is preparing to travel to the lighthouse. He's out now, looking to buy some horses."

"I will be careful," I whispered.

With my other hand, I stroked his cheek and smiled at him. I wanted to tell him about the poisoned apple, but I didn't want to worry him, so I remained silent.

"Where's Henry?" I asked, realising that he wasn't in the room.

"He's gone to buy some more medical equipment as he was running out." John squeezed my hand back and sighed. "I wish I could come with you and look after you."

I kissed his hand gently. "You need to rest here, John. I can't have you flaking on me."

He laughed softly. "That is true. Just keep out of trouble. I hear that Lady Felicity is onboard as well."

Inside, a smidgeon of rage erupted. "She is indeed, but I'm not sure why."

"Just be cautious, Mary," he warned, his eyes full of worry.

"John," I muttered, wanting to tell him that someone had just attempted to murder me.

"Something's wrong, Mary. I can feel it. What's happened?" he asked, his voice growing concerned.

"Someone just attempted to poison me with an apple," I stated bluntly.

My hand started to become clammy within his as I explained to him what had happened. He looked angry as he jumped from his bunk, trembling slightly, trying to regain his balance. He rubbed his face and then took my hand, leading me back to my cabin.

As we got there, the door was wide open. I knew I had closed it behind me, so someone had to have gone in there.

John also noticed the door was wide open. "Did you leave the door like this?"

I shook my head. "No, I remember shutting it behind me before coming to see you."

I held onto him, holding up his body weight, as we entered my cabin, searching for the apple.

The plate and the apple had disappeared, along with the

bowl of water and the wet cloth that I had left on the table.

I looked around the room, knowing deep down that someone had already gotten rid of the evidence. "It's gone, but it was there. There is still a bit of apple that I spat out on the table."

"Mary, I believe you. Who provided you with the fruit?" He asked, leaning against the wall for support.

"When I woke up, it was already on the table," I said.

He closed his eyes, clutching his stomach in pain. "We need to find out who gave you the fruit."

I looked at him, feeling guilty about removing him from his bunk. "John, you need to go back and rest."

He shook his head. "Not until we get this figured out."

"You're up?" A voice spoke from behind.

We both turned to see Tom smiling at us from the doorway. He then noticed both of our expressions, and his smile faded. "What's the matter?"

"Mary was nearly poisoned. Who gave her the fruit?" John demanded.

Tom shrugged his shoulders. "Lady Felicity, I believe. She offered to bring Mary a plate of fruit in an attempt to make amends."

"Make amends by poisoning me," I spat.

"How do you know the fruit was poisoned?" Tom asked, confused.

"The apple was black inside, and there was a pinprick in the skin with a black substance oozing out of it," I explained.

"Well, Miles has just gotten back with Lady Felicity now, if you want to ask her what she's playing at," Tom suggested, uncomfortable with the conversation.

"I will ask her. I will ask her right now," I growled, stomping towards the door.

"Mary, wait for me," John shouted.

I stopped and waited for John to drag himself out of the room. Tom grabbed his arm and supported his weight on his shoulders, helping him to the top deck.

I could see Felicity's arm around Miles's waist, her hand lingering near his hip, as she pointed to one of the horses tied up on the dock.

"That one can be mine," I overheard her say.

"Miles!" John called.

Miles and Felicity turned around. Her smile fell instantly at the sight of me as she saw that I was still alive.

"You should be sleeping, John. What are you doing to him, Mary?" Miles demanded.

I ignored Miles' remark and fixed my gaze on Felicity. "Did you place any fruit on my table?"

She nodded, faking a smile. "I did, indeed. I knew you'd be hungry when you awoke."

"What are you accusing Felicity of now, Mary?" Miles demanded, his voice full of venom.

"She poisoned my apple!" I shouted.

Felicity mocked a shocked look. "No, I did not. I was just trying to be nice, as you seem to hold a grudge against me."

"Mary, you'd better have some proof of this," Miles said through gritted teeth.

"I did, but someone took the plate away from me. The apple was black, and it tasted awful!" I snarled.

Miles laughed coldly. "Mary, it was most likely a rotten apple. You can't blame Felicity for that. She's done nothing wrong."

"Miles, I suggest you listen to Mary. The last time we didn't listen to her, all hell broke loose. I trust Mary more than I would trust a random woman who has pushed her way into our lives," John warned.

"You didn't trust Mary for a long time, John, until you began to fall for her, so don't tell me I shouldn't trust Felicity," he yelled back.

John shook his head in disgust and walked away, pulling me along with him. Felicity smiled smugly at me as she watched John take my hand. I wanted to punch her in the face. Tom stood there, unsure what to do and wishing the ground would swallow him up so he wouldn't have to deal with the situation.

"Mary, you need to stay on deck, as we are leaving soon," Miles called after me.

"I'm guessing Felicity knows the plan as well," I asked.

Miles rolled his eyes, bored with the accusations of Felicity. "Yes, she will be coming with us, like it or not."

I sighed and let go of John's hand. "Go and rest. I will be back soon, and I will come and visit you before I retire to my bunk."

John smiled and stroked my hair before leaving to go below deck. Henry appeared from the dock, holding a sack full of medical supplies.

"What is John doing out of his bunk?" Henry asked, annoyed.

"Mary summoned him to the top deck to accuse Lady Felicity of poisoning her with an apple," Miles stated.

"She did! Miles, why won't you believe me?" I yelled at him.

Henry gave me a questioning look. "Where has the apple gone?"

"Someone took it before I could show Miles," I stated. "I don't know where it is now."

"If it is discovered, I will be able to determine whether or not it has been poisoned. Tom, go through the food scraps we keep on board. I don't believe anyone has yet emptied it. Bring it to me if you find it," Henry ordered.

He put his hand on my shoulder and lightly squeezed it. He then shifted the sack to his other shoulder and descended the stairs below deck, leaving me alone with an irate Miles. For the first time since meeting Felicity, she looked scared.

I hoped Tom would find the apple, so Miles would know that I wasn't lying to him.

Tom also went below deck, obediently following Henry's orders, dragging his feet as he went. I turned around and stepped onto the plank, but before I could proceed, I heard Mark screaming from below the deck.

He appeared at the doorway, puffing for air and sweating profusely. "Captain! Mathew has vanished!"

"How?" Miles snarled.

With a suspicious expression on his face, he cast a glance over his shoulder at Felicity. That's all I needed to know—that Miles was not fully bewitched by her beauty. There was still a little of the Miles I knew left inside him.

"What do you mean he's gone?" Felicity asked, innocently looking at Mark with a fake worried look on her face.

"He isn't inside the hull. His chains are still there, but he's no longer there," Mark slurred, nervously looking around. "There's blood on the floor as well. It appears to be foul play."

"They've taken him," I stated, glaring directly at Felicity.

"But how exactly? Mark, you should have kept an eye on him!" Miles yelled.

"Please accept my apologies, Captain. I hadn't slept in more than two days. I must have dozed off," he begged.

"It's not Mark's fault. You should have transferred him to someone else so he could sleep," I scolded.

Miles fixed his gaze on me, his raging eyes boring into mine. "Don't even get started on me, Mary. We have no one to help us now that they have Mathew."

"I know where to go. Mathew told me last night," I admitted, not wanting to lead the party, but it looked as if I would have to.

"At least we have that in our favour," Miles remarked sarcastically. He then turned to Felicity. "I think it's best if you stay here, Felicity. It could get dangerous."

Her expression changed to that of a child who had just been told off. "But I'd like to accompany you. If it's going to be dangerous, why is Mary going?"

"Because I know exactly where it is," I spat.

"You are a noble lady, and you should not put yourself in danger. Mary is capable of looking after herself," Miles cautioned her.

"All right, I'll stay here," she sighed.

Looking grumpy, she folded her arms and began tapping

her foot hard on the wood, scowling at me as if I had just stolen her man.

"I will make it up to you, I promise," Miles teased, stroking her soft cheek.

She returned his smile and kissed his hand. "I'll be right here, waiting for you."

Another wave of jealousy washed over me as I saw them both smiling lovingly at each other, just as me and Miles used to.

"Come on. Let's go," I snapped and walked away, wiping a tear from my cheek as I walked down the plank to the horses.

The rest of the crew followed me, and I noticed that we had a few new members as well. Miles must have recruited them while I was asleep. There were seven new crew members. Some I recognised from the alehouse, but there were four that I didn't recognise.

The horses were all lined up, tied to a wooden fence that encircled the welcome signpost. I went with a pure white horse with a long grey mane. With its big brown eyes staring deep into mine, it appeared majestic and beautiful.

"Do you need a hoist-up?" Miles asked from behind me.

I nodded without looking at him and stepped into the foothold, waiting for him to nudge me. He grabbed my waist and hoisted me over, tossing my dress over after I sat on the saddle. The saddle felt cold against my legs as I held up the reigns, ready to go.

"Do you know how to ride a horse?" Miles asked.

"My parents used to be horse owners. I used to go horseback riding when I was younger, but it's been a while since I've done so."

"I'll assist you," he grunted.

With that, he hoisted himself over and gently pushed me up the saddle a little further. Felicity's gaze was on both of us as Miles wrapped his arms around me, gripping the reins tightly to keep the horse steady.

Her eyes were venomous. I could even see the veins on

her head protruding from her rage. A small part of me felt pleased with Felicity's expression, but another part of me felt these childish games were too exhausting to continue. I loved Miles, but if it meant giving him up so he could be happier with her, so be it. I didn't want to fight anymore, especially if it was going to cost me my life.

I moved as far away from him as I could on the tiny saddle that kept us so close together, close enough that I could feel his chest against my back. While Tom and Mark stayed on the ship to keep an eye on Felicity, the rest of us rode off up a small street lined with cottages.

It was another beautiful day, with the sun beaming down upon us and the air smelling fresh, and just for a moment, I felt happy in Miles's arms, forgetting about our quest. We trotted through the growing crowd of stallholders to a clearing surrounded by fields as far as the eye could see. Flowers burst forth from the grassy verges, sending clusters of colour in red, white, and purple our way. The view was stunning, with wildlife peering at us everywhere we looked. The galloping of the horses' hooves was like a heart rhythm, beating in time with ours.

"Are you comfortable?" Miles whispered in my ear.

"Yes, I am," I smiled and pointed up a long dirt track that disappeared into a group of trees. "It's this way. Mathew said to stay east."

We rode in silence, breathing in the fresh summer air. The wind blew through my hair and into Miles' face. He rested his head on my shoulder and then flicked the reins to get the horse moving faster. The crew kept up with our speed, with bits of mud flying everywhere from the horses' hooves.

The trees whizzed by in a blur, and some time passed before we saw the clearing leading to the lighthouse. The wooden structure sat on top of a hill, overlooking the sea. It was half-built, with bits of rubble and stone piled up next to it. Up ahead, I could see a small hut with a candle burning on the windowsill.

"Whoa there, girl," Miles said, pulling on the reins to

stop the horse. "We should leave the horses here."

He lifted his leg off the horse and jumped to the ground, making a loud thump. He then grabbed my waist and pulled me off the horse with one swift movement, as if I were a small rag doll. He held onto me a little too long, making me feel uncomfortable with the old emotions returning. I pushed him slightly and slipped out of his embrace. I noticed a glimmer of sadness in his eyes before it vanished, replaced by a small smile.

"We need to stay hidden, so he doesn't know that we are onto him," I said.

Miles nodded. "Let's stick to the trees and then crawl our way to the lighthouse. Are we ready?"

"Yes, Captain," the crew said in unison.

They drew their weapons and prepared to strike whatever monster was lurking inside the lighthouse. We made our way to the tree line, hiding behind each trunk as we scampered from tree to tree, trying to stay hidden. Miles' hands lingered on my waist, and I could hear his heavy breathing behind me. I ignored his feeble attempt to touch me and moved closer to the lighthouse.

As we crawled up the steep hill, the grass felt wet beneath my elbows, sending a chill through my bones. Thorny shrubs protruded from the grass, their tiny needles pricking my legs. A trail of long grass surrounded the hut and the lighthouse, providing us with a little more cover. From where we were, there was no sign of movement. Not even a bird squawk or the rustle of an animal could be heard. Everything lay dead silent.

"We should check the hut first," Miles insisted, moving faster than everyone else.

He cocked his pistol and ran to the hut's edge, kneeling in the mud to remain hidden. He motioned for us to follow him and then edged towards the front door, making sure not to make any noise. He pushed the door open slowly, aiming his pistol in front of him. I moved in closer, checking around to make sure there weren't any vines that could catch us this time. The hut appeared to be normal and empty. Except for the lit candle in the window, nothing seemed out of place. The rest of it was neat, and it didn't appear that anyone lived there. While the rest of the crew waited outside, Miles went through each room.

"No one is here," Miles said, gazing around the room.

"Miles, it appears that no one has lived here in a long time," I said while running my finger across a nearby table, gathering a cloud of dust on the tip. When I showed it to Miles, he agreed.

"Why is there a lit candle in here, though, if no one lives here?" one of the crew members asked.

"I'm not sure, but this doesn't sit well with me," Miles admitted, blowing out the candle.

"Come on. Let's check the lighthouse," I said and took off towards the lighthouse with everyone in tow.

Miles pulled me back behind him. "I'll go first. It could be dangerous. Stay with Bennett."

One of the crew members turned to me and smiled. "I'll look after you, miss."

Miles crept up the crooked stone steps and pushed the door open. The building was still under construction, but the bottom half had been completed. The majority of it was made of thick wood, with stone slabs running up the sides to strengthen the structure. A cluster of vines had begun to climb the sides of the lighthouse but had stopped halfway, dying off at the ends.

I yanked Bennett away from the vines and followed Miles inside. Miles stood in the middle of the lighthouse, stunned. Stone steps had been built into the wall, curling around and up until they reached the top. Because there was no roof yet, I could see the sky shining through the wooden beams and casting shadows across the cobbled floor.

A man's body hung from the middle beam. The holes which should have been eyes were fixed on Miles as he looked up, baffled and terrified of what was hanging above him.

"I don't get it," Miles muttered, feeling disturbed at the sight before him.

The eyes had been hollowed out, leaving a small red crust around the edges. His mouth was agape, tongue hanging out. From what I could see, he looked old, with a long mane of grey hair and a silver beard that touched his chest. His clothes had been ripped, exposing patches of his skin.

"Cut him down," Miles ordered, tearing his eyes away from the man.

Two men dashed up the stone steps to reach the man. One of them began to crawl across the beam in order to cut through the rope and free him. Miles watched as his men steadied themselves, careful not to fall from such a height.

"He didn't do this to himself," I pointed out.

"Well, that's obvious. We need to find Mathew as soon as possible. He would know what's happening," Miles said, his gaze drawn away from the body as the two men carried him back down the stone steps.

"Mathew could be anywhere at this point. He was kidnapped, but someone must have known he was on the ship," I locked my gaze on Miles, who knew exactly where I was going with this.

"Don't you dare, Mary. She has nothing to do with it. He must have been seen when we ported. Stop blaming Felicity," Miles snarled.

He shifted his gaze away from me and knelt beside the old man, checking his neck to see what rank he held. The ranking had been cut away, revealing his flesh underneath. Aside from the four men who stood around unfazed by what was in front of them, the new men Miles had requested stared nervously at each other. They spoke to each other in hushed tones, setting off my alarm bells. From where I stood, I watched them as they hunched together; It was as if they knew exactly what we were going to find.

"How come he hasn't turned to ash like the others?" Bennett asked.

"I'm not sure; perhaps they wanted us to find him this

way. I don't get it. He was a member of their group. Why would they murder him?" Miles looked around the lighthouse, perplexed.

"There's nothing else around here, Miles. We must return to the ship," I said as I took his hand in mine.

In a rage, he yanked his hand away from me. "Nothing adds up, Mary, and you just want to go back to the ship when we need to figure this out?"

"Whatever is going on, we cannot sort it out here. We need everyone to be present," I replied, unfazed by his sudden outburst.

He sighed loudly and rubbed his eyes in frustration. "I suppose you're right. It's just that every time we try and do something, someone is always one step ahead of us."

"So, that means that someone close to us is playing some sort of game, Miles. We cannot trust anyone."

"Let's get out of here. We've been away from the ship for far too long," Miles huffed, irritated that I was right yet again.

Outside, something dark drew my attention. I turned to see a man hobbling up the hill towards us, his face hidden by a cloak tied around his neck.

"Someone's on their way!" I hissed, pushing Miles into the lighthouse's corner. His team drew their weapons and crept behind anything that could conceal them.

Everyone was breathing heavily, fearful that a member of the cult was coming towards us.

"Captain! Captain! Captain!" someone yelled from outside.

I recognised the voice and emerged from my hiding spot to be greeted by a sweaty-faced Mark. I could tell he'd been running by the way he struggled for air. His face was flushed with exhaustion, and he clutched his chest, attempting to breathe and speak at the same time.

"Something has happened," he exhaled loudly. "Felicity is missing, and someone is attempting to murder us. I was able to escape, but I don't know about the others."

"Who is?" Miles demanded, his face flushed with rage.

"I'm not sure who it is. We need to go. It's taken me a while to get here, as I had to run all the way."

"Back to the horses, gentlemen!" Miles bellowed. "We must hurry!"

Everyone dispersed, running down the hill towards the horses, not knowing what we were about to get ourselves into.

Mark grabbed me. "I can't run anymore, Mary. Go without me, and I will catch up as soon as I can."

"I'm not abandoning you, Mark. Could you please run for a little longer?"

His eyes were filled with tears, but he nodded and followed me down the hill, puffing loudly. He continued to stumble, but he managed to keep his balance as he kept up with me. I sprinted down the hill, gaining speed as it became steeper near the bottom. When we arrived, Miles was already on the horse. He grabbed me right away, pulling me up with one arm.

"Bennett, take Mark with you!" Miles ordered.

The horses sensed our fear and began neighing loudly. Their hooves dug deep into the dirt, causing us to lose our balance on top. Miles whipped the reins, and our horse bolted, leaving the crew to fend for themselves.

"Miles, we need to wait for the others. We have no idea what we're getting ourselves into," I shrieked above the wind.

"Lady Felicity could be in trouble. I'm not going to wait," Miles growled as he whipped the reins once more to get the horse moving faster.

I wanted to say more, but I kept my mouth shut. I didn't want to aggravate Miles any more than he already was.

Is Felicity's absence proof that she's on our side? Is this a ploy on her part to make people think she's good? As we rushed towards the centre of the market stalls, questions raced through my mind.

"Miles, slow down. You're going to knock someone over!" I screamed.

He ignored me and continued on, drawing closer to the crowd, knowing that there were children present.

"Get out of the way!" I yelled.

As the horse bolted towards them, people began to look up, shocked. They pushed and shoved each other to get out of the way, terrified that we would mow them down. I could hear hooves galloping from behind us, getting closer. His crew was closing in on us as we entered the crowd and pushed our way towards the docks.

The ship was now within our line of sight, and from what we could see, it appeared to be normal. Miles yanked on the reins to slow the horse and then jumped off, leaving me alone. He dashed up the plank, shouting Felicity's name.

"This is not the time to be jealous," I muttered to myself as I dismounted the horse and tied her to the post.

I lifted my dress to make it easier to run up the plank, almost tripping over it in my haste to prevent Miles from doing anything stupid. As I boarded the ship, I noticed a body slumped against the mast with blood trickling down his arm. When I saw his fiery, coppery hair gleaming in the sunlight, my heart sank.

"No!" I yelled and dashed towards him.

He lay there motionless, with his eyes open, staring out to sea. An empty pistol lay in his hand with gunpowder smoke still blowing from its hole. A big patch of blood stained his right shoulder, increasing in size with each passing second. Floods of tears ran down my cheeks as I started shaking him to wake him up, but deep down, I knew that he was dead.

CHAPTER SEVEN

Death

"Tom, please wake up." I cried, clutching his body.

I stroked his chin and sobbed into his chest as his body lay limp in my arms. Mark could be heard limping up behind me, breathing heavily, but trying to get to me as quickly as his legs would allow.

"Mary!" he slurred as he attempted to kneel beside me and Tom's lifeless body.

"Mark, please double-check the others. Check to see if everyone else is all right," I sobbed.

"Yes, miss," he muttered, trying not to look at Tom's body and went off to find Miles.

The rest of the crew piled onboard, weapons drawn, ready to fight the attackers, but it seemed as if they had already left. Felicity was nowhere to be found, and I couldn't see anyone else either.

"Mary, you should come over here and take a look at this," Miles called out from the doorway leading below deck.

I didn't want to leave Tom alone, but I knew whatever Miles wanted me to see wasn't going to be good. His voice was filled with concern and worry, and he appeared to be on the verge of crying.

"I promise I'll be right back," I whispered into Tom's ear, knowing full well that he wouldn't hear me, but it gave me some comfort to speak to him as if he were still alive.

My eyes were filled with tears—tears for Tom's death, tears for the guilt of not being there to protect him—and my heart ached for him, knowing that he must have died alone. Miles took my hand in his and gently retraced his steps to where he wanted me to look. Halfway down the corridor, I realised that he was taking me to the medic's room, where John and Henry were. Because there was no noise in the room, my heart beat faster, pumping more blood through my veins. I let go of Miles' hand and dashed down the corridor, adrenaline coursing through my veins.

"John?" I shouted as I entered the medics' room.

John was nowhere to be found, and Henry lay unconscious on the floor, bleeding from a gash on his head. His glasses were square on the bridge of his nose, and he held a knife dripping with black goo in his hands. Mark was kneeling beside him, attempting to rouse him. There was blood all over the place and a small trail leading out of the medic's room, as if someone had been dragged out.

"Where's John?" I demanded.

Miles shrugged his shoulders. "I only know as much as you do, Mary. We are trying to wake Henry up so he can explain to us what happened."

He was trying hard not to cry, but a few tears had escaped and were slowly trickling down his cheeks as he stared at John's empty bunk.

Henry began to groan with each touch from Mark as he mopped up the blood from the gash and then bandaged it. His eyes popped open, and he began wrestling Mark to the ground until he realised who he was.

"Calm down, Henry. It's us," Miles said gently. "Tell us what happened."

Henry groaned and rubbed his temples. "Tom had found the apple I had requested. You can probably guess what happened next."

Miles kneeled beside Henry. "Tell me, Henry. Where's John?"

"They abducted him. I'm not sure who it was. I only know Mary was right about Felicity, and I believe it was her men who came for us. They took the diary Mary had asked me to read and smacked me over the head," Henry elaborated.

Miles looked taken aback by Henry's words. "That can't

be right."

"When are you going to admit that I was right yet again, Miles? Eh?" I yelled, rage coursing through my veins as I glared at him. "Look at what's happened. She killed Tom. She's kidnapped John and Mathew, and nearly killed Henry. You should have listened to me from the start."

Miles sat there, baffled. "But why would she do this?"

"All I know is that she is not to be trusted. We need to find John and because of you, Tom is lying up there dead. Let's not wait around for them to kill John as well," I growled.

"You cannot blame me for Tom's death!" Miles screamed in my face.

I shoved him away and retreated toward the door. "He was just a boy, Miles. If you think I was angry before, then you haven't witnessed anything yet. You better find her before I do, or else there will be nothing left of her by the time you get to her. There will also be a proper burial for Tom. He at least deserves that."

The three of them stood there silently staring at me, not wanting to aggravate me any further. Miles sulked in the corner of the room, knowing I was right and he was wrong. Mark stood up and joined me at the door, where he was awaiting his next orders.

Henry pulled himself up and sat shakily in his chair. "The diary didn't have much in it, apart from the events that took place at their monthly meetings. She described in detail how she got in, where she sat, and what they did there. The next meeting is today. I will be of some use to you if you would like me to join."

"We'll need every man that we have to get John back. Grab your things, but go slowly as you've been hit on the head," I cautioned him. I then turned to Miles, who was still sulking in the corner. "Are you coming, or are you going to stand there and sulk all day? You need to be a captain, Miles."

"I'm coming," he muttered, looking ashamed.

"Good. Then help Henry gather his equipment, and we shall use the horses to get to the manor," I said and then left the room while dragging Mark with me. I stopped him halfway up the corridor and whispered. "Before we leave, pick up Tom and put him in his bunk. When we return, we shall give him a proper burial."

Mark nodded. "Yes, miss."

When we got to the top deck, Mark went straight for Tom. With tears streaming down his cheeks, he gently picked him up and carried him over to me. Tom lay in his arms like a sleeping child. I would have assumed he was still alive if it hadn't been for the blood dripping from his shirt.

"Can't we use the locket to bring him back?" Mark asked.

I glanced at him, intrigued. "We will try it when we get back. But for now, he will be put in his bunk. We cannot waste any more time."

Mark did as he was told and took Tom below deck. I turned to face the remnants of Miles' crew, only to discover that the four men I had suspicions about had vanished, leaving us with even fewer men.

I stood there with my hands clasped behind my back, waiting for their attention to turn to me. "We will ride to the manor. We will defeat this cult of Elizabeth's, and we will bring John back alive. That is the plan, and we will stick with it. I need one of you to stay here and guard the ship. The rest of you will join your captain and ride with us to the manor."

Miles and Henry appeared, followed by Mark, in awe of my ability at giving commands. His crew turned to face him, and he nodded, pleased with my plan. They dispersed and mounted their horses, waiting for us to join them. One of them remained on the ship to protect it. I approached him and pulled up the hairline on the back of his neck to see if there was a rank there. There weren't any.

"Good," I smiled.

"Mary! Mary!" A voice that I recognised could be heard from the dock.

When I turned around, Carver and his men were galloping towards us on horses, their pistols drawn, and one of Miles' men in tow. He was still dressed in his captain's uniform, but he appeared to be much younger than the last time I saw him.

"What are you doing here?" I called as I ran towards him.

"William came and found us. We came as fast as we could," he shouted.

"We are in trouble - Mathew and John have been taken. Tom is dead, and we only have a few men left to take down this cult." I explained.

"It's a shame about Tom. I liked that boy. We shall stay and help you," he offered.

I shook my head. "I cannot let that happen. You are meant to meet my grandmother. You know what happens if you alter the course of history? If I hadn't been born, Elizabeth would still be alive and wreaking havoc on everyone."

Carver smiled. "I've already met your grandmother, Mary. We were together last night, but I will spare you the details. You don't need to know them. I will stay and help, and it looks to me that you will need all the help that you can get."

I patted his horse and grinned. "Thank you. Miles will fill you in on the plan, while I'll get everyone else ready."

He took my hand in his and kissed it gently. "Stay by my side, and I will protect you."

"I'm glad that you've returned. I need a friend around here," I replied, glaring over his shoulder at Miles.

He let go of my hand, allowing me to return to my horse. Miles had decided not to ride with me this time and had instead found a brown horse to mount. He looked upset, and I could tell he was still fighting back tears. As he guided the horse to the front of the line to lead his crew, I could see the guilt on his face. Carver moved next to him, and from what I could see, they began an intense conversation.

Bennett dismounted his horse and rushed over to assist me in mounting mine. He helped me up, and because of my dress, I had to side saddle. I knew it would be difficult to ride while side-saddling, but there was no way I could ride properly in this dress. I should have changed my clothes. I knew we were about to engage in another battle, but it was too late now.

"I've brought dynamite with me, in case we need it. My crew has it tucked into their trousers," Carver announced.

Miles smiled. "Good one. That will make it easier for us to blow up the place."

"I think ahead for such occasions," Carver chuckled.

"Are you ready, Mary?" Miles asked, looking up and noticing that I was side-saddling. "You can't go that way. You'll fall off if you don't have someone with you."

He scanned the crew and rested his eyes on Mark. "You can ride with Mary, Mark."

Mark nodded and got off his horse. He hopped onto mine with one big pull and curled his body around me to keep me from falling off. I wasn't sure if the horse could handle my weight and Mark's over-six-foot frame, but it seemed to be holding up well.

"Let's ride!" Miles bellowed and rode off through the narrow street.

The rest of us followed him, moving slowly through the crowd, trying not to bump into anyone as we went. People began to disperse as they saw us approaching. Everywhere I looked, there was a flurry of activity. There was so much life in the bay that it was difficult not to run into someone. Children chased each other around, smiling and playing games with one another while their parents shopped at the stalls nearby. My stomach grumbled loudly as the pungent smell of food wafted up into my nose.

As we passed, I grabbed a loaf of bread from a stall and immediately felt guilty about it. I was starving and didn't have any money to buy food, and I knew the rest of the crew would be as well. I ripped up large pieces of bread and passed them around. The crew gratefully accepted it and stuffed it into their mouths while still holding on to the reins.

We galloped through the extensive undergrowth and shrubs that nipped at the horses' hooves, over the steep hills and never-ending trees, and through the winding dirt tracks with multiple lines of cart wheels indented in them, to reach the manor house perched high on a hill overlooking the bay.

It took us more than a half-day to get there, but we rode with aggression and anticipation in our hearts, determined to find John and bring the cult down. Miles looked more like himself now rather than the sulking child he had been earlier. He even had a determined expression on his face as he led the way over a hill to the woods that surrounded the manor. He slowed to a trot as he waited for everyone to catch up.

"We're going to leave the horses in the woods and start walking from there," Miles ordered.

The woods appeared dark and foreboding, with vines growing down from every tree. I could see a sliver of darkening sky peeking through the gaps in the trees, signaling that time was running out. The ground shook beneath the horses' hooves, and twigs snapped under their weight. I could smell a hint of moss and the wet leaves that lined up in clumps around the trees.

Plants that were once vibrant and green were now a horrible shade of grey, lying lifeless and undisturbed until we trampled over them. Large, round mushrooms sprouted from the trunks, feeding on the bark. The trees twisted and tangled together as if they were embracing each other. A few of Miles' men became tense, twisting and jerking with each strange sound that came our way. Miles moved along the narrow, winding trail, the branches bending and snapping as he moved them out of the way. The darkening of the woods sent eerie vibes through the crew, stiffening their backs in fear.

"Let's leave them here," Miles said.

He dismounted his horse and tied it to a nearby tree before continuing on foot. He didn't bother waiting for anyone else and pushed his way through the shrubbery towards the manor. Mark stumbled as he got off the horse, falling backward into a tree and nearly knocking himself out.

"Go careful," I hissed as I jumped off.

He pulled himself up, using the tree for support, and pulled up his cloak's hood to conceal his face. We all gathered and began our journey toward the manor, terrified that we were about to walk right into a trap.

Miles was visible in the distance, slicing through some tree branches that were in his way. We had to sprint just to keep up with him. As he glared at the manor house through the gaps in the trees, I could see his eyes welling up with rage. The manor's lights streamed out through the windows and across the yard, casting shimmering shadows on the cobblestone path. The darkening sky appeared dull and cloudy, threatening us with rain.

"We need a plan," Carver announced.

"Mary, do you still have that key?" Miles asked, ignoring Carver's remark.

I nodded. "Yes, I do."

"Good. We will split up into four groups and attack from each side. We have to catch them off guard."

"We need to find John and Mathew first," I said.

"While I was away, I was able to learn a few things about the manor," Carver glanced at Miles before continuing. "From what I've heard from a few of the locals, there is a massive cellar beneath the manor that contains cells. If John and Mathew are still alive, that's where they'll be."

"Go on," Miles insisted.

"That's all I've discovered," Carver responded with a grunt.

"I know a few things," Henry called out as he pushed his way to the front. "According to the diary, there is another level beneath the cellar where they perform their rituals.

They first hold a meeting in the hall, and then everyone gathers down beyond the cellar."

"We should pick them off one by one and then strike the rest when they arrive at the cellar," Miles ordered.

"And how do you intend to accomplish that?" Carver asked, his brow furrowed.

"I don't know!" Miles spat and grabbed Carver by the collar. "I am just trying to do the best I can. I don't need you getting in my face about everything!"

Carver calmly grabbed Miles' hands and pulled them away from his collar. "You're the one who's in my face, not the other way around. We need a solid plan, Miles, not one you made up as you went along."

"Carver's right, Miles. We cannot mess this up," I admitted.

"At this point, what else can we do?" he demanded, exasperatedly throwing his arms up in the air.

"We need to tread carefully. John and Mathew's lives are on the line. We must wait until they are all together before striking, preferably when they are underground in the cellar. There should be only one way in and out, giving us the upper hand. Trap them in and blow the place up." I said,

Miles looked at me, impressed. "Alright, that's a better plan than mine."

I looked around at everyone's faces, hoping that they'd all live to see another day. "If Felicity is behind all of this, she knows what we're up to, and they'll all be on high alert."

"Who's Felicity?" Carver asked, bewildered.

"Miles took another woman on board who turned out to be evil and nearly poisoned Mary," Henry said.

Carver glared at Miles. "You just can't seem to stop yourself."

"Let's not go there right now," I intervened, averting a potential fight between Miles and Carver.

"Captain? I think the vines are beginning to move," Mark

trembled beside me.

I knew he was right even before I turned to see what Mark was looking at. It was happening again, exactly as it had at the cottage. The vines protruded from the trees, their vibrant green leaves dripping with black goo, threatening to drip onto our skin. The thorns grew in size, eventually becoming razor-sharp points as they moved towards us, gracefully twisting and turning around each other, slithering across the floor like serpents toward our feet. A fine mist began to form around the trees, swirling and moving with the breeze, its murky white colour camouflaging the vines and making it difficult for us to see.

My feet began to move on their own, dragging Carver along with me and away from the entwined ivy. "Everyone must move slowly away."

"Don't move too quickly because that's how the ivy hunts. It detects the vibrations caused by your footsteps. That was something I read in the diary," Henry explained.

Everyone suddenly stopped, and the vines began to retreat. Only our terrified, deep breathing could be heard. Henry was right, but we couldn't stay here like statues forever. We needed to get moving and save John before it was too late.

"I think the best thing to do is move slowly and stop when the vines start coming out again, or we can try to outrun them," I whispered.

Miles shook his head. "Let's stick with the first suggestion, Mary. On my count, everyone."

He quietly counted down while holding up three fingers. We began to tiptoe slowly towards the manor after he counted to zero. The vines began to pull away from the trees once more, coming to life with the sound of our footsteps. It was as if they had their own minds and could think for themselves. He motioned for us to stop, and the vines began to retreat to the trees.

"This is absurd. If we keep doing it this way, we'll be here all night," Carver snarled.

"What else can we do? The more noise we make, the

faster the vines will follow us. The poison nearly killed John. I can't afford to lose any more of my men," Miles stated.

"We fight back," Carver declared, drawing his sword and preparing to strike the ivy.

"We're going to make too much noise, and then we'll blow our cover. We must do it this way," I reasoned with Carver.

"It's getting too dark out here to be able to see anything soon. We have to fight back," Carver urged.

Then a thought hit me. I still had Miles's father's locket in my pocket. I used it last time when we were underwater and couldn't see. That was when I was with John, trying to save Miles' life. Now I'm here with Miles, trying to save John's life, and he could be already dead, but this locket could help us if only a little.

I pulled it out and showed Miles. "This can light our way."

Miles took it from my grasp and twisted the gyro around on the side of the locket. It began to open, revealing a bright white light that emanated from within and spread across the woods, lighting up every tree that surrounded us. The vines let out a loud, inhuman squeal and backed off, retreating up the trees to avoid the light of the locket.

"Do you remember Mathew telling us to fight their magic with ours?" I asked.

Miles looked at me, stunned by his father's invention. "Yes, I do."

"Maybe we could use this against them? This locket has the powers that Elizabeth wanted. There must be something in this locket that she needs, and maybe we could use it against them."

"But what could it be?" Carver asked.

"Carver, you were with her for some time. You must know something about this locket and why she needed it."

Carver paused and scratched his bushy beard. "I was bewitched, Mary. I can hardly remember anything."

"You must!" Miles hissed angrily. "This could help us."

"I told you, Miles, I can't remember!" Carver yelled, pushing him away in frustration.

"Leave it alone, both of you. We don't have time for you two to fight right now," I hissed at both of them, irritated by their childish behaviour. "We'll figure it out along the way. Carver, if you remember anything, then you need to speak up and not keep it hidden because it might come in handy. Now let's go."

I snatched the locket from Miles' grasp and held it out in front of me to illuminate our path. Every time we passed some ivy, it would curl inward and retreat up the bark of the trees, trying to escape the light. We were using light magic to combat dark magic, and it was working. Even though we had no idea how Miles' father had created such a device, we knew there was light magic contained within the locket. It could have been from Elizabeth's great-grandmother, but I couldn't be sure.

"Mary," Someone whispered from behind me.

I turned to see who it was, but all I could see was the breeze blowing through the trees. My heart raced as we trudged on in silence to the small clearing, where it reverted to a muddy track. Another whisper rang out into the night air, blowing with the breeze as if whispered right next to me. I couldn't tell if it was a man's or a woman's voice because of how the wind carried it, but I did know it reminded me of Elizabeth.

This time, I turned completely around to face the crew. "Who's calling my name?"

Miles and Carver raised their heads, frowning. "Nobody is," they said in unison.

"Someone is calling my name," I said.

"Mary," Another whisper rang out, but this time it was heard by everyone.

The crew sprang into action, unsheathing their swords and dropping into crouched positions, ready to strike. Miles glanced around, trying to find out where the whispering was coming from. Only the sounds of animals could be heard echoing throughout the woodland, sending off an eerie vibe that we were not alone. I could see Miles scanning the area, kicking through the bushes to make sure no one was hiding. Another whisper came, louder this time, and it was definitely a woman's voice. It was someone with a husky, seductive voice, calming us with its presence.

"Show yourself!" Carver demanded, his face growing tense.

CHAPTER EIGHT

Coming Together

A dense fog began to encircle us, nipping at our feet with its icy touch. The last time that this happened was when Elizabeth appeared. As the seconds passed, the fog became thicker, covering half of our bodies with its moisture. My heart began to race as the fog obscured the majority of the crew's terrified expressions. Miles' surprised expression was the last thing I saw before my vision blurred, but he wasn't staring at me; he was staring at something over my shoulder.

"MARY!" he shouted.

"Everyone, stand still. The fog is too thick to be able to see," Carver called out.

"What do we do?" Henry asked, his voice trembling with terror.

"Mary," a whisper called to me, but this time it was from behind me. I spun around, only to be met with a blanket of thick white fog. I shone the locket into the mist, illuminating it with its gleaming essence. A dark shadow stood within the thick blanket of white, showing no signs of life, and then suddenly vanished, leaving the fog swirling around where it once stood.

"There is someone else here," I cried out, my hands and legs shaking with fear. The fear of Elizabeth returning to taunt us again made me petrified.

"I know, Mary. I can see them," Miles hesitated. His voice shook slightly, hinting at his own fear. "What are they saying to you?"

"It's a woman's voice, and all she says is my name, nothing else. I think it might be... Elizabeth..." I didn't want to say her name, but I had a horrible sinking feel that she had somehow returned from the dead.

"It can't be. You killed her. We defeated her! She can't come back!" Miles growled, appearing through the fog with a scowl on his face.

"It's her, Miles. I can sense her," I sobbed.

"Where is she now?"

"She's gone," I said, pointing to where she used to stand.

"Did you happen to see her?" he demanded as he snatched the locket from my grasp and shone it into the fog.

"No, I didn't see her properly, but she was there."

"It couldn't be her if you didn't see her face, Mary. She's dead," Miles scolded.

"It was her, though! Maybe not in physical form, but it was her," I insisted.

"We need to move. If it was her, then she's trying to come back. We must act quickly!" Miles ordered and took off into the dissipating fog, towards the edge of the trees that surrounded the manor's land.

We hustled after him, tripping over every tangled root that poked through the mud. It was as if nature was conspiring against us, slowing us down.

From across the large garden that it occupied, the manor stood before us, tall and menacing. Freshly trimmed hedges surrounded an ornamental pond, with bits of shrubbery protruding from the surrounding area, making it appear slightly cluttered. The large lawns were abundant with wildlife and winding paths that led up to the manor house, surrounded by life-sized bushes that had been trimmed into different objects. Overflowing flower beds dotted the lawns, bombarding us with their sweet fragrance. The manor house looked beautiful, but the evil within it made it look dark and foreboding.

"There are two guards outside," Carver whispered beside me.

"We take them out," Miles grumbled, then cast a glance over his shoulder at us. "Carver, I need you and Bennett with me, and Mark, I need you to stay behind and protect Mary; I don't want her to see what we're about to do."

"Yes, Captain," they all said in unison.

Mark moved aside to let the crew pass, relieved that he didn't have to join them. We followed them, but stayed in the back, dodging and sidestepping the moist undergrowth to reach the lawn's edge. As we got closer, we could see people approaching the door, holding golden keys and dressed in brightly coloured clothing. With their smart, crisp outfits that would make a nobleman jealous, it appeared as if a normal-looking ball was about to take place.

"What's going on?" Carver asked as Miles peered around a freshly trimmed hedge, motioning for everyone to remain hidden.

"It appears that a ball is about to occur; are you certain that this is the correct location?" Miles asked, turning to face me.

I nodded. "Yes, this is the right place; they have the same key as we do."

"Perhaps we should have disguised ourselves a little more," Carver said as he looked down at his clothes.

Everyone who showed up to be let in looked so elegant and formal, with their powdered wigs and long lacy dresses, complete with matching suits, while we were dressed in filthy, scruffy clothes with years of stains on them. If we didn't change into something else, we would stand out from the crowd.

"We'll need a disguise if we're going to blend in," Carver whispered.

"I concur," Miles agreed. "We should take out a few of the new arrivals and take their clothes. Once some of us have disguises, we'll be able to let the others in through the back door."

"The carriages can be seen coming around the side of the manor. There's a small path that leads from the woods to the manor. The carriages can be intercepted there," Carver responded.

"All right, let's go," Miles moved away from the hedge,

leading us back to the woods without a moment's hesitation.

I could hear the crackling of stones being crushed beneath the carriage wheels as they moved one after another towards the manor. Horsemen flicked the reins subtly, causing the horses to speed down the winding track. Their top hats and dark overcoats stood out among the sleek-looking carriages, and they held a black whip in one hand and the reins tightly in the other, only easing on them if the horses were moving quickly enough for their liking.

"How do we intercept them without alerting the others?" I hissed as I watched carriage after carriage appear from the wooded area.

Miles sighed and shrugged. "I'm not sure."

"I've got an idea. Follow my lead," Carver said before disappearing into the darkness of the trees. He then reappeared when he realised no one was following him. "Follow my lead, I said. Come on, let's go."

This time we followed him into the woods, staying on the outline of the trees to find the path, hearing the sound of galloping hooves as we got closer to the carriages. It was now very dark and difficult to see; only the light from the carriage lamps could be seen, casting eerie shadows across the woodland area. I wanted to use the locket again, but I knew that would give us away.

"Carver, what are your plans?" Miles huffed as he tried to catch up.

"The last three carriages will be intercepted," Carver announced as he continued to move through the trees.

"Yes, but how will we do that without alerting the others?" Miles questioned.

"All you have to do is follow my lead, Miles," Carver called over his shoulder.

Carver made his way to the edge of the woods and then hid behind a tree to watch the remaining carriages creep by, quietly following the trail to their destination. Just as we were closing in on him, he picked up a large stick and held it above his head. I could see his eyes scanning the last of the carriages, attempting to time an ambush perfectly.

He waited for the first of the three carriages to approach our hiding spot side by side, and then threw the stick into the wheel, going straight through and hitting the futchel. The axle separated from the wheel with a loud snap. I'm not sure how he did it, but he perfectly hit the wheel to stop the carriage from moving. The coachman yanked hard on the reins to bring the horses to a halt and hopped off his dickey box to investigate the problem.

"What's the problem?" One of the other coachmen called.

The man sighed loudly. "The wheel is shattered. It'll take me a while to fix it, if I can fix it at all."

A woman in a huge heart-shaped wig poked her head out the carriage window, looking agitated. "What exactly is going on?"

The man raised his head from the wheel. "I need you and everyone else to stay in the carriage, madam. It's safe in there. It's just a technical glitch, nothing that I can't fix."

"Well, do hurry up, will you?" she snapped and disappeared back in.

The other coachman jumped off and joined him to figure out what was wrong. He was shaking his head and muttering to himself. "I don't think you'll be able to fix that tonight; I should take your passengers to the manor; if we push this carriage into the trees a little more, we should be able to get around it."

The third coachman got off to see what all the fuss was about, while the passengers complained about how long it was taking. I wasn't sure if the coachmen were involved with the cult, and I began to feel guilty that they, too, would have to be killed. I was hoping that we could spare them, but the look on Carver's expression suggested otherwise.

The man moaned aloud. "My master is not going to be pleased."

"Don't be concerned. We'll do our best to fix it," he

tapped him on the shoulder and bent down to inspect the damaged wheel more closely.

"What should we do now?" Miles hissed, growing impatient.

Carver pressed his finger to his lips to hush Miles and then crept out into the open, taking care not to alert the others. Miles saw what Carver was about to do and dashed out of the woods to meet him. I averted my gaze, not wanting to see what they were about to do, and instead imagined John's smiling face, hoping that it would keep my mind occupied. The sound of scuffling and haggard breaths stopped dead.

"Mary, you may now look," Mark murmured beside me.

When I opened my eyes, I saw Carver smirking. "Weak stomach?"

"Just a little," I mumbled, not looking down at the three bodies on the ground, which were now spewing blood all over the place.

"Let's surround them, lads. They need to take their clothes off first, as we don't want blood on them," Carver whispered.

Tiptoeing around each carriage, both crews awaited Carver's orders. I was surprised that even Miles was obeying Carver without complaining. He appeared tired and weary, and he most likely had no idea how to proceed with our plan. He was just going with the flow, which felt risky. John and Mathew's lives were in danger, and it was up to us to help them.

"One, two, three, go!" Carver yanked open the first carriage, then the others, opening the second and third carriages to a group of stunned passengers.

"Ladies and gentlemen, we are intercepting these carriages and will require your clothes, so please remove them on your way out," Carver scoffed.

They all looked at him, baffled, not knowing if this was real or some type of ridiculous joke. The look on Carver's face made it quite clear that he was deadly serious as he pulled out his pistol and aimed it at the first passenger's head.

"I demand to know who you are!" one of the male passengers said.

"You are not in a position to make any demands, sir," Carver yelled. "Now get out and give us your clothes and wigs, and you will not be harmed."

They slowly arose and edged out of the carriages, terrified and shaking at the sight of being surrounded by big, burly men armed with pistols and swords. Their flamboyant attire was definitely enough to blend in, and I was relieved to be able to change out of this filthy gown and into a nice silk one instead. There was only one woman among them, and she was dressed in a stunning lime green corset dress with white frills hanging from the sleeves.

Her grey wig was heavily powdered, with a few speckles falling gracefully onto her shoulder. Her face resembled a porcelain doll, and her shoes matched her gleaming green dress. She was about my size, which was ideal because I didn't want to be forced to wear a size too large again. The last time I had to wear clothes that were two sizes too big was when I was forced to wear Tom's clothes.

My thoughts turned to Tom and his poor slumped body within his bunk, and I realised that we were not only doing this for John but also for Tom and to avenge his death. The people who stood before me were a part of Tom's death, and they looked terrified by our appearance. I watched them stand there, petrified of what we were about to do, probably knowing that they were about to die, and even though I felt sorry for them, I was also smiling with pleasure.

"I said, take off your clothes," Carver repeated, still aiming his gun at the man's head.

He stood there, sweat streaming down his face and his body trembling with fear. "What are you going to do to us?"

Carver chuckled. "You're making this worse for yourself. Take off your clothes, or I'll shoot."

The man did as he was told and slowly removed his clothes, revealing his undergarments that had been incorrectly buttoned up underneath. He returned to his group after placing the clothes in Carver's outstretched hand.

I noticed the woman smirking as she looked at me up and down. "You're not going to take my clothes."

I approached her, returned her smirk, and yanked her wig from her head. She appeared shocked, then enraged as she attempted to reclaim her wig. I pushed her back into the crowd of passengers, who caught her before she hit the ground. As I placed the woman's wig on top of my head, I could hear Carver laughing behind me.

I smiled at her. "Now I look as ridiculous you."

She stared at me in disbelief. "You won't get away with this. She will know."

I grabbed her neck and yanked her head down, revealing her rank. She was ranked as air, the lowest of the ranks. The others followed suit, ensuring that they were all members of the cult. With the exception of the coachmen, they were all there, which sent a shiver of guilt through my body.

I turned back to face the woman. "Who are you talking about?"

"You've already met her. Every time you say her name, your blood runs cold. She is the one in control," The woman replied, her eyes glinting with mischief.

"What is her name?" I demanded, afraid she'd say her name, but needing to know if Elizabeth had returned or not.

"You don't need me to tell you who she is because you already know," she let out a horrendous laugh, shocking everyone with how loud it was.

"Does Felicity have any involvement in this?" Miles called out from behind me.

She raised her brow at Miles and then back to me. "So, you know Lady Felicity?"

"Yes, we do," I confirmed with a nod.

She took a step away from us, fearful. "We don't want to get into a fight with you if you're involved with Lady Felicity."

She removed her gown and handed it to me, revealing a jewel-encrusted corset beneath. She removed her shoes and pointed to mine. "May I borrow yours?"

I then nodded eagerly as I had an idea. "You certainly can."

Miles and Carver looked at me, perplexed. I drew them to one side and explained my plan to them. "All we have to do is make them wear our clothes and make sure the guards see them. They'll think it's us and shoot." I stated.

"Sure, but how do we get in after that?" Miles asked.

I gave him a sly smirk. "Miles, have you lost your mind or something? We'll sneak in and blend in with the crowd after the guards have gone to check."

"I'm not thrilled that someone else will be wearing my captain's uniform," Carver moaned.

"Then hide your clothes here and come back later. Simply ask one of the passengers to change into something else," I grumbled, becoming irritated by everyone's moaning. "They'll think they've killed us this way. Lady Felicity and a few of her men are the only ones who have seen our faces. They won't realise it's not us until it's too late."

"Mary, that's a great idea. Let's get them into our clothes and then release them. They will run straight towards the manor in an attempt to alert them," Miles stated.

We stopped whispering and returned our attention to the passengers. "We'll swap clothes, and then you'll be free," Carver declared with a sly grin.

They looked at him, unsure whether to believe him or not, but they knew they didn't have a choice given the number of guns aimed at their heads.

CHAPTER NINE

The Cult

Everyone had changed into each other's clothes in a matter of minutes. Carver grinned smugly as he hung his captain's uniform from a nearby tree. "No one will be wearing my clothes."

"Carver, stop being such a jerk and come on," I yelled at him.

He laughed and threw the coachmen's clothes at three of his men. "You will be our chauffeurs."

"Mary, you need to disguise yourself more, and so do I," Miles said, looking around for something to use when he noticed the powder on my wig. "We can use the wig powder to put on our faces, but you'll need something to stain your lips."

"I have something you could use," The lady took a shiny, round metal pot from her small bag tied around her wrist and handed it to me.

When I opened it, one side had a red paste and the other had a white paste.

She indicated the red paste. "That one goes on your cheeks and lips, and this one goes on your face."

She looked at me with desperate hope in her eyes. I knew that she was only willing to help if we spared her life. Her face said it all.

Miles dipped his finger into the white paste and began smudging it across my face. Carver smirked next to him as he watched Miles put on make-up. This was the first time I'd ever put on make-up. Knowing that my face was covered in white powder made me itchy and uneasy. Miles then applied the red stain to my lips, smiling with pleasure at the sight of my face.

"The red suits you," he said, admiring my lips.

I laughed at him. "I wouldn't know, as I can't see it."

Carver came up to me while still sniggering and poked my cheek. "It feels weird."

"You can stop sniggering for a start as you're next," Miles growled.

Carver pushed his hand away. "You're not putting that stuff on me."

"Yes, we are. If you want to blend in, then I suggest you start wiping this on your face. Just miss your beard though, as you don't want it in there," Miles suggested.

Carver sighed and snatched the pot from Miles' grasp. He scooped up a huge dollop from the pot and wiped it all over his face, narrowly missing his beard. With his ghostly features, he looked quite amusing, and he was well aware of it. He burst out laughing as Miles began smearing it all over his face. The rest of the crew got involved, and by the end, there was nothing left inside the pot. We all looked ridiculous, but we blended in just fine, which was exactly what we needed.

"What are you doing here?" The lady asked, intrigued.

"We've come to retrieve our friend," I stated. "Do you have any idea where he is?"

She cast a glance around at the others. "The prisoners?"

"Those two, yes. We're here to reclaim them."

"Then you'd better get moving. Their time is coming to an end," she warned.

"And what about Lady Felicity?" Miles asked.

"Her whereabouts are unknown to us. The head of the cult wears a cloak over their face, so we cannot see who it is, but Elizabeth is returning. There is nothing that you can do about that, and your friends are the ones that will be used as a gateway to bring her back," the woman sneered at me when she saw my expression. "Someone you care for, I presume?"

I ignored her last remark and entered the second carriage, while Carver's men pushed the first one out of the way. Miles joined me and placed his hand on my knee. "We'll get him back, I promise."

"Miles, if he dies, I will never forgive myself, nor will I ever forgive you. He's been your loyal servant for years, and you still didn't believe me or him about Felicity."

He moved his hand away from my knee and slid it to his side. "Mary, we don't know if she's evil yet. We don't know where she is. She, too, could have been kidnapped."

I squinted at him out of the corner of my eye. "Miles, you cannot be so blind. Henry has already informed us that the apple was poisoned by her. She tried to kill me, and you still believe she's good?"

"It could have been a mistake, Mary," he muttered.

"Your foolishness makes you look silly, Miles. You just can't seem to admit that you're wrong," I snapped.

He sighed loudly, irritated by my remark. "You're still young, Mary. You will understand someday."

"I understand that your feelings for her have clouded your judgement, putting your crew in danger and killing Tom in the process. That is something I will never forgive you for. His death is entirely on your shoulders."

"It was not my fault that he died!" he yelled.

"Don't you dare speak to me in that manner. You under-stand, as well as I do, that his death was entirely your fault. You can't deny that you made a mistake, and now is the time to rectify that mistake."

"Mary, I can't bring Tom back, as much as I'd like to," he muttered.

"Miles, we still have the locket, and I will do everything in my power to bring John and Mathew back safely. You promised Mathew that if he helped you, you would protect him. You couldn't even keep your promise."

"Mary, what do you want me to say? That I made a mis-take?" he spat.

"I want you to own up to your mistakes rather than hide behind them. Miles, you're a captain; act like one."

"Have you finished with your argument yet? It's getting

chilly out here," Carver said, poking his head through the carriage window.

"Yes, come in," I said, moving up for him to sit.

"For those of you who are dressed, get in the carriages. The rest of you follow on behind and wait until we have infiltrated the manor, then make your way in through the back. One of us will let you in when we are ready. Remember to place the dynamite in places where it wouldn't be found, and to my fellow cult members, you are free to go. It's getting cold out; you may want to shelter somewhere warm while we commandeer your carriages and clothes," Carver laughed.

He wasted no more time and got into the carriage, making Miles budge up next to me. I felt uncomfortable as his leg touched mine. A while ago, it would have made me have butterflies, but now my feelings for him were tinged with pity and shame. It was shame that he hadn't listened to us and instead followed his heart, resulting in a situation that could have been avoided.

Carver thumped the roof, signaling to our coachman that we were ready. As we sat back in our seats, I could hear the horses whipping and the carriage wheels turning.

"Are you sure you still have the key?" Miles asked.

"Yes, I have it, and the locket is still with me," I responded.

We sat in silence for the rest of the journey, listening to everyone's deep breathing as the carriage rolled towards the manor.

Carver smiled as he peered out the window. "Mary, it appears that your plans are working. They're sprinting towards the manor."

"We must hurry and get there before they do. Step on it!" I bellowed out the window.

The carriage accelerated forward, slamming us back into our seats. The trees whizzed past the window as we moved quickly up the rocky path. A full moon began to appear through the clouds, casting everything in a silvery light.

"No matter what happens, we stick together," Carver

said while looking me in the eyes. "This is a one-way mission. There will be no tampering."

"All I want is for John to get out safely," I muttered.

Miles raised his head, jealousy visible in his eyes as he looked at me from across the carriage. "You move on quickly."

"I believe you had a hand in it as well, Miles. You pushed Mary away to make room for Felicity. You don't know how to properly treat women," Carver stated.

"And you do?" Miles spoke up, raising his voice.

"I am far more knowledgeable than you. I wouldn't have abandoned her for someone else, pushing her into the arms of another man. You are a moron. You lost someone who genuinely cared about you for a woman who only left you when she got what she wanted," Carver exploded.

"Let's not argue about it right now," I sighed, looking out of the window. "Get ready. We have arrived."

Screams and shouts could be heard from the passengers as they ran across the lawn towards the manor. While our carriages pulled up next to the side of the manor house, the guards took notice of the screaming. They went in the direction of the shouting, leaving the front door open for us to enter. As gunshots echoed through the night air, we fled the carriage and ran towards the front door. The screaming stopped, with the stench of death in our nostrils. The air was tinged with the scent of gunpowder. It was hard to run in the woman's green dress, and the wig was so heavy, it felt as if it was about to fall off any second.

The large front door stood in front of us, with stone pillows supporting an arch decorated with delicate-looking flowers emitting a sweet scent. From the double doors, two sleek doorknobs protruded, with an iron keyhole nearby.

"Mary, your tactic worked. Their blood is now on their hands. We must act quickly. Where's the key?" Miles asked.

I handed him the key and took a step back towards Henry and Mark. I noticed a flurry of shadows from Miles' crew making their way towards the back of the manor. Everything was setting into place, while the guards were too busy hunting down their own. We made our way through the front door.

The entrance opened into a large foyer, with lavish styles visible from every angle. Thick red candles had been placed in gold candle holders in all four corners, illuminating the space. A stunning white crystal chandelier hung from the ceiling, casting a long rainbow glow across the walls. Miles led us into the foyer, concealing his pistol and sword beneath his costume. He returned the key to me and proceeded to the first double door.

The carvings on the door were exquisite, with large swirls etched deep into the oak wood, matching the design on the key. He opened the double doors to reveal a large ballroom filled with dancing bodies swaying in unison. Massive paintings in gold wooden frames hung on every wall, staring down at us. The paintings depicted elegant-looking male and female faces wearing the same outfit in each one. Their piercing eyes were fixed on us, watching our every move. Another massive chandelier spiraled down from the ceiling, emitting a golden glow that glinted off the occupants' clothing. Emerald, ruby, and amethyst colours flooded the room, along with glittery jewels that would make a pirate blush with envy.

Laughter and chatter filled the room, and three large carved wood chairs sat at the front, overlooking the guests. Three people dressed all in black sat in the chairs, their faces obscured by hoods, so we couldn't tell who was in charge. Our clothes blended in well, but we needed to do something rather than just stand there looking out of place, or we'd raise suspicions.

"We need to start dancing," Miles hissed next to me.

Before I could respond, he grabbed my hand and dragged me onto the dance floor. The crew immersed themselves in the dance floor, looking for lone women to dance with. I watched Carver become engrossed with a lady dressed in a red silk gown. I smiled and turned to face Miles, who was bowing in front of me. He took my hand in his and began swaying me from side to side. He grinned down at me, his face creasing.

As I returned his smile, I could see a glint of affection in his eyes. There was still something there, and we could both feel it as we looked each other in the eyes. Everything around us began to fade into the background, and it seemed as if there were only me and him in the room. Our bodies entwined, gracefully dancing around the room. An image of John's face entered my mind, my body recoiling from Miles's embrace.

"Everybody, settle down," a woman's voice spoke loud and clear from across the room.

When we turned around to see who it was, we saw one of the hooded figures standing at the front of the room, looking down at us.

"I just got word that our perpetrators have been killed. We no longer have to remain in the dark. There is no longer anyone looking for us," she stated.

Everyone in the room erupted in a loud cheer, celebrating our alleged deaths. From across the room, Carver smirked at me, knowing that our plan was working. Both of the other hooded figures stood up and clapped as they approached the first one.

"We've been waiting for this moment for a long time. Our leader will return to us, and we will hopefully be able to continue with our plan to take over the bay," the other hooded figure spoke up, this time in a male voice that sounded very familiar to me.

Miles cast a glance at me, recognising his voice but unable to place it. As I stared at all three of them, standing next to their chairs as if they were their thrones, an eerie feeling began to take hold of me, making me feel uneasy. They wore robes with the same gold design on the front as the key and the doors. The cult must have existed for a long time without anyone noticing, long enough to design an entire manor house in that time.

The moonlight poured in through the large triple windows overlooking the manor's garden, illuminating the cult leaders. They appeared evil and dangerous as they muttered to one another, while everyone else looked on in awe, wishing to be like them.

"Our prisoner is nearly ready for her arrival. He is the perfect match for her, and she will devour his body. He will spend eternity in the flames of our forefathers," The man boldly claimed.

It took everything I had not to run up to him and headbutt his masked face after hearing him talk about John like that. Nobody will hurt John, and I will make certain of it. Anger welled up inside me as I imagined all the ways I could rip his head off, but something else was bugging me, and that was his voice. I knew his voice from somewhere, but I couldn't for the life of me remember where.

"We'll meet downstairs in the chamber. It's almost time for her to return," the hooded woman stated. "It's now time to reveal ourselves, though most of you already know who we are. For those who don't know, we are the leaders. Our great leader, Elizabeth, is my older sister".

The hooded figures suddenly lifted their hoods, revealing their faces to the crowd. Carver let out an astounded gasp. Lady Felicity was the lady in the middle, which came as no surprise to me. Out of the corner of my eye, I could see Miles looking guilty, edging away from me as he hid behind someone taller than him. The second-hooded figure belonged to a man I didn't recognise. He had dark, piercing eyes and jet-black hair that glistened in the light. His skin was tanned, and his features reminded me of Miles. The third-hooded figure shocked me to the core. There he was, standing with a smile on his face and staring into the crowd.

It was Mathew.

CHAPTER TEN

The Truth

Not only was Felicity Elizabeth's younger sister, but Mathew was also a cult leader. Everything begun to make a lot more sense. They were always two steps ahead of us. It was Mathew who was running the whole thing, leading us around in circles, killing off his own to save the rest.

Then it dawned on me about Felicity's full name, Lady Felicity Amelia Shawl. Elizabeth's last name was Shaw. One of them must have changed their last name to conceal their identity, which also meant that Elizabeth was also noble. Unless it was Felicity who changed her identity.

Mathew, on the other hand, completely surprised all of us. He'd been playing us the whole time. We trusted him. Miles made a critical error, but so did I. Miles trusted Felicity, and I trusted Mathew. We'd both been duped.

"So, it's not just me who makes mistakes," Miles spoke into my ear, smirking.

I gave him a sidelong glance. "Don't rub it in, Miles."

Carver appeared beside us with Bennett. "We need to let in the others."

"We wait until everyone is going downstairs; otherwise, we will arouse suspicion," Miles whispered.

"Now, ladies and gentlemen, let's make our way downstairs. Leave your drinks here. We shall celebrate her return afterward," Mathew shouted across the room, his eyes narrowing on Carver.

The powdered-wig crowd made their way to the double doors. We blended in well, dispersing amongst the crowd and making sure our backs were turned away from Mathew and Felicity so they wouldn't recognise us. The crowd passed through another set of double doors across the foyer that led to the cellar of the manor.

From where I stood, I could see a set of stone steps winding down, with candles encased in glass sconces hanging on the walls. Miles took my hand and led me down the stairs with the rest of the crowd. Carver had gone to let the rest of the crew in through the back door, but Bennett and the others were still with us.

As we descended the stairs below, my stomach felt heavy. Everyone was talking about how much they were looking forward to Elizabeth's return. I could hear Felicity and Mathew talking behind us, putting me on edge. I stared straight ahead, petrified that they would recognise us.

"Are you certain it was them who attempted to attack the manor?" Mathew questioned, his voice trembling.

"Why? Are you concerned that they would discover your true identity?" Felicity laughed. "Mathew, you did an excellent job. You followed through on your end of the bargain, and I followed through on mine. Mary was the only one who was suspicious, but she is now gone. Elizabeth will be delighted."

"They were wearing the same clothes. Miles was among the dead. Everything is working out well," The other leader said behind them.

"They won't bother us any longer," Felicity reassured.

They remained silent for the rest of the way. We passed a small door on the right, which I assumed was where John was.

I pointed to the door quietly. "He could be in there somewhere. We need to go back and retrace our steps."

Miles nodded, and we carried on. Even though my heart was calling out to John, I knew that we had to bide our time. My heart was pounding so loudly in my ears that I was afraid the cult members around me would hear it. As the stairwell opened up into a large cellar, Miles' grip on my hand tightened, and he began to sweat.

The group dispersed into the cellar, encircling what appeared to be an underground well filled with water. The water in the large, circular well smouldered with a vapour that irritated my lungs, making me cough loudly. Except for me, no one else was bothered by the smoke. A cluster of ancient carvings engraved into the stone well pulsed a bluish colour, briefly brightening the room every time they flared. This area seemed more like an underground cave rather than a cellar of a manor. It reminded me of Elizabeth's island.

There were no chairs; there were only carved indentations where you could kneel in front of the well. Everyone found a kneeling spot and took off their wigs, placing them beside them and pulling up their hairline to reveal their ranks, but this time their marks began to glow the same bluish colour as the water well.

"I believe this is our cue to depart," Miles whispered.

He yanked on my hand, dragging d me back up the steps as the cult's last remaining members took their seats. The rest of the crew quickly followed, making sure the leaders couldn't see them.

"Let's move," Miles hissed.

We met Carver and the rest of the crew halfway up the stairs, waiting outside the door that could lead us to John.

"The place is ready to blow. I've put a few next to the entrance of the cellar, so hopefully they will be trapped inside when it blows." Carver announced, looking chuffed.

Miles smiled. "Well done, Carver. Let's blow them to smithereens!"

"Open the door," I said, growing impatient.

"It's locked," Carver said as he rattled the doorknob.

"Then kick it down!" I shouted at him.

He looked at me, shocked by my outburst. "Alright, calm down."

He pushed me out of the way and kicked the door. It didn't budge, but it made a very loud noise that could most likely be heard from the cellar.

"Come on, hurry up," Miles hissed angrily.

Carver groaned and tried again, this time more forcefully. The door collapsed inward, revealing a small corridor with stone-cobbled walls leading to another large opening.

I didn't waste any more time and dashed down the corridor, leaving everyone behind. The corridor led to a small room with another door. I booted the door open and my eyes went immediately to a large iron cage in the center. John sat in the middle of the cage, his head in his hands, quietly sobbing to himself.

"John?" I whispered.

When his name was mentioned, his head shot up. "Mary?"

I dashed towards him, arms outstretched, ready to embrace him. I noticed fresh blood dripping down his cheek as he put his arms through the cage to hug me. His right eye was puffy and black, and a large gash ran down the side of his arm.

"What did they do to you?" I sobbed as I stroked his cheek.

He appeared embarrassed as he looked down at the ground. "At least I'm still alive."

"That is true," Through my tears, I smiled. "A little battered, but still alive."

He smiled back at me. "It's nice to see your beautiful face again."

"Let's get you out of here as soon as possible," Carver said from behind me, making me jump in surprise.

When I turned around, I saw everyone standing in the doorway, waiting to come in. The first person I saw was Miles's envious face as he stared at me and John hugging through the bars.

"Someone is coming!" One of the crew members exclaimed.

"Hide!" Miles yelled and dashed behind the closed door, waiting for whoever it was to arrive.

"Where can we go? There is nowhere to hide!" Bennett hissed, his eyes wide with fear.

"Anywhere!" Miles growled.

Loud footsteps could be heard rushing up the corridor

towards us, causing everyone to panic. Bennett was right; there was nowhere to hide. We were all thinking the same thing, hoping that whoever was coming through that door would only be a few people, enough for us to take down. They would have seen the door that Carver had kicked in and come to investigate.

John kissed my hand and pushed me away gently. "You must leave, or they will kill you."

Carver then grabbed me and pushed me up against the wall as far as he could, breathing heavily in my ear as he stayed still while Bennett blew out the candles, leaving only one lit for us to see.

The door flew open, and three men I recognised as Felicity's guards barged in, their beady eyes scanning the room.

"They're here. I can smell their fear," one of them laughed. "Search the room and prepare our prisoner for Elizabeth."

The two other men moved in the direction of John. He stood in the middle of his cage staring at them with panic in his eyes. He took another step back, refusing to be taken.

"There's no point in you doing that," one of them chuckled as he plucked out a pair of rusty-looking keys from his pocket.

"The rest of you, on the other hand, are completely surrounded. Surrender by laying down your arms," The first man summoned in the darkness. He then resumed lighting the candles, revealing more cult members behind him. "You have two options: do it the hard way or do it the easy way."

Miles and Carver exchanged glances and nods. They slowly took out their weapons and emerged into the light, aiming their pistols at the cult members while smiling. While the rest of the crew joined them, I went to see John, who was cowering in his cage from the guard.

"Move," I yelled at the two cult members.

"They know you're here. There are too many of us for you to take down," The man with the keys said.

"The dynamite," Carver calmly whispered to Miles.

Miles nodded, knowing what Carver was about to do, and laid down his weapons on the floor, except for a dagger hidden in his boot. He motioned for the others to follow his lead. They exchanged puzzled looks but laid down their weapons next to Miles.

"That's better," the first man said, smiling. "Now you can join us for Elizabeth's return. I'm sure she'd be delighted to see you."

He turned on his heel and led us back down the narrow corridor, through the broken door, and into the cellar from which we had just emerged. When I turned around, I saw John being dragged from his cage and hurled up the corridor with force. He was then picked up, and a hood was placed over his face to prevent him from seeing what was about to happen.

"Bring him in when he's ready!" The first man called over his shoulder and closed the shattered door behind him. He led us down the steps, where everyone was expecting us.

"Do you honestly believe we didn't know what your plans were?" Mathew yelled at us from the front of the cellar as he stood next to Felicity and the other leader.

We were pushed in further, allowing the rest of the crew to come in behind us. When I looked over at Miles, I noticed that he was shivering. Carver stood next to him, looking bored, and Henry and Mark stood next to each other, unsure what to do next. Bennett stood beside me, gently rubbing my arm, trying to comfort me but knowing it was pointless. I stood there, stiff and terrified, staring at Felicity's evil smile, her icy blue eyes boring into mine.

CHAPTER ELEVEN

The Ritual

"We knew you were alive. You had a plan, but we have a much better plan. We wanted you to think that your plan was working, and we wanted to coax you here to see our great leader return to us. It'll be a huge slap in the face for you all after everything you all have gone through and the people you had lost to destroy her. Everything that you have done was all in vain, as now she will return to us, but this time she will be even more powerful than before," Felicity smirked.

All three leaders stood beside the well with their robes back on and holding three golden daggers topped with glittering rubies at the top. The rest of the cult members had each found a place to kneel, waiting for their leader's arrival. The area around us was glowing with a bluish hue, emitted not only from the well but now also from the backs of the cult members' necks, pulsing in time with one another.

"You slaughtered your own people just to get us in here?" Miles asked, looking appalled.

She giggled loudly. "They sacrificed themselves for Elizabeth. Don't forget that Mathew knew what your plans were, but what you didn't realise was that Mathew was giving you the details that I wanted him to give you. We wanted you here, and I especially wanted her here." She pointed at me before continuing. "I want you to see that your parents died for nothing, and to make this even more fun, we shall be using someone who you truly love to bring our leader back."

Her words stung.

Was she right about John being the one I truly love?

"She's not coming back," I exploded, shaking the very thought from my mind as I returned my gaze back to her.

She sighed and rolled her eyes. "I recommend that you look behind you, Mary. Whether you like it or not, this will happen."

I didn't want to turn around, but I knew I had to. Between Felicity's evil smile and Mathew's smug face, I wasn't sure which one I wanted to hurt more. I *trusted* Mathew. I protected him from the others, and this is what I got for it. The death of Tom fueled the anger inside of me as I turned around to see whatever Felicity was smiling with pleasure about.

"Mary, please don't turn around," Bennett urged.

"Let her. She needs to see the amazing job we have done for her beloved," The third leader chimed in, grinning from ear to ear.

Two men were holding up John, whose hands had been bound with the poison ivy that had nearly killed him previously. They had ripped open his shirt and carved strange symbols into his stomach that matched what was etched into the side of the well. He still had the black sack over his head, so he couldn't see where he was being taken. Blood dripped from his wounds and onto the floor, staining the stone a dark red. I could hear him groaning as they dragged him from the entrance to the well, where there was an altar table made from stone, ready for his body to be placed upon.

"What did you do to him?" I screamed, returning my gaze to Felicity's smug smile.

"I would have thought that was obvious, Mary," she then turned to John and ripped off the sack that had been covering his face. "Place him down on the altar."

John looked terrified as he glanced around the cellar before his eyes rested on me. "I'm sorry I wasn't strong enough, Mary," he croaked.

The two men lifted him and slammed him onto the altar, nearly knocking him out. Vines then began to protrude from the ground, slithering up the altar and wrapping themselves around his arms and legs like snakes killing their prey. He screamed in agony as a black substance oozed from the thorns, burning through his skin but avoiding the symbols on his chest.

"No!" I screeched and ran towards him, pushing a few cult members aside before being grabbed by Felicity's henchmen, who held me back.

John turned his head to face me, showing the extreme pain that he was in. His towering stature caused his legs to dangle over the edge of the altar, from which he attempted to kick his way free before another swath of vines appeared from the floor, tying him down once more.

Felicity held out her hands in the air and smiled at the cult members, who stared at her with admiration. "Let's begin."

Mathew moved around the well, quietly chanting under his breath, while Felicity closed her eyes and breathed deeply in and out. The third leader was standing in front of John, holding a gold dagger just above his stomach. John squirmed beneath the vines' grip, trying to break free, but he knew it was useless. They were too powerful. The cult members began swaying back and forth while chanting the same strange language that Mathew was chanting, gradually becoming louder. Miles looked at his friend with sadness and regret in his eyes, helpless, as the vines tightened their grip on him. He gasped for air, tears streaming down his cheeks as he stared at me with a mixture of sadness and sorrow in his eyes.

There was nothing I could do but watch John writhe in pain, and the symbols on his chest began to glow with the same bluish hue. The chanting became louder, and the vapour from the well became denser, making it even more difficult to see as the entire cellar began to glow blue, matching the colour of Felicity's icy-blue eyes.

I slithered free of the henchmen's clutches as they stared in awe at the blue hue rising and falling in time with

Felicity's breathing and returned to Miles and Carver.

"Something has to be done!" I whispered as I approached them.

Miles turned to face me. "Mary, what can we do? We are completely surrounded."

"You can't just stand there and watch them kill your best friend." I hissed.

"I've done some calculations," Henry appeared beside me, whispering. "There are enough of us, if Mary is included, to take them all down."

Miles shook his head in disbelief. "Mary will not be a part of this."

"I'll do whatever I want, and if I can help take them all out, you won't be able to stop me," I stated.

"You're so stubborn," he muttered, turning away from me and facing Carver instead. "What should we do?"

Carver stroked his bushy beard in thought. "Well, I'm not quite sure, but we need to do something as John is growing tired."

"You are the one with all the bright ideas, Carver. Think of something!" Miles growled, growing impatient.

I sighed exasperatedly. "You'll launch an attack while I set John free. You two must divert the leaders' attention. We won't be able to use the dynamite until we're safely out of here."

Carver agreed. "Sounds like a plan, but you've left something out. We don't have our weapons."

"Send two of your men to pick them up. No one will notice because they are too preoccupied with resurrecting Elizabeth."

"Alright." Carver then vanished into the crowd, only to reappear a few minutes later with a slew of weapons in his hands. He distributed them among the crew before placing a dagger in my hand.

"Consider this. Use it only if necessary," he whispered.

Felicity's bellowing chants caught my attention, making me jump. The ground beneath us began to vibrate violently. We didn't have much time left, and we were aware of it.

We only had a couple of minutes at most to set John free. The cult was too preoccupied with Elizabeth's return to notice us holding our weapons again, as they swayed in time with the brightening of the blue hue.

"Elizabeth, please come to us!" Felicity screamed, waving her arms erratically above her head.

Things were heating up as the blue hue around the cellar became brighter, and the cult members began to sway violently around, screaming their chants. As John tried to break free, his veins turned purple and erupted through his skin, making him look as if he were about to explode. The third leader pinned him down and held the dagger to his throat, ready to sever his neck if he retaliated.

"Sneak around the back of them, Mary. If you hunch down, they won't notice you, but please stay hidden," Carver insisted, his face solemn as he looked my way.

Before sneaking up behind his first victim, he took my hand in his and kissed it. Miles smiled sadly as he took one last look at me. He then approached Carver, raising his dagger beside him. A sadness eloped my heart. My feelings for Miles were still there, yet a creeping resentment had already begun to overtake my heart, causing a whirl of mixed emotions toward him.

"Mark, please follow me," I said in a hushed tone and dashed toward John, sneaking behind Felicity as she began to hover in the air, just like her sister had done weeks before.

Memories of Elizabeth hovering above 'The Drifter' as she screamed out her spells flooded my mind. Felicity was a lot like her sister; I could see it now. And it made me feel even angrier than before.

Carver was completely right. As Mark and I snuck up behind the third leader, no one noticed us. Before he could plunge the dagger into John, Mark grabbed his neck and threw him across the floor. This gave Miles and Carver the green light to launch their attack on the others.

Screams pierced the air, catching Felicity and Mathew

off guard. As they watched the crew fight back, their eyes widened in disbelief and fear as they realised that Elizabeth may not return as their leader.

I pulled out my knife and started cutting through the vines that held John down. The symbols on his chest stopped glowing and returned to normal, giving me a little reassurance that we had stopped Elizabeth from returning.

"Mary, watch out!" he shouted.

Mathew came after me, attempting to prevent me from releasing John. I used the altar to lift myself up and used all my strength to kick Mathew in the stomach before he could grab me. He flew backward and collided with the wall, collapsing to the floor in a crumpled heap.

"Cut him loose!" Miles shouted from the other end of the cellar.

CHAPTER TWELVE

Carver

When I looked up, Miles was wrestling with one of the cult members, and Carver was chuckling to himself as he launched another one head-first into the crowd. They appeared to be doing well, so I kept cutting through the vines to free John. Screams and bloodshed filled the cellar as gunpowder and violence filled the air.

Felicity ignored everyone and continued chanting loudly, still attempting in vain to bring Elizabeth back from the dead. When I looked down at John, I saw that the ivy I had cut through had grown back, wrapping itself around his body once more. I sliced through it again, this time faster, hoping to free him before it grew back, but it was pointless. Felicity's chanting accelerated the growth of the vines. As she stood over the well, arms outstretched, screaming into it with all her might, her eyes began to roll to the back of her head.

"Mary, just leave me. Go and help the others," John groaned.

"I'm not going to abandon you here, John," I yanked at the vines that were holding him down with gritted teeth.

"Felicity is the one controlling the ivy. Take her out," As the vines tightened around John's chest, he cried out, his eyes filled with pain.

Mark overheard John and made his way straight for Felicity, a determined expression on his face. As Mark approached her, she didn't bother looking up from the well. Instead, she motioned with her hand to her side and pointed to Mark. A large bolt of light emitted from her hand, striking Mark in the chest and instantly knocking him out.

"Mark!" I yelled and dashed over to him, hoping to wake him up.

As he lay motionless, blood could be seen oozing from the gash in his head. I dragged him away from Felicity and propped him up against the altar to keep him out of harm's way. I was terrified, but my rage propelled me forward, adrenaline coursing through my veins as I ran towards Felicity.

This time she looked up; her face was all contorted, and her eyes had turned jet black. She resembled Elizabeth in appearance. Even her hair was starting to turn black, just like Elizabeth's.

"You can't stop me now," she hissed and turned away from me.

I grabbed her by the neck and forced her to face me. "There will be no more bloodshed."

But she was no longer Felicity. She was transforming into Elizabeth, her sister. Her features had changed dramatically in a matter of seconds, and her hands had become old and gnarled. I grabbed her by the cloak and threw her towards the well, trying not to look into her eyes. She lost her footing and fell head-first into it, her screams echoing as she plummeted to the bottom. There was a huge splash, followed by silence.

I didn't have time to double-check that she was gone. I had to free John before the vines suffocated him. Without Felicity's influence, the vines had loosened enough for me to easily cut through them.

I hacked through them one by one, starting with his arms and legs. He snatched the knife from me and ripped through the rest of them with the last of his strength.

Before hopping down from the altar, he quickly hugged me. "Mary, you did it," he said, grabbing my head and kissing it affectionately.

"It's not over yet," I said and grabbed his hand, pulling him away from the altar. "Carver has the whole place rigged with dynamite. We need to get out of here before he blows the whole place up."

We joined Miles and Carver, who by now were sweating profusely and running out of strength as they pushed away one cult member after the other.

"Let's get out of here!" Miles ordered and gathered his men, while Carver continued to push the others away.

"Mark is by the altar. I need two strong men to get him and help him up those stairs." I ordered.

Miles nodded and motioned for two of his men to get Mark. I looked around and noticed that none of Miles's men had been killed, but Carver's men had been hit badly. Five lay motionless on the floor, covered in blood. I knew Carver was going to be angry that he had lost so many of his men, leaving him with only ten.

"Get out of here, you scumbags. I'm going to blow up this place," Carver declared as he fired his pistol into the crowd, covering himself in gunpowder. "Take everyone outside, Miles. When I'm finished, I'll come over and join you. Now get moving!"

Miles didn't think twice and led the way back up the stairs and into the foyer without looking back. The rest of them followed, leaving me and John behind with Carver. I knew that once he lit the dynamite, he wouldn't be able to get out of there alive. I knew it, John knew it, and Carver, by the look on his face, knew it too, but was trying to keep it from me. To save our lives, he was going to blow himself and the cult up. I looked at him, tears welling up in my eyes, knowing that this was the last time I'd see him.

Carver noticed me and gave me an odd look. "What are you waiting for? Leave right now."

"Are you sure?" I asked nervously.

His gaze darted between John and me. "Yes, I'm sure, Mary. Get out of here."

John pulled at my arm. "Come on, let's go."

I yanked my arm away and moved towards Carver, who then gently pushed me back towards John. "I promise you that I will return. Give me a few minutes," he then motioned for John to take me upstairs. "Carry her if you have to."

John nodded and reached for my waist. He threw me over his shoulder as Carver and a couple of his men pushed the cult's last remaining members away from the dynamite so he could light it. The last image of Carver was of him smiling at me as John rounded the corner and climbed the spiral staircase. I screamed the entire time as John struggled to hoist my body up the steps, where Miles stood fuming at the top.

"Hurry up! The place is about to blow," he growled.

"Mary, for once, just do as you are told. I don't have much strength within me to keep holding you," John pleaded as he placed me back down on my feet.

"Okay, fine," I puffed, my throat burning from yelling so loudly.

"I appreciate it," he grabbed my hand and rushed out the front door, with me stumbling behind, barely keeping up with him.

We huddled outside in a group, waiting for Carver. I could tell by the look on John's face that Carver's chances of surviving the blast were slim. As we all gazed up at the manor, waiting for his return, my heart yearned for my grandfather. To keep me calm, John came up behind me and wrapped his arms around my waist. We could hear a rumble beneath our feet, crackling through the ground like an earthquake.

It felt like time had gone into slow motion, with the first of the blasts being heard from inside the building, shattering the glass windows and throwing us backward from the force. A ringing in my ears began, blending everyone's voices into the background. I realised I'd fallen on top of John, who was shouting my name loudly, as a result of the blast. I couldn't hear him because of the deafening ringing in my ears. Flashes of light could be seen inside the manor as the dynamite began to detonate one after the other, completely collapsing the first floor. It lit up the night sky, all those colours of red, orange, and gold blending together as pieces of rubble flew towards us, forcing John to throw himself over me, trying to protect me from the explosions.

There was a moment of stillness before Miles staggered to his feet, dragging me and John with him. "Come on, we need to move back."

As they both dragged my body away from the manor, I couldn't move or speak. I didn't realise I'd been hit by a flying piece of debris until I looked down at my bleeding leg through the silk green dress. As the pain took hold, a scream escaped my lips, a burning sensation spreading up the side of my leg and into my stomach, making me tremble violently.

"She's going into shock!" John shouted over another set of explosions.

"I know. Take your belt off and wrap it around her leg to stop the bleeding," Miles ordered while holding his hand over my screaming mouth, trying to quiet me down.

John did as he was told and ripped his belt off, leaving no time to properly undo it. To stop the bleeding, he wrapped it around my leg and tightened it. Another explosion lit up the sky, ripping a hole in the manor's roof and scattering pieces of slate throughout the garden, smashing into the expensive-looking ornaments.

"Pick up her legs. We need to take her away from this." Miles yelled.

Before anyone could react, a figure appeared in the manor's doorway, staggering out into the garden and collapsing in a heap on the floor. As he tried to stand again, flames engulfed his back. He fell to the ground, allowing the blaze to spread further down his legs.

Through the pain and confusion of the explosions, I could see Carver attempting to flee to safety.

I smacked John on the arm in an attempt to get his attention. "Carver!"

When he looked over his shoulder to where I was pointing, he realised Carver was on fire. He bolted through the garden like a cheetah, ducking and avoiding falling debris as if it were nothing to get to him, forgetting his wounds in an instant as his adrenaline took over. Through my blurry eyesight, I could just about see John dragging Carver away from danger and to safety, where we were all standing, waiting for him. I plucked up enough strength, ignoring the searing pain in my leg, and stood up to make my way to them. Miles realised what I was about to do and gave me a helping hand by leaning most of my body weight onto him so we could both get to them. We left the rest of the men behind, with Henry bandaging Mark and the others standing around.

Bennett followed us, grabbing my left side as he went, helping Miles with my body weight, making it faster for us to get to Carver, who by now had been put out but had been considerably burned by the flames.

"Mary. Where's Mary?" Carver croaked through the smoke that was emitting from his body.

The flames had severely disfigured him, and his clothes had melted to his skin. I looked at him with tears in my eyes, knowing he wouldn't make it.

"I'm here," I announced. I then turned to look at both Bennett and Miles. "Lower me down to the ground."

They sat me next to Carver, who was staring at me with his right eye. His left eye had completely closed, and blood was streaming down his face. He had the aroma of a fireplace, and as I looked closely, I could see the burnt flesh beneath his char-grilled skin.

"You're in pain," he stated as he attempted to lift his head to get a better look at my leg.

I hushed him and smiled warmly, attempting to conceal the pain I was feeling. "I'll be fine."

"Unfortunately, Mary, I believe this is the end for me. I can feel myself fading," his voice slowed to a whisper.

"I know, I know," I softly murmured. "Try not to say anything."

"It's been a pleasure knowing you, Mary. I'm glad that you came back in time to save me from Elizabeth, and don't worry, you will survive. I just wish that I had more time to spend with your grandmother. She was an amazing woman. I now understand why I never came back for her and why she told you stories of what a terrible person I was," he coughed, spluttering up blood through his mouth. "I also wish that I could spend more time with you, too."

I stroked his forehead as tears streamed down my cheeks. "She will be told the truth. I promise."

CHAPTER THIRTEEN

Taken

As I sat there, my life flashed before my eyes, and he slipped away in my arms, his eyes closing for the last time. I knew I'd make it because Carver had met my grandmother just before he came to help us fight this battle. By blowing up the manor and trapping the cult within, he had saved everyone's lives. He was the true hero in this story. For many years, my grandmother had tried to track down Carver without any luck, and now I knew why. He died saving the people he loved.

My heart shattered into tiny little pieces as tears streamed down my cheeks. "I'm truly sorry," I spoke into his ear.

"I'm sorry, Mary. We must leave. Someone's coming," Miles urged, pulling at my arm.

I yanked my arm away. "We can't leave him to rot here."

"Mary, there's nothing we can do for him. He's gone. We need to get going. This place will soon be swarming with onlookers, and we must not be seen, or we will be hung."

I couldn't care less what happened. All I wanted was to avoid leaving Carver in a field where he could be blamed for the explosions and have his name branded, despite the fact that he saved many lives.

Miles looked at John and nodded, knowing exactly what he wanted him to do. They both grabbed me at the same time, and Carver's head slipped from my lap as I was dragged to my feet. I screamed in agony, my leg searing with pain.

"Sorry, Mary, but we have to get you to safety!" Miles thundered.

My body went limp, letting Miles and John carry me across the manor's lawn to the safety of the trees. I became silent and still, staring up at the stars that shone brightly down on us in the night sky. I was gradually losing everyone I cared about. My parents had died at Elizabeth's hands. I almost lost Miles, and now two of my closest friends, Tom and Carver, have died as a result of Elizabeth. Anger welled up inside me as I saw the many faces of my friends who had died bravely flash before my eyes.

It was all over now. The cult had been defeated, but there was a nagging feeling in the pit of my stomach that this was far from over. The survivors of Carver's crew trailed us silently, their eyes filled with pain and defeat that their captain had died to save the others. Their feet dragged across the ground, their hands dangling loosely beside them, as they looked back for the last time at their captain.

"We can't leave him there. He deserves a proper burial," one of them whispered to the others.

They nodded in agreement and slowed down behind us, letting the others walk on.

"Captain, Carver's men are going back for him," Bennett spoke up, breaking the silence between us all.

Miles cast a glance behind him. "Let them. They will join us shortly. If they are caught, then it would be their fault."

"Did Felicity steal your heart as well?" I snapped at him.

He lowered his gaze to mine, disappointed. "It is my responsibility to keep my crew safe. If they want to put their lives in danger, so be it."

"They'll be apprehended and hung," I sobbed.

He walked on with a shrug of his shoulders. "That isn't my issue. They no longer have a captain. They are free to do whatever they want."

This time, John looked over at Miles and shook his head in disapproval. "Mary is correct, Captain. If they are apprehended, we will have to intervene and help. They came to our rescue when we needed it the most."

As we approached the wooded area, Miles sighed loudly. "If we keep interfering in everything, this will never end. I didn't ask for their assistance. I just want to get my men to safety before we start another fight."

We returned to silence. No one dared to argue with Miles for fear of causing him to erupt. He appeared tired and weary as he continued through the trees towards where we had left the horses.

I could hear Mark behind me stirring from his slumber. "What happened?" When he realised he was being carried by four men, he groaned loudly.

"Mark, keep your head still. You've taken a blow to the head," Henry explained.

Mark nodded, still groaning. He fell back unconscious, becoming a dead weight in their grasp.

"I don't know how much longer I can carry him," one of the men said.

"We're nearly there," Miles called over his shoulder as the horses came into view.

The trees opened into a small, well-kept pathway that led down a short hill into an open area where the horses patiently waited for us. They looked up and neighed quietly as we approached, stomping their hooves, ready to make a move.

"Mary will ride with me," John announced, looking down at me and smiling.

Miles scowled when he saw John's smile. "She'd be safer riding with me because you're hurt, John."

"Captain, I'll be fine. She is riding with me."

"You two, stop fighting," I muttered, no longer concerned with who I was riding with.

As Miles and John hoisted me onto one of the horses, gunshots from the manor house rang out, followed by angry yells. Their heads both shot up in the direction of the gunfire and then looked at each other with worried expressions on their faces.

"We have to get moving," Miles said as he climbed onto another horse, allowing John to ride alongside me. "Return to the ship. We'll be safe there."

John nodded and mounted the horse, gently pushing me up the saddle to make room for himself. The others followed suit, eager to carry out their captain's orders. When I turned around, I saw two men throwing Mark over Henry's lap as he sat on one of the horses.

"What about the rest of them?" Bennett questioned.

"There is nothing we can do. We must keep moving. I can't afford to lose any more of my men tonight. If they are apprehended, we will devise a plan to get them out when the time comes. But for the time being, we need to lay low," Miles stated. "Let's ride!" he added, and with that, he rode his horse back down the path to the ship.

The horses' hooves echoed through the night, frightening sleeping birds from their nests. The sun began to rise with dawn slowly approaching over the horizon, casting a bright orange across the sky. As we rode in silence, my head fell against John's shoulder, his left arm tightly wrapped around my stomach, making sure I didn't fall. The pain in my leg was beginning to go away, and I wasn't sure if it was a good or bad thing or if I was losing too much blood. I didn't care if I lived or died at this point, and even though we had defeated the cult, it felt as if it had all been for naught.

The horses sped through the woods, causing the dead leaves to fall gracefully to the ground from the trees. We rode past the ivy, but this time, it didn't come alive and try to snare our feet. The sound of birds tweeting and the rustling of the trees blended into a natural sound that relaxed my body as I tuned into their harmony.

A strong burning odour wafted through the trees towards us, reminding us of our narrow escape to freedom. Carver's men had most likely been apprehended as convicts by this point, leaving us alone to defend ourselves. I couldn't just sit back and watch something bad happen to them. I knew it would be immoral; we had to do something to set them free.

"We can't let them die in the hands of the authorities, John. They will be hanged because of this. They came to help us, not to get blamed for everything. We must help," I pleaded.

"I understand, Mary, but we have to follow the captain's orders. Let's return to the ship first, and then we'll make a plan to help Carver's men."

"Miles is trying to get away from this. We can't sit back and let Carver's men take the fall for this. What would happen to them?"

John sighed and yanked on the reins to slow down the horse. "They would be taken to the holding cells and, most likely, hanged the next day. If we are to assist, we must act quickly. We only have two days," he explained.

I nodded. "Once we return to the ship, we must speak with Miles and persuade him to help them."

I shifted my gaze away from him and out into the woods, soaking in the early morning sun. We passed the wrecked carriage that we had dumped earlier, with the bodies of the two men still lying in the same position we had left them in. Carver's clothes were hanging on a tree next to the carriage, where he had placed them with pride.

"John, stop for a minute," I said and pointed to the clothes. "I want Carver's clothes."

John smiled. "As you wish, Mary."

John quickly pulled on the reins to slow the horse as it galloped up to the tree. He reached out and grabbed the clothes from the branch, gently placing them on my lap before returning to the path to catch up with the others. Everything that Carver had owned was all there, including his large gold buckled belt. His captain's hat had been slightly flattened but could be easily mended by someone who knew how to sew.

"Why do you want them?" He asked as he guided the horse back onto the track.

"I'm going to have them made to my size so I can wear them. He was my grandfather, and I will wear them with pride." I murmured, looking down at the royal blue doublet.

"I'm sure that's what he would have wanted. Hush now, Mary. Try and rest, as you're going to need it," he whispered into my ear before kissing my head.

He was right. I needed to rest. I needed to heal, not only from my leg but also from the trauma that I had endured from losing two of my closest friends.

CHAPTER FOURTEEN

The Unwanted Surprise

I must have followed John's advice because I awoke with the sun streaming down on my face as the ship came into view. John's eyes twinkled in the light as he smiled down at me. As we got closer to the ship, he cuddled my body even tighter, his head nestled into my neck.

He jumped down and wrapped the reins around a pole closest to the ship. Everyone else had dismounted and boarded, leaving us on the dock alone. The dock began to come alive as morning residents emerged from their homes, anticipating the start of the market. It was another beautiful day at the bay, but there was a lingering darkness nearby, something neither of us had noticed. I sensed someone watching us from the shadows but dismissed it, thinking I was being overly paranoid. Everyone had long since gone, buried beneath the ruins of the manor, never to be seen again.

"Come, my lady. Let's get your leg tended to," John said, holding out his arms to catch me as I slipped off the saddle.

"It's not as bad as it used to be," I tested the pain by leaning on it, but there was nothing there. "As you can see, I'm not in any pain."

John gave me a dazed look of bewilderment and lifted my dress to examine my wound more closely. "That's not possible."

"What's happened?" Miles called from the ship as he made his way down the plank toward us.

"Captain, something strange has happened. Mary's wound has healed completely. There's nothing there any-more," John explained and dropped my dress to cover up my leg.

Miles paused, scratching his chin. "That is not possible. She had a lot of blood loss."

"Well, I'm fine now," I said with a smile. I was a little confused as to why my wound had gone, but I felt relieved to not be in pain anymore.

"I'd like Henry to examine your leg. Something doesn't seem to add up here," Miles said as he led me up the plank and onto the ship.

"Where's Mark? Is he going to be okay?" I asked as we headed below deck.

Miles nodded. "He's going to be fine. Henry has patched him up, and he's now resting."

As we walked past Tom's cabin, I was struck by an unearthly feeling that caused me to stop just outside his door. Miles and John came to a halt as they realised I was no longer following them.

"Mary, what are you doing?" John asked, perplexed, before realising it was Tom's cabin. He nodded, understanding what I was about to try and do. Before Miles could join me, John shook his head and placed his hand on his chest. "She wants to give it a shot, just like she did with you."

"Oh, I see," Miles muttered in amazement as I disappeared into Tom's cabin, where he lay peacefully in his bunk.

As I stared at Tom's ghostly features, tears streamed down my cheeks. He was far too young to suffer and die. He was killed while bravely defending the ship by Felicity and her men. I took out the silver locket and placed it on top of Tom's heart, just as I had done for Miles when he died, hoping it would work again for Tom.

"Please work," I murmured as I stroked Tom's cold, waxy cheek.

I couldn't do it for Carver because I knew it wouldn't work for him. I knew his future, but I didn't know I'd be there to see him die. I was glad I was there because I now knew how he died and not the story my grandmother used to talk about Carver abandoning her to raise her child alone. He died saving everyone's lives, and annihilating the evil that had infiltrated Stone Hill Bay.

I walked away, kissing Tom's limp hand and leaving the locket to do its work.

Outside, John and Miles were quietly muttering to each other until they noticed me emerge from the doorway.

"Let's get you to Henry," John gave me a weak smile and took my hand, leading me the rest of the way to the medic's room.

He knocked and walked right in, directing me to an empty chair in the corner. Henry sat in his chair, nib in hand, writing in a leather-bound book.

He spoke without looking up. "How are you doing, Mary?"

"I actually feel quite good," I stated.

He peered over his book this time, looking me up and down. "That's quite unusual. When I last saw you, you were screaming in agony. Let's take a closer look."

He set his book down on the desk and gently grabbed my leg, lifting it onto his lap as he kneeled to inspect my now-invisible wound.

"There's a bowl of water and a cloth over there, John. Can you bring it over?" he asked.

John did as he was told and came over with the bowl. Henry wasted no time in removing the dried blood from my leg, revealing only healthy skin.

"This makes absolutely no sense," he muttered to himself.

"It's completely healed," Miles said as he looked down at my leg in disbelief.

"Mary, what did you do?" Henry asked, confused.

"I haven't done anything, Henry. I only remember being in pain, and then the pain was gone," I said, shrugging.

He lowered my leg again and sighed deeply as he repositioned his spectacles on his face. "I'm at a loss as to why this has happened. Perhaps it's a miracle."

"Is it possible that it was the locket? I kept it tied around my leg after we changed into our other clothes, and it was close to my leg. Miles, since the locket can bring people back from the dead, it stands to reason that it can also heal wounds," I said, impressed by my own suggestion.

"I suppose that makes sense," Miles muttered.

"That's the only explanation I can come up with."

Miles cocked his brow. "If it was the locket, why didn't it heal you when you were injured on Elizabeth's island before?"

"Miles, I'm not sure. I'm not an expert on everything," I growled, irritated by his constant questions.

He looked surprised at first but then smiled. "Okay, miss stroppy. Calm down."

Our conversation was cut short by a loud knock at the door. Bennett appeared with a grim expression on his face, holding a crumpled-up piece of paper.

He handed it to Miles. "We've got a problem."

Miles' face shifted from confusion to fear as he read through it, his eyes quickly scanning the words.

"How is this even possible? She should be dead," his words were barely audible. "I don't believe it."

"What's going on?" John questioned, approaching Miles and peering over his shoulder at the piece of paper.

"She's alive and unharmed," John fumed. "It was all for nothing!"

Bennett noticed my expression and explained. "Felicity is still alive. She was rescued by the authorities, and we are now wanted for murder."

"Where did you find this?" Miles asked, his hands shaking with rage.

"They have been put up everywhere. The word has spread. We need to make sail and get away as far from here as possible. Felicity wants our blood, and she's going to do everything in her power to get it."

"We can't just run away. What about Carver's men?" I asked.

"They are as good as dead, Mary. Even if we wanted to

set them free, we won't be able to get anywhere near them without being recognised," Miles said.

"No one knows what we look like yet," Bennett hesitated for a second but then carried on. "It would be risky, but we could pull it off."

"Bennett, don't be a jerk. We cannot put ourselves in danger for the sake of a couple of men," Miles snarled.

As he sat there sulking, I gave him a dagger stare. "They helped us, Miles. They were putting themselves in danger because of us, but they still did it, and you don't want to help them because it would put you in danger? Stop being so pitiful."

"What do you propose we do? Sneak into the cells and break them free without anyone seeing us? That place is heavily guarded, and we would be shot down within seconds. I have my men to think of."

John shook his head. "Mary's right, Captain. We cannot stand by and let them hang for something that we did. It's immoral, and you know it."

"So, what are we going to do?" he yelled, becoming enraged as we all stared at him, waiting for him to come up with a plan of action.

"We storm in and take them back. We also finish the job of taking out Felicity before she brings her sister back from the dead," John said, ignoring Miles's glares.

"We can't just storm in, John. That's a ridiculous idea," Miles growled.

"Miles has a valid point. Besides, Felicity will now be heavily guarded. We won't be able to get close to her," I confessed.

"Then we do what we do best. Sneak," John stated.

"There are some underground tunnels that connect the jail to the townhouse where Felicity lives. We could move around unnoticed, sneak in, and help them," Bennett elaborated.

Miles gave him a look. "How do you know that?"

"I used to play in them when I was younger. I'll probably still remember my way around."

John smiled, knowing that this was going to go according to plan. "See, Miles. We can sneak in."

Miles pursed his lips and threw his hands in the air like a scolded child. "All right, but this has to be meticulously planned, and we can't afford to make any mistakes."

"This time, we won't make any mistakes," I agreed, looking around at everyone's tense expressions.

"Let's round up the men. We're going in," Miles said.

"Shouldn't we wait until nightfall?" Henry asked.

He shook his head. "No. They will be ready for it. We attack during the day. They won't be as well prepared this way. We need to get out of these ridiculous outfits. The first cabin has some spares." He then turned to look at Henry. "You'll be staying here, Henry. You can sew Carver's old clothes into Mary's size while you wait for us. I'm guessing that's why she's clutching them so tightly to her chest."

I nodded. "Yes, it is. You know me so well."

He laughed softly. "I know you better than you realise," he then clapped his hands together. "Gather the men. We need to change and prepare."

Bennett stopped us by raising his hands. "Shouldn't we move the ship to a safer location first, then return in boats?"

Miles paused for a moment before responding. "It's better to be safe than sorry. We'll drift just offshore, far enough away that the ship can't be seen, and then return on boats."

"We should keep a few men, including Henry, behind to guard the ship," John said, stroking his chin in thought.

Miles headed toward the door. "Prepare the ship, gentlemen. We are going into battle."

His footsteps echoed up the narrow corridor to the top deck as he walked away. We turned to face each other, knowing that this could be the last time we saw each other alive. We all knew it was going to be dangerous and possibly a trap set by Felicity, but we had to give it a shot.

"Come, Miss Carver. Let's get you out of that outfit," John smiled and extended his hand for me to take.

I accepted his hand, and he pulled me up from the chair and led me out of the room, leaving Carver's clothes with Henry. Bennett tapped an unconscious Mark on the shoulder before following us out.

CHAPTER FIFTEEN

Lust And Love

We arrived at the first cabin and stood outside the door, glancing at each other. Bennett realised he wasn't wanted there, so he murmured something under his breath and awkwardly left to find the others.

John turned to face me. "After you, Mary." He then pushed open the door and led me inside.

I stood there staring at him as he ripped open the chest full of clothes and threw them one by one onto the floor, looking for something in my size.

"Ah, yes!" He said, holding up a white linen shirt that appeared to be my size. He grinned as he held it up to me. "This should fit you."

"Thank you," I muttered as he handed it to me.

He then returned to the chest and looked for a pair of trousers for me to wear. He found a brown pair with a small rip down the side and tossed them to me.

"I'll keep wearing these shoes. They're very comfortable." I stated.

He shook his head. "No. Please wait here. I've got something for you. They'll be in your size."

He exited the room, leaving me befuddled and dazed. I wasn't sure what he was going to bring until he appeared a few moments later holding a gleaming pair of black thigh-high leather boots. The silver buckle on the side gleamed in the sunlight streaming in through the window, and they appeared to have been worn only a few times. He placed them gently in my hand and took a sheepish step back.

"Who do these belong to?" I asked curiously.

"They belonged to my late wife before she passed away.

I kept them, as they were the only thing I had that belonged to her. I want you to wear them now. They belong to you." He explained.

I stared at him, dumbfounded. "I cannot wear these, John. These are your wife's. I'm not your wife, so I have no right to wear them."

"I know you're not my wife. You are so much more, Mary. I thought I knew everything about love, but then you came along." He averted his gaze, embarrassed.

"You don't mean that, John. You loved your wife, and you still do."

"I love my wife, but I now realise that I wasn't truly in love with her. In a different way, I adored her. My feelings for you have progressed beyond friendship and what I once thought to be love. Every time I look at you, my entire body tingles. I have to be close to you, Mary."

"What does love mean to you?"

"That's a discussion for another day, I think," His lips curled into a small smile as his brown eyes crinkled, showing me the love that he had for me through his eyes. "I'm not going to let out too many secrets."

"Full of secrets, but unwilling to share anything with me," I smirked playfully.

He took a step back and sat on a chair in the corner. He crossed his legs and folded his arms in defence, looking nervous about what he was about to say. "Look, Mary, we both know we despised each other when we first met. You were too stubborn and wouldn't listen to my orders, but as time passed, I began to admire the traits that had previously irritated me. Your stubbornness turned you into a strong-willed woman, and your willingness to fight for what was right made me love you even more. I have never met a woman like you before, and no, it wasn't love at first sight; that only exists in mythical tales. It was your fierce and determined personality that caught my heart. So, there you have it."

I grinned at him. "That wasn't too hard to say, now, was it?"

He leaned forward in the chair, eager to know my thoughts on him. "And how about you, Mary?"

I chuckled as I tapped the side of my nose. "Wouldn't that be telling?"

"I know you love me, Mary, but I'm not sure why you don't show it. Women are more emotional than men, but you appear to suppress your emotions."

He was right. I was in love with him, but I lacked the courage to express it. I loved him so much that it hurt when he was taken away, and I had no idea where he was or if he was still alive. He was also right about when we first met. He scared me with his masculine ways and abrupt behaviour, but they are now his best qualities. It seemed strange that all we needed was a little time together for our hearts to align, but I also had to admit that my feelings for Miles were still very strong, albeit in a different way. I thought I loved Miles, but I realised it was just lust. What I felt for John was not the same as what I felt for Miles.

John got up from his chair, shaking me from my thoughts. He approached me, drew me away from the wall which I was leaning against, and kissed me softly but firmly on the lips. I tried to get away at first, but he wouldn't let me. Instead, he drew me in closer, wrapping his arms around my waist, stooping lower to match my height. His entire body engulfed mine, leaving me with no room to breathe.

Although his embrace was warm, I could feel the roughness of his chapped lips. I gave up trying to pull away from him and allowed him to open his mouth slightly, enticing me in. This was the first time I'd ever been kissed properly, and it was nothing like I'd expected. I never imagined that my first kiss was to be with a much older man, but here I was, with his hands wandering to places that should have been off-limits to such a man like him.

He drew away, a cheeky grin on his face. "I had a feeling you had feelings for me somewhere in there. I might have to do that every time I want some emotions from you."

Bennett burst through the doorway, noticing us immediately. He looked away, embarrassed that he had caught us. "So that's why it's taking you two so long to change."

"We will be there in a moment," John said, not bothering to look his way.

"You need to hurry up. The captain is waiting, and he's starting to grow impatient," he called over his shoulder as he disappeared up the corridor.

John smiled down at me and gently turned me around to face the wall. He untied the laces on the back of my dress one by one, making my entire body tremble with anticipation. My dress sagged and slipped off my shoulders, exposing my snowy-white skin. He then tugged it downward, allowing it to fall to the floor as his fingers stroked the back of my neck and then moved down, tracing my curves and hips. A low moan escaped my lips as he kissed my neck slowly, holding my arms behind my back so I couldn't stop him.

"Let's get you dressed," he whispered in my ear and then dropped my hands, so I could move freely again.

He took the shirt and drew it over my head, his fingers brushing against my chest as he went. I wanted him to do more, but I knew it wasn't the right time. He stepped back and let me put on my trousers before picking up the boots for me to put on.

"Perfect," he said as he stood there admiring my new outfit.

"Your turn," I teased.

He wasted no time and ripped his shirt off with one swoop of his hand, dropping it in a heap on the floor. His body was toned, muscular yet soft, which I preferred. He snatched a shirt from the chest and pulled it over his head, covering himself back up. He then drew his trousers down, displaying his physique for me to admire. His skin was much darker than mine, most likely due to the amount of time he spent working in the sun.

"Do you like what you've seen so far?" he asked as he

pulled a new pair of black leather trousers up his thighs.

I nodded eagerly. "Yes, I do."

"Is that all? Do I need to go back over there and get some more attention from you?" he joked. He finished putting on his boots and drew me closer, but this time he kissed my forehead and then let me go. "Let's not keep our captain waiting any longer," he said and led me out of the room.

Tom's cabin caught my eye. I immediately pulled away from John and gestured to the cabin. "Before we go, I need to see if it has worked," I muttered.

He waited in the corridor as I entered Tom's cabin, knowing, with a sinking feeling in my stomach, that it hadn't worked. He was still in the same position I had left him in, but he had turned a deathly pale colour. The locket shone brightly in the candlelight of the room.

"Why didn't it work?" I whispered to myself as I stroked his cold cheek. "He deserves to live."

When John heard me blubbering quietly, he burst into the room and hugged me tightly. "I'm truly sorry, Mary," he repeated in my ear; his words comforting me as he squeezed my body against his chest.

Tears streamed down, soaking John's clean shirt. As I slumped into him, he nuzzled his head into my neck, swaying my body back and forth. It felt like an eternity before he finally let go of me and picked up the locket, twirling it in his hand.

"I'm curious why it didn't work," he said as he placed it in my hand. "I'm sorry, Mary, but we better get going. Miles is waiting for us."

I nodded, wiping the tears from my eyes. He gently kissed my hand and led me up to the main deck. The first thing that I saw as we entered onto the deck was Miles glaring at us as he leaned against the middle mast, waiting impatiently for us to appear.

"There's a time and a place for it, and it's definitely not on this ship!" he spat.

"Miles, we were only getting changed," John retaliated.

"From the look on Mary's red face, I'm sure there is more to it than that," he growled, eyeing my face and body for more signs.

"Stop being jealous, Miles. You lost her when you decided to choose another woman who turned out to be just as evil as your deceased wife," John scoffed.

Miles shot daggers at John, his face growing purple with rage. "That's a low blow coming from you. You fell for Elizabeth first."

"Will you both just stop? We are wasting time," I snapped at them both.

Miles scratched the back of his head, embarrassed by his outburst. "Err, yes. All right, everyone, gather around!" he called out as he waved his hands around, motioning for everyone to come closer. He paced up and down the deck, looking around at his men. "Bennett will show us the way through the tunnels, but we must remain vigilant. We have one advantage: no one will recognise us just yet. There are no drawings of us, and no one recognises our faces. We can move around freely for the time being, but Felicity will be on high alert and will use her guards to find us. First things first, we need to move this ship to a safe place. Let's get a move on!"

Everyone dispersed across the ship, preparing it for sail before Felicity dispatched her men. The men set out to work, climbing up and down the rigging, and securing the sails, while John took his place at the helm, ready to steer the ship to safety.

"Do you belong to this crew, Mary?" Miles questioned, his brow furrowed as he leaned in closer, his hands still behind his back.

"Indeed, Captain," I muttered.

"Then I suggest that you get to work and stop dawdling around," he ordered.

I didn't respond, but I moved away from him to climb the rigging to the crow's nest. As I climbed higher, away from the din below, my thoughts turned back to Tom. It was now my responsibility to keep an eye out for danger. Tom had taught me everything I needed to know about the crow's nest, and as I climbed in, I was reminded of him and his boyish ways. This was the closest I'd ever come to him again.

CHAPTER SIXTEEN

The Return of Elizabeth

From where I stood, I could see the endless blanket of blue ocean meeting the horizon as far as the eyes could see. The bay grew further away from us as John steered the ship around the bay's corner, where a small, rocky island lay just off the coast, hiding it from sight. I climbed back down the rigging to where John was standing, retrieving the boats we'd need to get back.

"While we're gone, four of you will stay here with Henry and guard the ship. Make certain that no one boards. The rest of you will board the boats," Miles demanded and jumped into the first one, dragging me along with him. John noticed but said nothing. He continued to push each boat out and began lowering them into the waters below. He was the last to leave, inspecting the ship to ensure that everything was in order before climbing down the rope and onto the boat.

As he stepped aboard, the boat rocked slightly. His balance was off, causing him to stumble on top of Miles. A chuckle escaped my lips as Miles' face shifted from surprise to annoyance, pushing John from him while John grumbled under his breath, attempting to regain his balance.

"John, just sit down, will you? You're going to capsize us in a minute," Miles growled, becoming even more irritated with him as he swayed the boat back and forth, looking for a seat.

He smirked as he sat down between me and Bennett. "Please accept my apologies, Captain."

Miles let out a deep sigh, trying not to laugh. "Now, everyone, grab an oar. Let's get moving. I'm hoping you've all remembered your weapons."

A few of the men nodded, while the others and I double-checked that ours were loaded and ready for whatever came our way. The metal felt smooth beneath my fingertips as I reattached the pistol to my belt. Miles then yanked something from beneath where he sat and tossed it into the middle of the boat, narrowly missing John's head by inches.

"Put these on. There should be some in the other boats as well. I want everyone to put one on," he said as he wrapped it around his shoulders.

I picked one up and examined it. It was a monk cloak with a white rope to tie around the waist. I wasn't sure where Miles had nabbed these from, but it was a good idea to stay inconspicuous.

He noticed the surprise on my face and decided to explain. "I took these many years ago after a raid on a monk's monastery went horribly wrong. I figured they'd come in handy if we ever needed to flee. Nobody ever bothers a group of monks, so we're safe."

"Good idea, Captain," Bennett said, pulling up the hood to cover his face.

The others followed suit, covering their faces so no one could recognise us. Even though we stood out from the crowd, Miles was right in saying that no one would bother a bunch of praying monks. They would turn a blind eye and go about their business as usual. The only person we had to avoid was Felicity.

The waves slammed against the sides of the boats, rocking us back and forth as we tried to stay on course. I couldn't see the ship anymore as it vanished behind the rocky outcroppings, leaving us to fend for ourselves. Part of me wanted to stay onboard and avoid putting myself in danger again, but the other half of me was determined to free Carver's men. I wanted my grandfather to be proud of me and see that my strong and willing mind was a result of his faith in me.

John jolted me from my thoughts as his hand slipped beneath my cloak to hold my leg. He grinned, casting a glance in my direction while the others carried on rowing. At the corner of my eye, I could see Miles watching John carefully, his eyes narrowing into slits as he noticed John rubbing my thigh.

I felt guilty, but then the memory of Felicity came back to me, filling me with rage. Miles didn't care about my feelings when he dribbled over Felicity's feet in front of me. He was the one who put everyone in danger by ignoring me when I knew Felicity was evil and trying to poison me. So, what was it about being with John that made me feel so bad?

I had repeatedly saved Miles' life, but he pushed me away in favour of someone nobler. I also saved John's life by refusing to give up and hunting down the cult in order to free him. But as I sat next to John, my thoughts turned to me and Miles and what it would have been like if I had gone through it with him.

What if things had been different?

Miles' expression showed that he still had feelings for me, and I could tell that seeing me with John hurt him a lot. I shifted my gaze away from Miles and toward John. The sun shone brightly in his eyes, turning them a light brown rather than the typical dark brown they usually were. The stubble on his face aged him in a good way, as it made him look manlier and sculpted his face perfectly. His tanned skin glistened with sweat as I sat there admiring his handsome face. He noticed and winked at me, turning my cheeks a bright red.

"There is no need for you to be embarrassed, Mary," he smirked. "I enjoy seeing you admire me now and then. It demonstrates that you have feelings."

He squeezed my thigh and laughed a deep, throaty laugh, turning Miles' face even uglier with rage.

"You weren't supposed to notice," I explained, looking away.

"People will notice, even if you try to hide it, my dear

woman. Humans notice everything, even if they are unaware of it at first. Do you really believe that none of us could see the way you look at him? Your eyes tell us more than your facial expressions," Bennett laughed.

Everyone stared at me, nodding in agreement with Bennett, and my face turned crimson.

"Oh," I muttered, averting my gaze from all of their stares.

"It's pointless for you to try to hide your feelings for John in front of us," Bennett stated, gesturing toward John.

John gave Bennett a look to silence him and took his hand off my leg. "That's enough, Bennett. Everyone knows that Mary and I have feelings for each other. Let's leave it at that."

"Hoods up, everyone. We're here," Miles ordered, trying to hide the pained look on his face as he stared ahead.

We approached the dock with the scent of dead fish wafting up our noses. Moss grew around the dock's posts, emerging through the waves. The waves pushed us deeper under the dock than was necessary, guiding the boats through driftwood and rubble that the tide had brought in. Miles grabbed the rope and tied it to the side of the boat to keep it from drifting away. It thudded against the rocks beneath the dock, tempting the boat to sink.

"Arm yourselves, lads. We're going in. Bennett, lead the way," Miles stepped off the boat and onto a shoddy ladder attached to the dock's side. We followed him up and formed two lines, our hands clasped together as if we were praying. Miles led the way, standing at the front of the two lines, and headed into the centre of town.

Everyone's attention was drawn to us, but none of them bothered to approach as we silently moved through the crowd. The plan was working; we were ahead of schedule, giving me just enough time to grab an apple from one of the stalls. As I hid it beneath my robe, John cast a glance my way and chuckled to himself.

We kept our heads bowed and moved slowly, weaving

through everyone to get to the town hall, where the sewage drain would be. I peered through my hood to see where we were going and noticed that a few of Felicity's men were surveying the scene, keeping an eye out for us. My heart thumped, making me nervous about the prospect of being apprehended, and hung alongside the rest of them. I thought back to Mark and was rather glad that he was resting in his bunk, as I knew that he would insist on coming with us.

That's what Felicity's men were looking for. Mark would have stood out like a sore thumb, jeopardising our position and sending us straight to the gallows. Everyone here knew how to fight, and while I was the weakest member of the crew, my mind was the strongest, which was exactly what Miles needed. He needed a woman's point of view, and it was me who saved everyone's lives that day when I destroyed Elizabeth, ridding the world of her and her evil ways.

We crept down an alleyway into a courtyard surrounded by tall, stately buildings with high-top chimneys towering over us, belching out black smoke. A stone water fountain with marble gargoyle ornaments stood in the centre of the courtyard. There was no one else here. The guards stood on the outskirts of the courtyard, immersed in looking for us in the throng of people, leaving us to sneak into the tunnels without being seen. As we got closer to the fountain, our steps echoed across the courtyard, bouncing off the perfectly sculpted marble building in front of us. It was the drain system that we were looking for. It was made from rusted iron and branded with the cult's mark.

Miles looked at it, perplexed. "It has cult markings on it. What does this mean, Bennett?"

Bennett looked down at it, horrified. "I had no idea that these tunnels belonged to the cult. I was only a child when I played down there."

"Does this mean the cult is older than we first thought?" I asked.

"I'm not sure, but I do know one thing for certain: we can't trust anyone. If Elizabeth's cult has a tunnel system beneath the jail and town square, we can only assume that the authorities are also a part of the cult," Miles stated.

"Let's get it open before we get caught," John said as he bent down to remove the drain's head.

Miles noticed him struggling and kneeled beside him to assist. "We must tread carefully and stick together, despite our differences. Agree?"

"Agreed," John tensed up as he tried to pry open the drain cover.

It eventually gave way, causing John to fall backward and land on his back, still holding the cover.

"I'll go first to make certain that the coast is clear. Don't come down until I tell you to," Miles gave me a stern look before leaping into the hole, pistol drawn and ready to fire. I took a step back and waited for Miles to call us down.

"Quartermaster, someone is coming this way!" one of the crew members hissed behind me.

John started to panic and called down to Miles, but there was no response. He shrugged his shoulders. "So be it. Everybody, get in now."

He grabbed my shoulders and pushed me down into the hole. I fell in and landed awkwardly on my ankle. I let out a small yelp as I scurried away to make room for someone else to pass through. They appeared one by one in the tunnel, leaving only John to pass through. John's legs appeared first, followed by his body. He dangled from the hole, reaching for the cover to replace it.

"Could someone please hold me up?" He yelled as he struggled to keep his grip on the opening.

One of the crew members stepped forward and took hold of John's feet, balancing them on his shoulders as John drew the cover back over to cover our tracks.

John lost his balance, tumbling off the man's shoulders and landing hard on the floor. He smacked the floor in frustration and stood up. "Thank you, Billy," he grumbled as he glared at him.

Billy averted his gaze from John, embarrassed. "I'm sorry, sir."

John brushed himself down and then looked around, observing the old tunnels. They were made to perfection, with carvings that matched the cult's symbols strewn across the walls and etched deep into the surface. Even though there were no candles to guide us, there was a source of light. The symbols were casting their blue glow across the stone floor.

"This place is strange," John said, turning in circles, admiring the tunnel.

"I remember this now," Bennett muttered under his breath as he traced his finger along one of the glowing symbols. "I used to like how these would glow, but I had no idea what they were."

"That is, until now," Billy murmured as he watched Bennett stroke the symbol on the wall with care.

Miles appeared from around the corner; his face flushed with rage when he noticed us standing around. "I told you to wait up there until I said the coast was clear."

"Yes, we are aware of that, but someone was approaching, and I had to make a quick decision, and I chose to get everyone in the tunnel before we were seen," John explained.

"You've gone against my orders, John," Miles snapped, approaching us with a thunderous look in his eyes.

"I had no choice but to get everyone to safety, Miles. It was a spur-of-the-moment decision. Either get caught and imprisoned or escape and carry on with our plan."

"If you disobey my orders again, I will relieve you of your duties."

I stepped in front of Miles, locking my gaze on him. "This is not the time to start this. Set aside your differences and work together to bring down the largest cult the human race has ever seen. Keep your opinions to yourself and start acting like our captain instead of allowing your jealousy to take over."

Miles returned my stare and took a step closer to me. "Step carefully, Mary, or you'll be kicked out of this crew and out on the streets. Your feelings for John are clouding your judgement."

"Back down, captain," John growled, appearing beside me with a glare in his eyes.

Miles turned to John and sneered. "You're the one who should be doing as I say, not the other way around." He then glanced over his shoulder at his crew and said, "Let's get moving." He turned on his heel and walked back down the way he came, with a strut in his stride. It was as if he enjoyed talking down to me and John.

While the rest of the crew followed their captain, John drew me to the side. "Mary, ignore him. He's just envious. He'll settle down."

"He shouldn't be speaking to you like that when you've made the right choice."

He nodded. "I know, but let's just try to stay on his good side for the time being."

He took my hand in his and followed the others, who had vanished around the corner. The tunnels were identical to each other, but Bennett knew where he was going. He checked for markings that he had left on the wall as a child so he wouldn't get lost. We had caught up with the rest of them as they turned another corner into a larger tunnel, etched with more symbols to light our way.

This tunnel was a little different from the others in that it had two small openings that led into another set of tunnels, most likely leading to different parts of the bay. We passed them and continued on our way until we were interrupted by voices coming from the top of the tunnel.

Bennett looked up, terrified. "Quick. We must hide."

With a panicked look in his eyes, he pushed Miles backward, ushering him back the way we came. Miles drew his pistol while peering over Bennett's shoulder to see who was approaching us. Bennett pushed us inside one of the small openings to another tunnel as the voices grew closer and clearer.

"Find them," the voice of a woman hissed.

As I heard her voice echoing down the tunnel, my blood ran cold. My body began to shake violently as she continued to speak in hushed tones to whoever was with her. When John noticed my trembling body, he gave me a concerned look and mouthed her name to me.

I barely managed a nod as I said her name. "Elizabeth."

The expression on Miles' face said it all. He appeared to be both terrified and enraged. They all did. Bennett was shaking his head in disbelief, refusing to believe it was her, but my gut instinct told me it was her in the flesh. All the time and effort spent tracking her down and destroying her was for nothing. The countless deaths that had happened because of her would most likely happen again if we'd let her live.

Another voice rang out through the tunnels; this time it was Felicity's. "We are doing everything that we possibly can to hunt them down, but their ship has vanished and there's no sign of them anywhere. I think they've gone into hiding."

"Well, I suggest that you have your men search the entire bay; otherwise, I shall hold you personally responsible if this goes wrong. I'm not fully formed yet, and it's going to take time for this to work. If they are still out there plotting against us, we don't have time to mess around. She's destroyed me once, Felicity. She can do it again if we don't remain vigilant."

They both walked past our hiding spot, unaware that Elizabeth had just given us the power to destroy her once again. If she wasn't yet fully formed, then this time it would be easier for us to take her down. She appeared to be the same as the last time I saw her, but she was much frailer, giving us an advantage. Her obsidian black eyes scanned the tunnel as she sniffed the air loudly. She was still wearing the same tattered red dress she wore previously, but this time it hung from her body rather than hugging her curves. She looked older. Her jet-black hair was greying in places, and the skin on her face peeled with each word she spoke.

But it was Felicity's expression that shocked me the most. Her youth and beauty had vanished, making her look just as old as Elizabeth. One side of her face was mangled with burned scar tissue from the explosion caused by Carver, and the other was wrinkled. She wasn't the Felicity we remembered. She had transformed into a blonde version of her sister with the exception of her eyes, which had remained the same icy blue instead of turning the deep, dark black colour that Elizabeth's had.

"That will not happen, Elizabeth. I've sacrificed my beauty to bring you back, without the assistance of anyone else. Mary won't be able to get anywhere near you. This place is heavily guarded, and I'm sure that they are long gone by now. I have the authorities working for me, and they are out there searching for them. I told the authorities some stories about them being pirates and destroying my home and wanting my valuables, while I was presenting the biggest ball that the bay had ever seen. They bought it."

"Good, we need as many people with us as we can get," Elizabeth said.

Their voices trailed off, leaving us with as much information as we needed. We all breathed a sigh of relief at not being caught and stepped back into the tunnel. We were all in shock, unable to speak for some time, scared that they would be able to hear us.

Eventually, Miles was the one who spoke first. "I did not see that coming."

"Let's not panic just yet. We took her down once; we can do it again," I said, ignoring the heavy, dense feeling in the pit of my stomach.

John nodded in agreement. "We now have a competitive advantage. Elizabeth is unaware that we know she is alive and that she has also provided us with information on how to destroy her. We now know that the authorities have been fed a slew of lies and believe we are the bad guys."

"We can discuss it later. We need to get moving before we are noticed," Miles stated.

"It's too late. I can hear them approaching," Bennett hissed in fear. "Come on, let's go. We must get moving!"

He bolted, leaving us behind until we realised what he was saying. The voices became more audible as they echoed back down the tunnel towards us. We needed to move quickly without being noticed.

"Tread quietly," I whispered to everyone as we tip-toed as fast as we could around the corner and out of their sight.

Bennett was waiting at the other end of the tunnel, ushering us to hurry up. We moved quickly yet quietly as the voices grew nearer. As we approached a panic-stricken Bennett, he pointed up above him to a drain cover that looked identical to the one we had come through.

"The cells are above us." He whispered.

"Is there another way in? I need to know how many guards there are before we go in." Miles asked.

Bennett shook his head. "There could be, but this is the only way I know that leads to the cells."

"We must act quickly. They'll be here in a minute," John stuttered, becoming agitated with the sounds of Elizabeth and Felicity approaching.

"We have to take a risk then. Weapons at the ready, I'll go up first, and then you will follow," Miles ordered, cocking his pistol back, ready to fire. He then looked at Bennett. "Help me up."

Bennett kneeled to allow Miles to climb on his back and hoist himself up. Miles then slowly lifted the drain cover, being careful not to make any noise. He peered through the slit he had made, fully lifting the cover, when he realised there were no guards nearby. The cells were empty.

"They aren't there. Where else would they be?" he questioned Bennett, looking down at him.

"There's another set of cells on the opposite side of the building. They could be in there." Bennett replied.

"How do we get there from here?"

"I'm not sure. Our safest bet would be to climb up there

and get to the other cells."

"They're almost on us; get moving!" John snarled.

Miles didn't argue and hoisted himself all the way to the top, disappearing through the hole. Everyone waited in line, while the voices of Elizabeth and Felicity could be heard just around the corner. John grabbed my hand and lifted me up, allowing me to grab the edges of the hole and pull myself up. John was the last to arrive, giving us only a few seconds to replace the cover before Elizabeth and Felicity appeared from around the corner.

"What was that ruckus?" Elizabeth shouted loud enough for us to hear her through the drain cover.

Fortunately, they didn't notice the drain cover move as their voices trailed off once more, this time at the other end of the tunnel. John stood up, exhaling a sigh of relief. He was perspiring profusely, with tiny trickles running down his brow and glistening in the candlelight of the jailhouse. On each side of the room, there were four empty cells lined with rotten-looking straw. A plate of mouldy food sat in one of the cells, attracting the attention of rodents. Because of the salty sea air, the iron bars had rusted and could be easily bent to break someone free. There were doors on either side of the dingy-looking room, leading into two narrow corridors.

"Where from here?" Miles asked.

"I'd say we keep to the left. So, we should go through that doorway," Bennett said, pointing at the left door.

"Why do we have to stick to the left?" Miles asked, his brow furrowed.

"The other cells are on the left side of the building, next to the gallows. So, it makes sense that we keep to the left," Bennett explained.

Miles nodded and motioned with his hand for Bennett to go first. With our weapons drawn and determination in our eyes, we set off through the left doorway, hoping that whatever was on the other side wouldn't expose us to the guards.

The corridor was dark, with only a few small candles affixed to the wall to guide us. Miles' hands were trembling as he followed Bennett closely. The rest of us stepped back slightly in case something came our way. My thoughts returned to Elizabeth and Felicity. If Felicity had died in the explosion for which Carver had heroically died, Elizabeth would not be alive. Fears from the past began to resurface, leaving me feeling empty and numb inside. I didn't have the energy to destroy Elizabeth again. I nearly died the last time I tried to kill her.

As we approached the other door, everyone slowed down. It was painted a dark red with a gold-gleaming handle that reminded me of Elizabeth's gown. The door matched the rest of the corridor's decor, which was various shades of red and gold, as opposed to the jail cells, which had dingy wooden walls and mouldy straw on the floor. This section of the building appeared elegant and sleek, most likely for the nobles who visited here.

"What's behind this door?" Miles asked.

Bennett hesitated with his hand placed on the handle, ready to open it. "I'm not sure, Captain. The only way to find out is to open it."

Miles pushed Bennett aside and pressed his ear against the door to listen. Within seconds, his eyes grew wide as he backed away, terrified.

"Someone is coming," Miles hissed in fear.

"We can't hide. Gentlemen, hold your ground," John gave the order as he drew his pistol from his belt. With terror and fear etched on our faces, we stared at the turning door handle. The door clicked, and a man dressed like a judge in a white powdered wig and a long scarlet robe with a black girdle entered the corridor, looking startled when he saw us. Bennett slammed the door behind him as John grabbed him and dragged him into the corridor.

He pushed him against the wall with his collar and hissed in his face. "Say anything, and I'll kill you."

In defence, the man raised his hands, pleading with us not to hurt him. John's grip loosened slightly, but his hands remained around the man's neck.

"I'm going to ask you a few questions, and you'll answer them." John forewarned.

The man nodded but remained silent, terrified that John would kill him.

"Good," John said as he let go of him, "Where are Carver's men imprisoned?"

The man shakily pointed at the door. "Through that door, it leads to the cells. They are being held there, ready for the court to decide the outcome. I've just come from there."

"So, you decide their outcome?" I asked behind John.

The man peered over John's shoulder at me and slowly nodded, knowing what I was going to say next.

"You will set them free," I said sternly.

He shook his head. "I'm afraid I can't do it. I've already given them their punishment. They're getting ready for the gallows."

John grabbed him once more and threw him against the wall. "You're going to set them free. They haven't done anything wrong. It was us, not them, who blew up the manor. There was a reason why we did it."

"For what purpose? Lady Felicity was almost killed by you. She is a well-respected member of the court."

John laughed. "Do you have any idea who she really is? She's a member of Elizabeth's cult."

The man looked at John, puzzled, but with a twinkle in his eyes. "The witch?"

"Yes. Elizabeth's sister is Felicity. Elizabeth is currently in the tunnels beneath us, plotting to take over this court-house." John elaborated. "Felicity has deceived you all. We blew up the manor to prevent the cult from resurrecting Elizabeth."

"Sir, we are not evil. We're attempting to keep Elizabeth from taking over the bay. I've already destroyed her once, and I intend to do so again. You must release Carver's men. They have committed no wrongdoing," I stated.

"If what you're saying is true, then how long do we have?" he asked.

"A day at most," I said.

"What makes you think I should believe you?" he questioned John with scepticism in his eyes.

"Let me put it this way. If you don't believe us and have us hanged alongside Carver's men, you'll have no one to defend you or the bay when Elizabeth and her cult take over, enslaving everyone and killing innocent people who defy her," John replied, smirking.

"Or you could believe us and release Carver's men, allowing us to continue destroying Elizabeth and her cult before she becomes too powerful to be destroyed. We overheard her saying in the tunnel that she was still very weak," Miles said, joining in with John.

The judge stroked his chin in deep thought. "I usually go with my gut instinct, and my gut tells me to trust you. I'll accompany you to the cells and free your men. You must remain in the shadows because you do not want people to know who you are."

John took a step back and extended his hand. "I'm John, the crew's quartermaster. This is Miles, our captain, and this is our crew."

There was a slight glare from Miles as John shook the man's hand. "My name is Edmund Lawrence. Judge Lawrence."

"Take us to our men," Miles said as he pushed open the door for Edmund.

Edmund did as he was told and opened the door, leading us into a large, brightly lit room full of chairs stacked on top of one another. The room was the same colour as the corridor, with a splash of dark red and gold and the smell of dampness. A dusty-covered chandelier hung from the ceiling, swaying slightly in the breeze from an open window opposite the door.

"This used to be the courtroom, but it was moved to the other side because it was too small for the number of convictions that were taking place," he explained before turning right and entering another corridor through another door.

We passed a door on the right as we rushed through the corridor. Miles stopped and pointed to it. "Where does this lead?"

Edmund retraced his steps and started opening it. "This will take you to a storage room. It's chock-full of previous convictions as well as information on the law and bay rules."

The door refused to budge. He tried again, shaking the door handle. "That's unusual. I believe it has been locked."

John ushered him out of the way and proceeded to test himself. While twisting the door handle, he slammed his shoulder into it. "It's not locked. There is something against the door on the other side."

He shoved the door again, and this time it opened. He pushed whatever was on the other side of the door away, allowing us to go in. He was the first to notice it, coming to a halt just outside the door, his eyes wide with fear. He couldn't speak, but he had a familiar expression on his face that I recognised.

"What is it, John?" Miles asked, placing his hand on John's tense shoulder.

He still didn't say anything or move. He just stood there, mouth agape, staring at whatever was behind the door.

CHAPTER SEVENTEEN

Sister's Strength

"Get out of the way." Miles pushed John to the side to get a better look at what he was afraid of.

The same expression that had appeared on John's face had now spread to Miles's face like a disease. Edmund looked at them both, unsure what was going on. I moved Miles to the side and peered in, knowing deep down that I had seen something similar before based on the expressions on both of their faces.

There in the corner, propped up against the wall, was what appeared to be one of the guards. He had been half-drained. One side of his face was normal, but the other appeared to have been melted away by something or someone. His legs had been keeping the door closed until John shoved them away with force. The last time we saw something like this was when Elizabeth began draining people in order to become healthier. This was her doing, and we all knew it.

"Edmund, I think you should come take a look at this. Maybe you'll believe us now," Miles said as he stepped aside to allow Edmund to look.

As he took a step forward, Edmund's eyes twitched from side to side at each of us. He was trembling uncontrollably, and dribbles of sweat were dripping down his face.

His eyes widened in terror as he looked at the guard slumped in the corner, then back at us in disbelief.

"What happened to him?" he stuttered.

"This is exactly what she does. If she's doing it now, she's already getting stronger. Who knows how many more she's drained?" Miles said with a raised voice.

"We must keep moving. Let's close this door and get out of here," Bennett muttered, becoming increasingly agitated with each passing second.

We shut the door and walked away from the half-mutilated corpse, saying a quiet prayer under our breaths.

Edmund stopped and turned to face us. "I now believe you. What can I do to assist?"

"Please keep us safe. Lock this place down without Elizabeth and Felicity knowing," John stated.

Edmund nodded slowly, deep in thought. "I can keep you safe, but I don't want to be involved in murdering someone; otherwise, I'll be just as bad as the convicts I've sentenced."

"You can either think of this as murdering someone or you can think of this as saving hundreds of people's lives by taking two people down," I stated, bluntly. "She must be destroyed."

"How about Lady Felicity?" He asks. "She is a noblewoman with a large following. She has numerous assets all over the country. If she does not return, someone will notice. Can't we spare her and instead sentence her?"

I glanced at Miles and John, waiting for their approval. They both nodded, so I carried on. "She can be sentenced, but we will need to make sure that she's either fully locked up or dead, depending on the sentence you give her."

"I may not be the one to sentence her, but I will see that it is done correctly," Edmund responded with a look of determination on his face.

The men exchanged handshakes before we continued up the corridor to find the others. Edmund didn't stop for a second to see who was behind the next door; instead, he stormed into the room and began to look around.

"Sir, are you alright?" a voice rang out from across the room.

I peered around the door and saw two men standing guard at the entrance to the next section of the building. The room was large and had the same decor as the first one, but there was no dampness in it this time.

Edmund nodded and moved closer into the room, waving his hand behind him for us to follow.

"These are my guests, and they will be treated as if they were noblemen. Do you understand me?" Edmund spoke sternly, his voice shifting to a much more instructive tone.

"Who are they?" the guard questioned, his weapon raised.

"You are just a guard. You don't get to ask questions," Edmund snapped at him.

Before speaking, the guard's eyes twitched from one person to the next, observing us intently. "Lady Felicity has requested that she be notified if any new guests arrive here today. What should I say to her?"

"Let me remind you, sir, that I am the judge of this high court, and you must obey my orders. You will not inform Lady Felicity that I have visitors; otherwise, you will end up in a prison cell. You must notify me once Lady Felicity has returned. In fact, I'd like to have this place secured. No one, including her, goes in or out. Do not make it obvious that the court is under lockdown, and refrain from gossiping as well. Do you understand?" he demanded.

He stood up straight with his hands clasped behind his back, trying to intimidate the guard by making himself appear taller.

The guard saluted and returned the weapon to his belt. "Yes, sir."

"Felicity should not be trusted. Keep her occupied until I return," Edmund then motioned for the guards to move out of his way with a wave of his hand. They exchanged nervous glances before stepping out of the way to let us pass, but they kept a close eye on us as we entered the cell room.

The room was much larger than I had anticipated. On each side, there were six cells with exhausted-looking prisoners. The room had the same earthy odour as the previous one, and straw lined the floor, soaking up the urine from the prisoners. The cell bars appeared to be newer and tougher than the previous cells I had seen. I immediately recognised Carver's men in the room's final cell. They appeared tired and haggard as they sat on the floor, waiting to die. They didn't bother looking to see who had entered until Miles shouted after them. They turned their heads to the sound of Miles' voice, getting up when they realised who we were.

"We thought we were going to be goners," one of them said as we made our way to them.

Edmund pushed his way through and took a position near the front of the group. "Open this cell," he gave the order to the two guards, leaning against the back wall, looking bored.

One of them looked at him, puzzled, but did as he was told and handed Edmund a bunch of keys.

"I instructed you to open it," Edmund ordered, his tone aggressive.

The guard shrugged and turned away from Edmund. He rummaged through the keys until he found the one he needed and unlocked the cell. The men each smiled eagerly at the crew, a look of relief on their faces.

"Welcome to the crew," Miles said, shaking one of their hands.

"What's the plan now?" John asked, nervously peering over his shoulder at the door.

"Captain, Elizabeth and Felicity are on their way for the men!" Bennett hissed as he stormed into the room, panic setting in.

"Quick, Edmund, where can we hide?" Miles demanded.

Edmund looked around for a hiding spot and noticed a door at the far end of the cell room. He indicated it with his finger. "Quick. Get in there quick."

He yanked open the door and ushered us all in, including Carver's men, who looked terrified at the prospect of Elizabeth's return. Edmund pressed his finger to his lips and hushed the guards, who stared at us blankly. He then drew the door close, enough to cover us but open slightly so we could hear their conversation. The prisoners stood in their cells, interested in what was going on, their eyes filled with excitement over potential bloodshed.

Elizabeth rushed into the room. Her face filled with rage once she noticed Carver's men had vanished. She hissed as she pointed to the empty cell with her gnarled finger. "Where have they gone?"

Felicity staggered into the room, looking even worse than the last time we saw her. She appeared old and frail, whereas Elizabeth appeared young and full of energy. She was no longer recognisable, with the body of an elderly woman, as she walked over to stand next to Elizabeth.

"Lady Felicity?" one of the guards asked with a face full of fear as he stared at her decrepit face.

She nodded, her face solemn. "It is, unfortunately, me."

Elizabeth smirked. "She looks different, doesn't she?"

The guard nodded slowly, returning his eyes to Elizabeth. "Who are you?"

Her eyes narrowed into slits as she stared at him, unable to believe he was defying her. "I'm her sister, so you will do as I say."

She then returned her attention to the empty cell, twirling the keys around her finger as she spoke. "So, I'll ask you again. Where have Carver's men gone?"

His eyes twitched slightly in the direction of where we were hiding, but he remained silent, not wanting to offend his judge. Elizabeth didn't notice and kept twiddling the keys until they fell to the floor with a thud. Felicity clung to one of the cell's bars, attempting to keep herself from collapsing. I could hear her muttering something as she struggled to breathe.

Elizabeth turned to her. "What did you say?"

"They've gone, I said. I think I need to go somewhere and rest," she puffed.

Elizabeth grabbed her arm and whispered something in her ear before she could leave. Felicity nodded, her shoulders drooping from exhaustion. She stayed by Elizabeth's side. Whatever Elizabeth had said to her had caused her to stay rather than go off and sleep. Elizabeth was draining her, and she knew it. The prisoners remained silent, petrified that her attention would turn on them.

She returned her gaze to the guard. "I'm going to ask you one last time, and if you don't answer, you'll pay the price," she said while staring at the two guards. "What happened to them?"

"They've been set free," he stated.

Felicity's head jerked up. "Why? They blew up my manor. They were sentenced to death by hanging today."

"All I know is that they were set free just before you arrived. We have no idea where they are right now," he elaborated.

Elizabeth's lips twitched slightly with a small smile. "If they were released just moments before we arrived, they would have passed us on their way out. You're deceiving me, sir," she jabbed her finger into his chest.

As her eyes began to turn black, a fearful expression spread across his features. "I'm speaking the truth, miss."

"Then where have they gone?" she growled as she moved closer to both of them.

They both looked at each other, unsure what to do or say, but they knew that if they told the truth, they would not only be in trouble with the judge and could be hanged but they would also be killed by Elizabeth herself.

"We are telling you the truth, madam. We have no idea where they have gone," the guard stuttered.

His hand slowly moved to his pistol, ready to strike her if she lunged at him. She noticed and smiled sweetly. "That's of no use here."

He returned her smile, unsure of what she meant, and reached for his pistol. She held her breath and let him shoot her in the chest. As she stood there, evilly smiling at him, a black-looking substance began to appear through her red dress and spread slowly up her chest.

He stared at her, terrified and puzzled as to how she hadn't died. She took a step towards them, playing on their fear.

The black substance from her chest started protruding towards the two guards; its jittery insect-like movements sent chills up my spine as I watched it edge closer to them, who were rooted to the spot. While Elizabeth stood there giggling like a little girl, the strange and squirming black goo slithered and slimed its way onto one of the guards, attaching itself to his chest and face.

It got into his mouth and down his throat, causing him to gargle loudly. His arms were at his sides, and his pistol was still in his hand. The other guard attempted to flee, abandoning his friend to die, but the goo was too fast for him. It snagged his arms, wrapped itself around one of his wrists, and drew him back to his friend. His scream pierced our ears as we watched on in horror. One of Carver's men started to move towards the door, his weapon poised.

John grabbed his arm and pulled him back. "We cannot do anything for them. If you step in there, she will kill us all."

The man nodded and took another step back, turning his head away so he wouldn't have to watch Elizabeth sucking the life out of them. Screams from the prisoners echoed around the room as they stood there watching the horror that was taking place, inches from their cells. This was the first time I'd seen her do something like this, and while it was terrifying to witness, she never ceased to amaze me with her abilities.

"Elizabeth, stop. That's enough. Let them live," Felicity shouted.

She clutched her chest, gasping for air, trying to remain standing, but she knew that she was losing her strength to her sister.

Elizabeth chuckled to herself. "You're going a tad soft at your old age."

"That's not funny. You've taken too much of my youth. You need to stop, or you will kill me."

Elizabeth turned to her sister, her grin spreading from

ear to ear. "I'm not yet fully regenerated. You promised me your health so I could return, Felicity."

"I know, but this is too much. I didn't expect this."

"It's too late now. You cannot go back on your promise."

She returned her gaze to the two guards, who were beginning to look old and shriveled by this point. She was sucking the life out of them, stealing every ounce of their youth so she could grow stronger.

"We cannot allow this to happen," I snarled.

Miles grabbed me from one side and John from the other, both holding me back. "Mary, don't start. We cannot do anything for them," Miles growled in my ear.

He was right. If I went out there, guns blazing, then I may as well just kill the rest of them myself, as Elizabeth would finish them off anyway. I heard a thud and looked over Edmund's shoulder to see the two guards slumped on the floor, completely drained. Only shriveled skin and bones remained. Her body had completely absorbed their flesh.

"You might as well finish me off," Felicity hissed, her legs buckling under the strain of her weight.

She landed hard on the ground, and Elizabeth rushed to her side, pulling her back up to her feet.

"Felicity, you'll make it through this. You're more than capable. You were created for this purpose," Elizabeth said as she cradled her in her arms.

Felicity looked into Elizabeth's dark, menacing eyes. "I wasn't made for this, Elizabeth. I did it out of love for my sister."

Elizabeth's lips curled into a small smirk. "That's what you want to believe, Felicity. I, on the other hand, like to think of you as my backup plan. Now get up; we have work to do."

Felicity shook her head. "I can't. I'm out of energy."

Elizabeth let out a loud, exasperated sigh and drew Felicity's head towards hers. "Stay still."

Felicity squirmed beneath Elizabeth's grip, but Elizabeth

kept a firm grip on her head. "What are you going to do to me?"

"I'm going to do something I should've done a long time ago. I will become a part of you, and you will become a part of me," she said, leaning in close to Felicity's face.

"This is too much! I wish I had never brought you back. You will not take over my mind as well as my strength!" she huffed, trying to get away from her.

Elizabeth dug her nails into Felicity's sunken cheeks, while the rest of us watched on in horror at what she was about to do to her sister. Her mouth opened wide, revealing her blackened teeth. Her eyes turned upwards, towards the back of her head, as a low hum began to emanate from her gaping hole. The black substance we had seen before returned, slowly wrapping itself around Felicity's drooping body. After a few seconds, it had completely engulfed her, while something resembling mist began to emerge from Elizabeth's mouth and seep into Felicity.

"What's she doing to her?" Edmund hissed, appearing beside me.

"I don't know," John stuttered, turning white as the black substance began to retreat from Felicity's body and disappear back into Elizabeth, revealing Felicity's new features. Her face had shifted slightly, resembling Elizabeth's, with jet-black eyes to match. Her hair had darkened and grown longer, similar to Elizabeth's. Her hands, like Elizabeth's, became more gnarled and claw-like.

But then, in a matter of seconds, her face returned to normal, to her youthful self, as if nothing had happened. She blinked slowly before rising and looking around. She then raised her hands and turned them outward, admiring them. "It's strange to be in two bodies at the same time."

Elizabeth cracked a grin. "Felicity, you now have my strength. Make good use of it."

She nodded eagerly. "You are me, and I am you. We are united as one."

I took a closer look at Elizabeth through the door crack and noticed that she had aged. Her hair had turned dark grey, and the wrinkles on her face had deepened, giving her the appearance of an old hag rather than the beautiful woman she once was. She had given Felicity not only her strength but also her youth, and I didn't believe she was meant to do so. She hadn't noticed yet, but if she did, I didn't want to be there to witness her rage. Felicity leapt to her feet and extended her hand for Elizabeth to take. She accepted it gratefully, and Felicity gently drew her to her feet. She stumbled and staggered a little before staying upright as Felicity held her up against one of the cell bars.

"I'll be a little shaky for a while until I regain my strength. I need to feed," Elizabeth mumbled.

Felicity nodded, giggling. "Let's hunt."

CHAPTER EIGHTEEN

Body Swap

Felicity helped Elizabeth to her feet and ushered her towards the door. She winked at the prisoners over her shoulder, startling them with her mocking grin.

"I'll be back for you all later." She chuckled and threw Elizabeth over her shoulder in one swift movement.

She disappeared through the door, leaving the mess of the two guards behind for someone to find. She didn't care if they were caught, which made me feel even more on edge than I already was. The shared power between them could take anybody down, and now that Elizabeth's power was growing rapidly, nothing would be able to stop them.

John and Miles breathed a huge sigh of relief beside me and opened the door. A strong sense of confusion clung to all of us, not quite knowing how there were now Two Elizabeths roaming around instead of one.

Was Felicity still Felicity, or had her sister completely taken over her?

"Check the guards to see if they are alive," Miles ordered.

Two men approached the guards, checking their necks for a pulse, but with them being half-drained, neither of them was likely to be alive. One of the men looked up and shook his head, indicating that they were both dead.

Miles nodded. "What should we do now, then?" he asked, looking around at his men.

Edmund's face was as white as a sheet as he looked around at everyone going about their normal lives, seemingly unaffected by what had just happened. "How come everyone is acting as if what just happened is normal?" he demanded.

I gave him a weak smile. "This has happened before, Edmund. Although it is horrifying to witness, we have grown accustomed to Elizabeth and her evil ways."

"She has to be stopped," he said while pacing the room with his hands clasped behind his back again.

"She will be stopped, but we need a solid plan. There are two of them now, which I didn't even think was possible," John said as he took my hand in his, giving it a gentle squeeze to reassure me.

Edmund noticed and smiled my way. "I see."

"I don't understand. Is Elizabeth acting through Felicity as well as herself, or did she just give her some of her strength?" Bennett asked.

"I'm not sure, but we need to round up the guards and take them both down. We can't let them leave," Miles explained.

Edmund agreed. "I'll go this way and start on this side. You guys begin on the other side. Take this so they know you're with me." He placed a medallion in Miles's hand.

"What exactly is it?" He questioned, his gaze drawn to it.

Edmund's eyes twinkled as he approached the door. "Every judge receives one. It's to show our identity as we move around the building."

Miles nodded and gathered his men. "Okay, let's get started. Keep an eye out for both of them, everyone. We don't want them to figure out what we're up to."

Edmund cast one last glance behind him before disappearing through the door. "Best of luck."

Miles pointed to two of his men. "You two follow him. Make sure he's safe."

The rest of us followed Miles into another room through the door on the right. This one was completely empty, giving us an eerie feeling as we walked through it, looking over our shoulders every few seconds to see if anyone was following us. Miles drew his gun and knelt in front of the door. He pressed his face against the keyhole, peering through it to see what was behind it.

"Anything?" John asked eagerly.

Miles rose to his feet and nodded. "At the end of the corridor, there are two guards. Come on, guys."

He flung open the door and displayed the medallion to the guards. As we approached them, they both looked at him, puzzled, and reached for their weapons.

"Don't be scared. We are not here to cause you harm. We need your help," Miles said, putting his pistol away to show them that he was being truthful.

They exchanged glances and gradually lowered their weapons, but kept them close by in case they needed to defend themselves. Miles held out the medallion in the hopes that they would recognise it.

"Where is Judge Lawrence?" The guard asked, his gaze fixed on the medallion.

"He's gathering up all of the guards to take down the witch. She's here now, and she's taking you all down one by one," John explained.

One of the guards raised an eyebrow. "What witch?"

"I'm sure you'll recognise her name, Elizabeth Shaw. She's returned," Miles chimed in, watching their expressions intently.

With a terrified expression on his face, the first guard turned to his friend. "We have to get out of here."

"Stand your ground, gentlemen. No one is going anywhere. We cannot run away from this," Miles warned. "Follow us; we need as many of you guys as possible."

The guard took a step back and drew his friend with him. "We can't stand up to her. She is far too powerful. What makes you think we'll be able to kill her if she can defy death and return?"

"We've got her," John said, pointing at me. "Elizabeth was once destroyed by her. She's capable of doing it again."

They were both taken aback when they saw me. "How is that even possible? Look at her. She's tiny."

I nodded, triumphantly. "I did, but we don't have much time. She's growing stronger by the second, and she's using your fellow men's lives to become whole again. We must hurry."

After a moment of hesitation, they nodded and pulled out their weapons, ready to fight. "Show us the way."

"Are there any more guards in this part of the building?" Miles asked.

One of them shook their head. "It's just us over here. The rest of them are guarding the cell room and gallows out back."

"Right, follow me then," Miles said, and he turned on his heel to go back the way we came to find Edmund.

A penetrating silence filled the air as we moved quickly into the cell room and through the other door where Edmund had left us. As we passed through the cell room, I noticed that Elizabeth had finished off the other prisoners, their carcasses strewn across the floor. John grabbed my hand and ushered me in front of him while he defended the rear of the group, his eyes scanning the rooms as we passed through them. I was scared yet determined to finish her off - for good this time. I could smell her rotting flesh in every room, and I knew that she had been there, hunting down her next victims to drain.

"Where's the gallows?" Miles hissed over his shoulder.

"Through those doors over there," the guard pointed to the far end of the room, where there was a set of double doors leading into a courtyard outside.

Miles dashed towards it, but before he could open it, one of the outside guards slumped against it. The sound of his body hitting the door sent a wave of shock through all of us. We could see the terror on his face as he stared at us through the frosted glass of the small window on the door before being dragged away, screaming at the top of his lungs.

Miles pressed his face against the small window, his gaze fixed on the courtyard. "They're both out there, along with Edmund and a few guards," he then drew back from the window and pulled out his pistol and sword. "Prepare your weapons, gentlemen. If you can, shoot at both of them."

"Mary, do you still have the locket?" John asked.

I patted myself down and found it in one of my pockets. I held it out to John, but he shook his head and put his hand on top of mine, closing my fingers around the locket gently.

"Keep it. I want you to promise me that you will use it to go back to where you came from, if necessary," he whispered, his eyes pleading for me to agree. "If this becomes too dangerous, then I want you to leave. Don't hesitate, just go. I can't watch another person that I love die, so please just do as I say."

I wrapped the chain around my wrist and nodded. "For you, I will."

He gave me a warm smile and kissed my hand. "See you on the other side." With that, he dropped my hand and ran through the door with the others, leaving Miles alone with me, his face tense and solemn.

"He's right, Mary. Do as he says. We could all die today, and I wouldn't want you to be a part of that."

"Why do you care?" I asked.

He laughed softly. "My love for you won't ever change, Mary. I still care about you. People make mistakes all the time. That's what makes us human."

"I can't do this right now, Miles. We have a witch to destroy," I muttered, leaving him in there on his own while I went outside and joined the others.

As he followed me outside, his shoulders sagged from my rejection. I could feel the hurt and sadness resonating in him. His eyes were wet, but I couldn't tell if he was trying not to cry or if it was due to the bellowing wind outside whipping at his face.

I turned my attention away from him and toward the carnage in front of me. Elizabeth and Felicity were backing into a corner, away from our pointed swords and loaded pistols. The fear on Elizabeth's face was comical to me, but Felicity's face remained neutral. There was no emotion there at all, which made the hairs on the back of my neck stand on end. She stared at me with her piercing blue eyes, unblinking and evil. She was not the Felicity that I knew. She was something new, something different, with a mixture of Elizabeth inside of her.

The wind blew into us, whistling through the courtyard. The gallows' noose swung freely, making a loud creaking sound as the doors we'd just exited banged against each other. The sun shone over the building, casting strange shadows across the mossy yard. There was a stack of barrels and crates in one corner.

"I didn't expect to see you so soon," they spoke in unison as they glared at me.

"If I have to keep coming back to finish you off, Elizabeth, so be it," I snapped.

Both of them let out a low, gurgling chuckle. "I see you've made your decision between these two. You've taken long enough." They grinned like a Cheshire cat, tilting their heads in unison. "What if I take both of their lives, and you have to choose which one lives?"

Their faces began to twist into hideous, shriveled old women as they moved quickly toward us and reached out their hands. They grabbed Miles and John's chests and ripped a hole in each of them, pulling out their hearts in one swift movement and throwing them to the ground.

No sound came out, but I knew that I was screaming as I watched both of them slump to the ground, a dazed expression on their faces. Their eyes were full of sadness, staring at me before their life drained from them, leaving their faces emotionless. Everything slowed to a blur, with my surroundings fading into the background. It felt as if my own heart had been ripped out, too.

The screams and moans coming from the crew shook me back to reality as they jumped away from Miles and John in shock, while Felicity and Elizabeth laughed hysterically at them. My heart leapt into my throat as I watched the two men I adored, lie motionless on the ground, their eyes fixed on the sky.

"Mary, you have two options," Elizabeth huffed, her

strength dwindling once more. "Let us go, and I'll let one of them live."

"If you force us to stay, they will both perish. You have a choice," Felicity smirked.

"Do as they say, Mary. Allow them to go. At the very least, we will have one leader back," Edmund raised his voice behind me.

I glared at them both. "If you think that I will abide by your rules, then think again."

I pulled out my pistol and shot Elizabeth straight in the heart. She stared at me, her mouth agape, while Felicity clutched her body to stop her from falling.

"Stand your ground! Take Elizabeth to the gallows," I screeched at the crew.

They hesitated slightly, but then regrouped, forming a semi-circle around me. Felicity's mouth fell open as the men cornered them again, grabbing Elizabeth by the arms and legs and yanking her from Felicity's grasp.

I kneeled to Felicity's level and stared her down. "You take my men, and I'll take the only person you've ever loved and destroy her right in front of your very eyes."

"You wouldn't dare," she hissed as she looked me dead in the eyes.

My lips formed a sneer. "Watch me."

I stood up and left her there with three other men holding her down. She tried scratching her way free, but it only made them hold her tighter as Elizabeth was dragged across the courtyard to the gallows. Her feet smacked against the wooden stairs leading up to the noose. Her hair blew away from her face in the breeze, exposing the fear she was desperately trying to conceal. She used her body weight to try to escape the crewmen's grasp, but it was futile. She knew she didn't have the energy to fight anymore.

"You can't escape me," she gasped as one of the men tied the noose around her scrawny neck.

I smiled sweetly at her. "I always win, Elizabeth. I suggest that you remember that next time you try to return," I then turned my attention to Felicity. "Watch your sister's life wither away, Felicity. You took my men away from me, but I will find a way to bring them back. I still have this." I pulled out the locket and held it up so they both could see it.

Felicity brightened into a grin as she giggled behind me. "It only works once on someone, you fool. Your young man over there has been brought back to life before, so it won't work for him. You've only got one chance with John, and it may not even work for him either, but I can bring them back, Mary. I have the power to bring them both back if you let us go."

I paused, knowing that Felicity was likely right and that it might not work for either of them. I knew I couldn't let them go because they'd wreak havoc on the bay, but I also couldn't let John and Miles die. Felicity looked at me intently, trying to figure out what I was up to, hoping that I would believe her and let her go.

Felicity's smile faded. "If you let me go, you can take my sister's life," she pleaded.

Elizabeth's head shot up as she locked her gaze on her sister. "You're willing to take my life so you can live?"

"You took more than was necessary from me. You made me look old so you could regain your beauty. I'll never forgive you for that," she spat.

"Enough of that, both of you," I yelled angrily. I then directed my attention to Bennett, who was standing next to Elizabeth. "Bennett, get ready to open the hatch."

Elizabeth's eyes began to glow a bright red, ignoring my comment and focusing instead on Felicity. "I was going to spare you because you're my sister, but after what you've said, Felicity, I've changed my mind."

Felicity's eyes widened in terror as a black mist shot straight across the courtyard into Felicity's stomach, causing her to fly backward into one of the windows behind her. The men who had been holding her down collapsed, stunned.

"Do it now, Bennett!" I screamed, not wanting to see any

more of Elizabeth's enchantment.

Her eyes returned to normal, but this time they were blue as she raised her hands in protest. "No, wait. I'm... "

Bennett quickly drew back the lever, allowing the hatch to open and Elizabeth's body to fall through. The rope made a snapping noise as the weight of her body tightened the noose around her frail neck. She clung to the rope, scratching furiously, attempting to escape as her legs spasmed, kicking and flailing around. We stood there in awe, watching her body slowly come to a standstill as every last bit of her strength faded, leaving it swinging side to side in the wind. Her head stooped, falling sideways, her eyes wide open, and a black substance frothed from her mouth.

CHAPTER NINETEEN

Repercussion

"Aren't Elizabeth's eyes brown, not blue?" one of Carver's men questioned.

"I noticed that, too," I muttered, perplexed as to why they had changed colour.

We were so preoccupied with Elizabeth's death that we didn't realise Felicity had escaped through the broken window and into the courthouse until one of the men spoke up behind us. "Mary, she's gotten away."

"Go find her," I yelled at each of them.

They dashed away, leaving me alone in the courtyard with Elizabeth's swinging body and Bennett, who stood there staring into Elizabeth's eyes, a look of concentration on his face.

"Bennett, help me with Miles and John. We must at least try to bring them back," I called to him.

He shifted his gaze away from Elizabeth's dead eyes and toward me, where I was attempting to drag Miles's body over to John. "Her eyes are different, Mary. They appear to be Felicity's rather than hers," he muttered, stroking his chin in thought.

"We'll think about it later, Bennett. For the time being, I need your help," Miles's body was becoming increasingly difficult to drag. I puffed breathlessly, hoping Bennett would get the picture and come over to help.

He finally came over, picked up Miles' arms, and dragged him to John with ease. He then grabbed their hearts from the floor and pushed them back into each of their chests as if he was just picking up a rock. It hadn't fazed him in the slightest.

There was no sign of life in them. If this didn't work, I'd lose them forever, and I couldn't bear the thought of it. I pushed the thought to the back of my mind, and, with determination in my heart, I took out the locket and placed it on John's heart, hoping it would bring him back, just as it had for Miles.

"How long does this take?" Bennett whispered, staring intently at John.

I shrugged my shoulders. "I'm not sure. Hopefully, it will work quickly if it works at all."

"What if it doesn't work? Who's going to become captain?" he asked.

I turned to him and gave him a small smile. "It would be the next in command, Bennett. We'll figure it out when it comes down to it, but for now, let's just focus on bringing them back."

He turned his gaze away from me, nodding. "Alright, but there is something that's really bugging me, Mary."

"I know what you're about to say. Elizabeth's eyes are not her own. They are Felicity's," I let out a loud sigh, not knowing what else to say, but we both had the same idea. Elizabeth had switched bodies with her sister. We killed the wrong sister, and if that was so, then Elizabeth had escaped in a new body and would now be unrecognisable to everyone. She could cause so much more harm, and no one would realise that it was her.

"You have the same conclusion as me, don't you? I can tell by the look on your face," he muttered, his face twisted into a frown.

"We've killed the wrong sister," I admitted.

"What should we do?" he asked, nervously.

I looked him dead in the eye and smiled. "We will do what we do best and hunt her down. She thinks that she has won, but she doesn't realise that we've found out about what she had done. She killed her sister in order to escape and live."

He returned my smile, a glint of excitement in his eyes. "Mary, I believe you should become captain. You've got the brains for it. Most of the time, you know what you're do-ing."

I shook my head. "You might think I've got everything figured out, but deep down, Bennett, I'm just as scared as the rest of you. I'm not sure what I'm doing."

I returned my attention to John, focusing on the blood patch on his shirt that had begun to fade beneath his skin. "I believe it is working, Bennett."

Bennett laughed as he clapped his hands together. "Brilliant. Let's hope he doesn't wake up in a bad mood."

I kept my mouth shut and watched as John's fingers twitched. His eyes began to flutter, and the blood stain that had previously existed vanished. I kneeled and lifted his shirt, looking for a wound, but all I found was a small scar just above his heart.

"Are you checking a dead man out?" John joked as he opened his eyes.

I jumped up, my cheeks flushed with embarrassment. "No. I was looking for a wound."

He sat up, pulling his shirt back down and rubbing his eyes with the back of his hands. "I feel terrible. Where's the captain?"

"Miles is lying next to you, John. His life was also taken," my voice quivered as I tried to hold back tears.

When John noticed, he leapt to his feet. "He's already been brought back once, Mary. It's not going to work this time."

"We have to try," I whimpered, snatching the locket from John's grasp and placing it on top of Miles' heart, as I had done with him.

John took a step back from me, baffled by my outburst. "I had no idea he meant so much to you after what had happened."

"He will always mean a lot to me, John. That won't ever change. He was the first person who helped me when I first came here. Don't forget that."

"I understand, Mary, but I don't want you to get your

hopes up. According to his father's diary, the locket only works once. He's been resurrected before. It will not happen again."

As I lowered my gaze to Miles's serene expression, tears streamed down my cheeks. "So, what do we do now that we don't have our captain? We can't simply leave him here."

John kneeled beside Miles and bundled him into his arms. "I shall carry him back to the boats. It's my duty to do that."

"There has to be another way to bring him back," I wept as I watched John struggle with Miles's weight.

"There is no other way, Mary. This is it for him," he muttered, looking down at his captain's face with tears in his eyes.

Bennett cleared his throat and wrapped his arm around my shoulder in an attempt to console me. "At the very least, John is back."

He was right. I would have been devastated if I had lost both of them to her. John kept me sane, and I knew he'd look after me, but Miles was the most enjoyable part of my life. He'd made things simpler for me. When everything was falling apart around me, he stayed by my side. He was a breath of fresh air for me, and despite the fact that he had thrown me away for a noblewoman who had turned out to be as evil as her sister, he knew that he had done wrong and wanted to make amends.

And as I look at him now, I know that my love for him won't ever diminish. His beautiful face will forever live within my memory, and I would never want it to fade.

I trailed John as we walked through the double doors of the courthouse, where we ran into Edmund. He was flushed and sweating, and he slowed down as soon as he saw us walk in.

"We can't find her. She's nowhere to be found," he coughed loudly, trying to catch his breath, and then continued. "We've searched everywhere, and I even have all the guards searching the courthouse for her."

I sighed loudly, frustrated with Edmund's response. "Edmund, she's probably not in the courthouse. She's probably gone to the tunnels below to escape without being seen. Use your intuition. You're a judge, for goodness' sake."

He was taken aback, but quickly masked it. "I hadn't considered that."

He walked away without looking back. I could hear him huffing and puffing as he dashed down the corridor and out the beautifully carved wooden door.

"I told you that you would make a good captain," Bennett whispered in my ear.

My lips curled into a small smile. "I guess you're right."

We continued on, making our way through the courthouse's winding corridors and dusty rooms until we reached the entrance and came to a stop. Miles' arm slipped from John's grasp and swung back and forth as John tried to adjust his body position. My heart yearned to take his hand in mine, and if Miles could see me now, he would have smirked, knowing that I still had feelings for him.

"We cannot carry a body out in broad daylight. We need a plan." John said, placing him down on the cold marble floor.

"Take him through the tunnels. Bennett can show you the way. I will wait here for the others to return. Look after him, John, and make sure he's put into his cabin," I said.

"I'm not going to leave you here on your own, Mary. It's far too risky," John responded.

"Someone needs to remain here, and I don't know my way through the tunnels. Bennett does," I explained, but I knew that it was no use trying to explain to a stubborn man like him. "I'm staying here, John, and there's nothing that you can do about it."

I could feel the anger welling inside him from the way he looked at me. "Why do you have to be so stubborn all the time?"

"It's just the way I am, John. Now go, before someone sees us. I'll wait here, and you can come back for me if the others don't, or if you see Edmund, then please tell him to come here. If no one comes back, then I'll make my way back to the ship."

John nodded slowly, unsure of whether to leave me or not. "Hide in the shadows and make sure nothing happens to you, Mary. She could still be here."

"I'll be fine. Just go, John," I said, ushering them both towards the door.

I wanted to stay behind and grieve alone, so no one could see me. I didn't want anyone to know that I still had strong feelings for Miles, and I especially didn't want John to see me cry.

John took my hand in his and drew me closer, embracing me with his long, thick arms. He placed his finger beneath my chin and gently lifted my face to his, kissing my lips. They felt warm against my cold, chapped lips, sending a tingling sensation all the way through my body.

He drew back his head and smiled down at me. "Be safe, Mary."

He then motioned for Bennett to help him with Miles's body and left quickly via the left door, leading to one of the drain covers that led into the tunnel system below us. I touched my lips as I watched them leave, shocked yet happy. John gave me one last look over his shoulder, grinning from ear to ear, and then disappeared with Bennett.

A wave of emotions washed over me, and I couldn't stop shaking as a result of the kiss. I sat down on the hard, cold floor and closed my eyes, remembering John's warm embrace. My mother would have been pleased that I had found an older man, but my father would have been furious if he had known that John had already touched me in ways that only a married couple should touch.

I adored him. That was all I knew, but love was a strange feeling, and I couldn't quite wrap my head around the idea of being married and forever playing by a man's rules. In that way, I was similar to my mother. My father would say that I, like my mother, am too stubborn for my own good, but I'd rather have a level head about myself than follow another man's rule.

It took a while for anyone to come through the foyer to see me. Edmund peered through one of the doors and smiled at me as I sat in the corner, rocking back and forth, grieving for Miles.

"There you are," he called out to me and came over to where I was sitting. "We haven't found her yet, but the men have spread out to cover more ground."

"Edmund, she's cunning. She'll find a way to hide in plain sight and laugh at us while we're frantically searching for her."

He exhaled a sigh. "I understand, but for the time being, we're doing our best. The guards are returning to secure the courthouse, and the crew will continue to search for her, even if it takes all night."

"Why should you bother looking for me when I'm right here?" a woman's voice shouted from behind Edmund.

We both looked up to see Felicity, who was standing in the back of the foyer with six courthouse guards, smiling at us. Her piercing blue eyes stared at us both as she folded her arms with a sneer.

"What's going on here?" Edmund demanded to the guards.

They stood next to Felicity, their faces expressionless. They were ready with their weapons, waiting for her command. When no one responded to Edmund, she chuckled.

"Bring them to me," she hissed, but this time her voice sounded more like Elizabeth's than her own.

They did as they were told and came for us with their weapons raised. Edmund's eyes were filled with fear as he tried to scarper away. One of the guards yanked his arm back, dragging him to Felicity, who stood there with her hands on her hips, smiling wildly at him. I didn't bother moving. I didn't even flinch when two men grabbed my arms and dragged me in front of Felicity. Her face twisted and contorted into Elizabeth, and her eyes darkened. She glared at us, her eyes twitching from me to Edmund, looking us both up and down.

"The roles will be reversed, Mary," she sneered and clicked her fingers.

I was grabbed from behind again and forced to stand straight. "What is that supposed to mean?"

She let out a small giggle, covering her mouth with her hand like a child. "You'll see."

She then turned on her heel and sauntered off towards the door that led to the courtyard outside, motioning with a flick of her fingers for us to join her. The guards picked up a moping Edmund and dragged him away, his heels scraping across the marble floor. I shook off the guards' forceful hands and walked willingly to wherever Felicity was taking us.

Her hair had begun to darken, resembling Elizabeth's scrawny colour rather than her own. I wasn't sure if Felicity was Elizabeth, but I knew it would be revealed in time. There was something strange about the way she walked, tip-toeing around excitedly as if she were about to embark on some thrilling adventure.

"Are you going to intrigue me with what you have planned for us?" I called after her as she moved gracefully through the corridor.

She stopped skipping and turned to face me. "That would be spoiling the fun, Mary," she said while tapping the side of her nose.

I didn't waste my time arguing with her. Instead, I followed her out into the courtyard, where she began to dance around the gallows with her hands wide open as if she were in a slow dance with someone else.

"Take Edmund to the gallows," she sang while skipping around him, taunting him with her eyes.

The guards tugged on his collar, leading him up the wooden steps to the noose. He began to cry, tears falling down his red, puffy cheeks. They pulled Elizabeth's body from the noose and placed her on the ground. Felicity laughed to herself as she watched Edmund thrash around, attempting to break free from the noose that was being tied around his neck. Two more guards rushed up to him and restrained him, while another tied his hands with rope and wrapped the noose tightly around his neck.

"You cannot do this to me! I am the judge of this county. You do not take orders from her. You take orders from me!" he cried, his shoulders shaking with fear, while his legs could hardly hold him up. "Mary, do something!"

"Elizabeth, please don't do this. You don't need to kill him," I pleaded.

"But, why not? He's going to be the message that I'm going to leave for your friends to find," she laughed. She then patted my shoulder and said, "Thank you for calling me Elizabeth and not Felicity. I'm sure you're well aware that she's dead and that I swapped my soul with hers."

"That is, if you have a soul, Elizabeth, which I don't believe you do. You're the epitome of evil!" I raised my voice a little, trying to hide the terror I felt within.

Her brow furrowed as she looked at me. "Mary, you don't appear to be upset about the situation. The man who helped you today is going to be hanged, and you appear unconcerned about it."

I raised my eyes to Edmund, who was now sobbing uncontrollably. A wet patch formed at the front of his trousers and trickled down his leg as he stared at me, pleading with his eyes for me to stop her, but I knew it was pointless. There were too many guards and a vicious witch who I couldn't persuade to let him go, even if I begged them.

"I'm sorry," I mouthed at him.

Felicity returned her gaze to Edmund and smiled at him. "You are relieved of your duty, Edmund."

I looked away, not wanting to see any more bloodshed. I felt sorry for Edmund as he stood there on top of the gallows, waiting for his life to be taken away by some evil force, and I knew that I was next in line.

The guard pulled the lever, and Edmund let out an ear-piercing scream before dropping through the hatch, his neck breaking instantly on impact. There was a moment of silence as we all stared at his swinging body slamming against the gallows' side.

"Well, that was no fun. It was too quick," she moaned.

"I suppose it's me next," I muttered.

She took her gaze away from Edmund's swaying body and turned her head towards me, her eyes scanning mine for any sign of fear, but there was none. Being around her made me feel deflated and exhausted. Her evil had sucked every ounce of happiness from me, leaving me hollow and empty, so I didn't care if she was going to take my life as well. I just wanted it to be over, and while my thoughts turned to John, who was now safe aboard the ship, I couldn't help but think about Miles and his peaceful body lying in his bunk.

"How come you'd say that, Mary?" she smirked at me, jolting me back to reality. "I have something far more exciting in store for you. You'll accompany me. I won't kill you just yet. Please remove your belt."

"My belt? Why?" I asked, baffled.

"Just do it, Mary, and stop asking me questions," she growled.

I had a plan, and I hoped that John would understand when he saw it. Without Elizabeth looking, I pulled out the locket and placed it into the belt underneath the pistol so she couldn't see it.

She turned back to me and stood there, watching as I untied my belt and let it fall to the ground. She then picked it up and tossed it next to the gallows, along with the hidden locket. She took the bait, and I had to conceal a smile to not give away my plan. I wanted John to find the locket so he could use it for the ship to make it go faster in case she took me across waters. That was the only plan I had, and I hoped that John would use his senses to see what I was trying to do for him.

The guards of the courthouse surrounded her, waiting for their next command. She must have used a spell on them to get them to work for her instead of Edmund. They wouldn't have murdered their own for no reason without intervention from Elizabeth, just like she did with using my grandfather against me to try and kill me.

"Why can't you just finish me off? Stop playing games with me," I snarled at her.

She stopped inches from my face, staring deep into my eyes as she spoke. "I'll do what I want with you, Mary, but for now, you will come with me. The others will probably try and look for you, but with my brilliant plan, they will be led astray."

I bluntly nodded. "Okay, then."

Her face sagged into a scowl. "Why are you acting this way? You're supposed to be afraid of me."

I gave her a weak smile. "This is what happens when you take all the love I had out of my life. You've killed my grandfather, my parents, Tom, and now Miles. I have no one left."

"You still have John," she said.

"For now, which I'm sure that you will destroy as well. If you are trying to get a rise out of me, it will not work. You've won, Elizabeth. I have no fight left. Take me wherever pleases you."

"Yes, it appears to be the case. Come on, we've got work to do," she muttered. She then turned to face the guards with a sinister grin on her face. "Knock her out. I don't want her to be able to see where we're going."

Before I could respond, one of the guards smacked the back of my head with his pistol, instantly knocking me out, sending me into a black oblivion.

CHAPTER TWENTY

John

The creaks and groans of the ship kept John on edge as he leant his arms against the ship's side, looking out to sea. He was anxiously awaiting Mary's arrival, but as the tide receded and the hours passed, he became too impatient to wait any longer. He gathered the crew and made a plan to return to the courthouse armed and ready. A horrible feeling pricked his instincts, and he knew Mary was in danger.

She hadn't returned with Edmund, and he hadn't seen her for hours. Something had happened; he knew it deep down in his heart. Felicity was also missing, and he had a horrible gut feeling that Felicity had something to do with Mary's disappearance. Miles was safe in his bunk, so he had no reason not to return to find Mary. He summoned the men and jumped back into the boat.

"Am I allowed to come?" Henry asked.

John nodded. "I may require your assistance on this journey."

Henry climbed into the boat and sat alongside John. They rowed back to the bay in silence and tied the boats back up. John wasted no time and dashed through the stallholders, unconcerned about who saw him. He was aware that they were still being pursued by authorities as a result of Miles's stupid mistake, but he couldn't let them waste any more time than they had already wasted by waiting for her.

The crew followed him up the stone steps to the courthouse and barged in through the thick double doors. The empty foyer sent shivers up John's spine as he looked around for any sign of where Mary could have gone.

"Spread out and look around!" John yelled, his voice

echoing off the room's marble pillars.

Fear of losing her made his heart race, and he felt sick to his stomach. He couldn't let her go now, or ever. He'd lost too many people he cared about in his life, and he couldn't bear the thought of losing Mary as well. He watched as his men scattered, entering every door in the foyer and leaving no room untouched.

Before he spoke, Henry stood beside John, breathing heavily. "Do you believe she's dead?"

A jolt of fear ripped through his heart as he heard the word dead, making him dizzy. "I'm hoping not."

Henry's gaze was drawn to the door, which was being pushed open by one of the crew members at breakneck speed.

"Quartermaster! I've discovered something," he yelled before disappearing through the door once more.

John snatched Henry's arm and dragged him along with him. "Come on, come on."

They both threw open the door with the palms of their hands at the same time. The crew member had waited in the corridor for them to show them the rest of the way.

"What is it?" John asked.

"I think it's best that you see it for yourself," The crew member muttered and pushed open the next door that led to the gallows.

The first thing John noticed was two legs dangling from the noose. He sped up, hoping it wasn't Mary. Edmund's purple-looking face came into view, his body still swaying slightly in the breeze, and his heart calmed a little, knowing that there was still hope for Mary being found. He felt sorry for the man, but he didn't have time to mourn his death.

"I've found this. It belongs to Mary," The crew member said, holding up her belt and a loaded pistol. "She's either dead or she has been taken by Felicity."

The locket fell out of the belt and landed on the floor, making a loud clang. John bent down and picked it up, running his thumb over the smooth metal.

"We must find her. I want this whole building to be searched from top to bottom," John ordered.

"I don't believe she's dead, John. If she had died, Felicity would have paraded her body around for all to see. She's taken her somewhere, and we have to figure out where," Henry stated.

John agreed. "You're right. Two places come to mind. The manor house or Elizabeth's island, where she lived."

Henry yanked his arm and drew him to the door. "Let's start with the manor house because it's closer. We need horses."

CHAPTER TWENT-ONE

The Power Unfolds

I awoke with a pounding headache and something on my face. It felt like a coarse fabric sack wrapped around my head, forcing me to gasp for air. I could hear thrashing waves and birds screeching high above my head. My hands were tied behind my back with what felt like rope, and my legs were also tied together.

My fingers brushed up against something hard, and upon closer inspection, I realised we were on a boat. My stomach churned as I realised we were on our way back to Elizabeth's island, where she had been hiding for all those years.

"She has awoken. Remove the sack," Elizabeth demanded.

As the mask was removed, sunlight shone into my eyes. My instinct was right. We'd made it to Elizabeth's island.

As I looked around, my mind was filled with memories of the place. The cave's entrance had shrunk due to rocks that had fallen from the dynamite Tom had placed the last time we were here. The body that had previously hung on one of the hooks was still there, scaring onlookers away with its decomposing skin. The spires from the cave's ceiling had fallen into the water, protruding like teeth. The rest of the cave had been left untouched, and I could see the lantern we had used previously near the cave's entrance.

"Why have you brought me back here?" I asked.

She smiled at me. "I have something planned for you, Mary, but first I have some guests arriving. You see when you blew up the manor with my followers trapped inside, you didn't actually kill any of them. You only trapped them in there until the authorities dug them out. Your grandfather's actions were pointless, and he died for no reason. He was far from a hero. He was a moron to believe he could destroy us by blowing up a building."

Anger began to form within me. "He died doing something good, Elizabeth. Maybe you should give it a shot."

"Why should I do that when I'd rather be feared? You'll find out soon enough why we are here," she stated.

When I looked at her, I noticed a glint in her eyes, which told me that something terrible was about to happen. "What exactly do you mean? What do you intend to do?"

"You'll sees" she smirked as she repeated herself.

We approached the hooks protruding from the rocky wall, and she stood up, swaying the boat slightly as she stepped off.

"Take her to the cell and tie her up. Make sure she can't get away," she directed the guards.

I exhaled a sigh. "You don't need to grab me. I'll gladly come."

Elizabeth glared at me. "Bring her this way."

The guards picked me up from the boat and threw me to the ground. As they dragged me through the next cave, pain seared through my hip. Elizabeth moved quickly, her footsteps echoing around the small cave that her ancestors had carved out many years before her.

"I want to know what you're going to do to me," I demanded.

She glanced at me over her shoulder and winked. "You'll see my way of thinking soon, Mary." She then stopped and pointed to an oval-shaped entrance with iron bars sticking out from it as a door. "This is where you will stay for a while until my guests arrive."

I didn't argue as one of the guards unlocked the cage door and pushed me inside. He quickly locked it back up before I could escape, but I didn't bother moving. Instead, I sat in the middle of the cell and looked around. Moss grew around the stone walls, and little trickles of water dripped down, keeping the ground moist. I could still see the chisel marks indented in the rocks from when it was first built. I brushed my fingers lightly over the marks and smiled to myself, which made Elizabeth uncomfortable as she stared at me through the bars.

"Why are you smiling?" she asked.

I returned my gaze to her and gave her the biggest grin I could muster. "I was admiring this place's handy work."

She looked at me with a puzzled expression before shrugging her shoulders. "I'll see you shortly."

She walked away, followed by the guards, leaving me alone with my thoughts. She could tell I wasn't bothered by her presence any longer, which, I'm sure, scared her a little. I didn't give a damn anymore, and she knew it.

The cell was gloomy and lonely, with no light. I sat in the dark, my bum turning numb and wet, waiting for her to return. That's exactly what she desired. She intended for me to be scared and lonely while I waited for her. I knew I had to remain calm and diligent, not showing any signs of fear at what she was about to do to me. I didn't want to be carved open the way she had done to John. I also didn't want her to wreak havoc on my body in any way. If she was going to kill me, she needed to do it quickly so that I could get out of this nightmare.

Time passed slowly as I walked up and down the cell, bored out of my skull, until two guards appeared with a lamp to usher me out. I was grabbed from behind once more and dragged through the tunnel that led into a large cave that I had previously visited. I knew where this cave led, and I was certain she was about to cast a witchcraft spell on me.

As we entered the cave, I could see the bodies that had come to life and attacked us from the last time I was here back in their original position. They were bending at an impossible angle to form a circle above our heads. Miles' father's body was also there, looking exactly the same as the last time I saw him. These bodies had been nailed to the cave ceiling, preserved with some slimy substance, and their eyes had been pried open to stare down at us. This time, there was something different about the cave. It had an altar table in the centre, with Elizabeth standing behind it, arms outstretched, greeting me.

A crowd gathered in a semi-circle around Elizabeth, dressed in black robes with the symbol on them that they had worn at the manor house. They prostrated themselves before Elizabeth as if she were a goddess. I ignored the knot in my throat and continued to watch them, hoping that among them were John and the crew, ready to charge in and save me.

As we approached the altar, I was forced to lie down on top of it in front of a beaming Elizabeth. My heart pounded as the guards separated my arms and legs, tying me down to prevent me from moving.

Elizabeth smiled at the audience and hushed them. "Greetings, my friends." She approached the altar table and pointed at me. "This is a very special day. Before you is a woman who has attempted but failed to kill each and every one of us. She will not stop until she succeeds, so we must stop her. By using a part of my mind, I will turn her into one of us. Her mind will entwine with mine, and she will start to see our way of life."

"Why can't we just kill her?" someone shouted from the crowd.

"There is no greater victory than having an enemy begin to think the same way you do. We can use her to bring John and the others down, and we will take what is rightfully mine. The ship is going to be mine. We're going to be unstoppable. We will be feared. We are going to rule the ocean."

The crowd erupted in a loud cheer, followed by a frenzy of chatter and excitement. Her words echoed in my mind, sinking into the fact that I would carry a piece of her within me, altering my perspective on life. This was the worst thing that could have happened to me. Terror and fear swam through my veins, clouding my vision, as all I could see was Elizabeth smiling as the crowd cheered for her. I didn't want to be the same as her. I didn't want anything to do with her. My legs began to shake uncontrollably, and my hands became slippery and sweaty, causing the rope to become slightly looser than before.

"Settle down, settle down," she said, waving her hands at them to take a seat. "Let's not waste any more time and begin the greatest victory in history!"

She returned to her original position beside me, holding her arms out and her palms facing the ceiling. A small smile played across her lips as she began to quietly hum something to herself that I couldn't quite understand. Her followers joined in, their heads bowed to the ground, and they began to chant slowly, in time with Elizabeth's humming.

I felt terrified as the sound of their voices pierced my ears, causing them to throb with pain. I wriggled free from my wrist restraints and attempted to sit up until the guards noticed my struggle and rushed over to restrain me once more. Elizabeth bent down, inches from my face, and breathed a strange black mist into my mouth while they held my face still. Her mouth opened wide, and her teeth grew into sharp, elongated pinpoints as she lowered her mouth onto mine, sinking her teeth into my cheeks. I kicked my legs and arms, struggling to break free, but she latched onto me, forcing her teeth into my flesh even more. I could feel my heart rate increasing, and the effects of adrenaline started to kick in rapidly. My stomach churned with whatever was coming out of her mouth, burning my insides.

Tears streamed down my cheeks, and the force of her claws digging into my forehead began to burn my head. The chanting became louder with each breath I took through Elizabeth's mouth. Something caught my eye out of the corner of my eye as a blur of a white shirt passed quickly through the crowd of robes. Nobody had noticed it, but it was as obvious as day. The blur slowed as it approached the altar table, standing next to an oblivious Elizabeth. Her mouth was still on mine, and her eyes were closed, not noticing the strange blur.

It stopped and smiled at me, revealing a pair of pearly white teeth just inches away from my face. "This will be over soon. Hang in there, Mary."

I immediately recognised the voice and sprang up, throwing Elizabeth off in the process and watching her crumple to the floor in a heap. Her teeth had left puncture marks on my cheeks, which bled profusely, mixing in with my tears.

"I had a feeling you'd do that," the same voice spoke into my ear.

I looked around for the source of the voice, but no one was there. The strange blur had vanished. I recognised the voice and knew who it belonged to.

It was Miles.

After hearing Miles' voice again, something inside of me shifted. I felt energised, and my adrenaline was pumping through my veins like crazy. But there was also something else going on. I felt strong and powerful.

I looked down at a stunned-looking Elizabeth. She stared up at me from the floor with a puzzled expression on her face. When her eyes widened in surprise and fear, I knew something had gone wrong with her plan.

"What have I done?" she whispered to herself.

I ripped the ropes around my legs and then snapped the ones around my wrists in one swift motion, surprising myself with my strength. The cult members became quiet and stopped chanting, staring at me in awe, while Elizabeth tried to scramble away. I jumped off the altar table without thinking and grabbed her by the neck, holding her up like a ragdoll.

"What did you do to me?" I snarled.

She clawed at my arms, trying to break free, but I couldn't feel any pain. I couldn't feel anything but anger and frustration. She gurgled as I tightened my grip around her neck. Her eyes were popping slightly out of their sockets.

She stared at me, terrified. "Please stop."

I realised that my newfound strength was killing her, so I let her go. She collapsed to the ground and began to cough and sputter, grabbing her neck in defence.

I glared down at her. "Answer me."

I had no idea what was going on, but whatever Elizabeth had done to me had made me stronger and more fearless. I wasn't sure if I still had any emotions. All I could think about was power.

She was sobbing as she looked me in the eyes. "It wasn't supposed to happen like this."

I kneeled to her level and screeched in her face. "What have you done?"

She started to shake, realising what she had done. "The spell has backfired. You have part of my powers, but not part of my mind."

With what had happened, it began to make sense. I could feel her power within me, but I wasn't thinking in the same way she did. I was still myself.

I stood up, a small smile playing across my lips as I marveled at my newfound strength. Miles' earlier remark became clear to me. He wanted me to push her away for a specific reason and at the appropriate time. He knew I'd be startled by his voice and used that to his advantage, allowing me to have her power but not her mind. I had the best of both worlds and was still able to think for myself.

CHAPTER TWENT-TWO

John's Words

The man who sold the horses to them last time looked at them confusedly as they returned for more. He didn't ask why they needed more and gave the crew the rest of them, leaving him with none left over.

"This has been a good business week," he said as John handed over a sash full of coins in exchange for the man's horse's reign.

"You just never know. We may return for more," John grunted.

The man's face became solemn. "I won't have any more until the following week. Return at that time."

John mounted the horse and rode away without saying anything else, leaving the man to count the sash of coins with glee. The crew trailed him, with Henry attempting to catch up to John's horse. "What if they aren't there, John?"

John slowed slightly, allowing Henry to ride alongside him up the muddy lane into the countryside. "After that, we'll return to the ship and set sail for Elizabeth's island."

"At least an afternoon ride to the manor is required. She could be in perilous danger if she isn't there," Henry yelled over the galloping.

"Then we must hurry, Henry. We cannot waste any more time," John shouted over his shoulder and whipped his horse to make it go faster.

He left them behind and continued down the winding path leading to the manor. He pushed his way through the brambles and thorns, which scratched the horse's legs. He rode past the wrecked carriage, which had accumulated a thick layer of dirt on its roof. He was thinking about Mary as he pushed the horse to gallop even faster through the overgrown woodland. He knew he shouldn't have left her with Edmund at the courthouse. He should have been more obstinate and dragged her back to the ship with him. This was his fault, and if she died, her blood would be on his hands, leaving him with no other option but to take his own life. He couldn't live without her—not now and never again. He had to find her, no matter how long it took.

Another hour had passed, and the sun was beginning to set, casting a reddish glow on the manor as it came into view. He slowed the tired horse to a trot while waiting for the others to catch up. Henry was the first to appear, followed by the others and a tired-looking Bennett.

"Should we start referring to you as captain?" one of the members of the crew asked.

A wave of guilt washed over him as an image of Miles, lying in his bunk, flashed through his mind.

Miles had died while rescuing Mary and his crew. He's now gone, leaving me to guard his father's ship and crew.

He should have been happy because he had wished for his own crew, but the guilt gnawed at him, and he missed his old friend. When this was all over, he knew he'd have to do everything he could to bring his friend back, but for the time being, he had to act as captain.

John shifted his gaze to the crew. "This crew's second in command is me. The time has come for me to step up and take over as captain. I never intended for this to happen, but I will take my rightful place as your captain."

"Aye aye," they all chorused.

A smile formed on John's lips as he guided his horse back around to the manor. "Follow me, gentlemen."

Instead of the manor, there was only an empty shell of what it once was. The manor was long gone, full of crumbling walls and rubble pushed into three separate piles. The front door's pillars remained standing, but the door had been blown off its hinges. On the first floor of the building, one window had been smashed through, scattering shards of glass across the gravel.

"I don't think she's going to be here," Bennett said, appearing beside John.

"If she's there, then she would be in the cellar," John clicked his tongue to move the tired horse forward. "Let's go and see."

Two soldiers appeared as they approached the wreckage of the manor, keeping a wary eye on them. Henry and Bennett exchanged nervous glances. John ignored his crew's nervous glances and continued towards the two soldiers.

"Hold up there. This is private land," one of the soldiers shouted.

"We want no quarrel with you, sir. We are looking for a young woman who's accompanying Lady Felicity," John said.

He reached for his pistol slowly, making sure the guards couldn't see it. The others watched him and quickly followed suit, knowing that things could turn ugly.

The soldier looked at him with suspicion. "Lady Felicity isn't present. She resides in her townhouse. The woman you're looking for could be there."

"Thank you very much for your time, gentlemen. We shall now be on our way," John bowed his head and began to back away from them until the soldier grabbed his reins and pulled him back.

"You haven't explained why you want to see Lady Felicity," he questioned, his gaze scanning John's for clues.

John cleared his throat loudly, unsure of what to say. Bennett looked at John and decided to speak up instead. "The lady in question has something of his that he would like back. His grandfather's pocket watch. It's of sentimental value."

The guards took a step back and began whispering to one another. The buttons on their bright red tunics glistened in the fading sunlight. They wore identical black trousers tucked into thigh-high black boots. They had clean, shaven faces and no dirt on them, giving the crew a scruffy and unkempt appearance. Their gazes shifted to

John and the crew every few seconds as spoke to each other in a hushed tone, careful of them not to overhear. John kept his hand on his pistol in case the soldiers started a fight, but he knew they wouldn't because they knew they were outnumbered.

One of the soldiers nodded before returning his attention to John and the rest of the crew. "Alright then, you should be on your way now. This is a restricted area. Remember that for the next time you decide to come round these parts."

"I appreciate your time, gentlemen," John said as he led his horse away from them and rode back towards the woods.

The horses puffed loudly, growing tired. They slowed to a trot, unwilling to move any faster. The men had worn them out from the journey, getting to the manor in half the time.

The sun was setting slowly over the horizon, and John knew that they were running out of time. His heart quickened at the very thought of Mary being in the hands of Felicity. The woman was as conniving and manipulative as her sister, Elizabeth.

As their horses trotted across the immaculately clean lawn, the crew murmured amongst themselves about what to do next. The soldiers kept a close eye on them, unaware that they had just come across a group of convicts wanted for destroying the manor house. Fortunately for the crew, the news had not spread as far as the manor.

"Where to now, Captain?" Bennett asked.

As he stared at the locket in his hands, John thought long and hard. Mary wouldn't have left it behind for any reason, and she'd hidden it in her belt out of sight of Felicity. He remembered Elizabeth's eyes being blue rather than her usual obsidian colour, before hanging her. Felicity's eyes were blue, which could only mean one thing. Elizabeth had swapped bodies with her sister, leaving her sister to die instead of her, suggesting that Mary had been taken by Elizabeth in her sister's body rather than Felicity herself.

Elizabeth's cunning plan paid off, as she could now use her sister's nobility to get what she wanted. Another thought occurred to him that he should have had before coming here, as they'd wasted time coming here when they could have gone straight to Mary if he'd used his head.

"Why do you think Mary has hidden this locket?" John asked as he held it up for everyone to see.

Henry grabbed it and examined it more closely. "Doesn't this locket belong to the ship?"

John nodded, realisation dawning in his mind. "Yes, it does. For some reason, she had left it for us to find, and that was because she wanted us to use it on the ship to get to her faster."

"We should have thought of this before, Captain." Bennett grimaced.

John slowed his horse to a halt and fixed his gaze on Bennett. "I realise that, Bennett, but I can be quite slow at times." He clicked his tongue again, causing the horse to move. "Let's return to the ship."

CHAPTER TWENT-THREE

The Chase

Elizabeth's expression was a mix of terror and admiration. Her chest moved quickly as she breathed, and I could see her shoulders shaking. My blood was drying around her face, and her razor-sharp teeth drew back into her gums, returning to normal. Her black, wiry hair was disheveled and wild, and her skin started to sag from her cheekbones, making her look old and weary. She grabbed the edge of the stone altar table and pulled herself up, keeping an eye on me in case I approached her.

The power within me was stirring, wanting to break free and wreak havoc on the cult. It was difficult to keep it under control, and I wanted to use every ounce of my power on Elizabeth, but I knew that if I did, I'd be no better than she was.

She noticed my struggled look and spoke sternly to me. "You must control it, Mary, or it will control you."

"If I wasn't controlling it, then you would be dead by now, Elizabeth," I spat.

She looked at me with fear in her eyes. She wanted to say something but instead bit her tongue, not wanting to anger me any more than I already was.

"You will allow me to leave this place and not come after me," I demanded as I stepped closer to the exit.

"I'm afraid that I cannot allow that to happen. You're too dangerous to be freed, Mary," she stated.

I glared at her. "Then what are you going to do?"

"The spell must be reversed. You can't have my abilities. I'm not going to let it happen." she stammered, trying to keep her voice steady.

"And what happens if I refuse to let you take it back?" I scowled at her.

She tried to hide the shocked expression on her face, but I saw right through her. I smiled at her, letting her know I was aware of what she was thinking.

"Guards!" she yelled.

The guards grabbed my arms and pulled them apart, stretching my body out, making movement more difficult. I struggled to get away. My frail, womanly body couldn't fight back against the strength of two men, yet the power within me could.

"Keep her still," Elizabeth ordered.

Something began to stir inside of me. It felt like a powerful force was forming within me, pushing its way through my veins and absorbing the strength of my arms. I shoved the guards back, causing them to fall into the crowd. Elizabeth looked at me, bewildered, as I moved away from her and toward the exit.

"Go after her!" she screamed.

Her face turned bright red with rage, and bluish veins appeared on her brow. Her hands began to clench, eventually forming fists. I could sense her power brewing within her as if it were mine. It was like a big fireball of orangish-red light inside her heart, glowing like a lantern.

"I can see your power now," I said, amazed.

As she looked down to where I was staring, her face twisted into a scowl. "My power doesn't belong to you, Mary! Give it back!"

"I'm sorry, but no," I grinned at her before turning on my heel and sprinting to the exit before I could get apprehended again.

I rushed into the next cave while the guards stood up and brushed themselves down, still dazed from my push. As I rounded the corner into another cave, I could still hear Elizabeth screaming at the guards. I had no idea where I was going, but anywhere was preferable to being anywhere near Elizabeth. I kept running, adrenaline coursing through my veins, mingling with the power within me -

a dangerous combination. I felt sick and scared of what was happening to my body.

What if this was turning me bad, like Elizabeth?

My greatest fear was becoming like Elizabeth. Aside from rage and resentment, she was emotionless. She had no feelings for anyone, not even her sister. She was full of arrogance and greed, and that was something I would never want to be.

The tunnels became pitch-black, making visibility impossible. My hands shook as I felt my way along the mildew walls, looking for a place to hide. I needed to keep moving, but the fear of being caught and drained by Elizabeth slowed me down, with images of her sucking the life out of me running through my head. I needed something to guide me—a source of light.

Symbols and words that I couldn't understand began to form within my mind, glowing. My mouth began to move on its own, hissing strange-sounding words into the darkness. I couldn't make out the jumbled sounds coming from within, but my mouth made them perfectly. My hands began to glow a strikingly bright blue, casting a calming glow across the cave's damp walls.

In my mind, I could hear Elizabeth's words. I used her spell to create a source of light. I not only had her power, but I also had her spells. An ancient language was resurrecting deep within me. Words spilled from my lips, rolling off my tongue, and my hands glowed even brighter.

I was astounded, but also excited, by the possibilities of my newfound abilities. I could put this to good use. I could finally get rid of Elizabeth for good. I could feel my entire body working tirelessly, my calves bursting with energy and adrenaline coursing through my veins, propelling me to run faster than I had ever run before. The intensity and perfection of skipping and jumping over every fallen rock that would cause a normal person to trip and stumble made me feel alive.

The tunnel began to blur as I gained momentum, my

steps pounding in time with the sound of my heartbeat. I didn't know where I was running, but I knew I had to get away from them as soon as possible, and it was working. I looked behind me and saw nothing. The guards had long since vanished. As I forced my legs to go even faster, my muscles screamed at me to slow down.

"Mary, stop!" a male voice rang out in the empty tunnel.

I ground to a stop, nearly falling head-first into the wall due to the speed I was running at. Shock pulsed through me as my mind caught up with the fact that it was Miles's voice that I had heard.

"Miles?" I called out into the darkness.

A low snigger rang out behind me, forcing me to turn around to find out what was making the noise. He stood there with his hands on his hips and his lips pursed, staring at me. He didn't appear to have changed since the last time I saw him. His enticing smile made my stomach flutter. He was surrounded by an aura that made him glow a pure white. He was breathtaking, and my mind quickly switched from survival to love, showing me I had retained my emotions, unlike Elizabeth. I was still a human being capable of feeling love. When I looked into his bright green eyes, I saw a soul similar to mine. He was like a magnet, drawing me closer to embrace him, but I knew that I shouldn't.

He looked down at my glowing hands and laughed. "Using her powers wisely, are we now?"

"What's happening here, Miles? You're meant to be dead," I said, ignoring his remark.

"It's rather complicated, Mary. I'm torn between the afterlife and this world. I cannot move on as I have unfinished business here, and I don't want to leave you alone."

I gave him a grateful smile. "You annoy me even in death, but I'm glad to see you."

He was right. I didn't want to be here by myself. I needed a friend, and even though he was supposed to be dead and I could have hallucinated him, he was there to keep me company, which I appreciated.

He flashed his pearly white teeth at me. "I'm delighted to be of assistance to you."

"Can anyone else see you?" I asked.

He shook his head. "Only you can see me, which makes it rather amusing for me because if anyone else saw you right now, you'd look like you're talking to yourself."

My lips twitched, and I had to purse them to stop myself from smiling. "What should I do, Miles? What should I do next?"

His face grew serious. "The guards are out looking for you now. You need to get off this island. Your plan for John has worked, and they're out searching for you now. They're on their way here as we speak. Get to the beach, and they will find you."

"How do I get out of these caves? I have no idea where I'm going," I said.

He moved in closer and took both of my hands in his. "If you close your eyes for a moment, you'll hear something important that will help you find your way out of here." He took a deep breath and closed his eyes while still holding my hands. "Close your eyes and pay attention."

I closed my eyes and strained my ears to listen. All I could hear was my breathing and the faint sound of footsteps. "I can only hear footsteps."

He shook his head. "Listen again."

I did as I was told and ignored the approaching footsteps, instead focusing on the more distinct sounds of the cave. I could hear a low, rumbling sound to my right in the distance. It sounded like a thunderclap resounding across the sky. My mind was tuned into the strange sounds of the cave, and I could now feel the vibration of the ground that I stood on running up my legs.

"It sounds like thunder. Is that what I'm meant to be hearing?" I asked.

He looked into my eyes and smiled warmly. "Well done, Mary."

"What is it?"

He pressed his hand against the damp cave wall. "It's a waterfall. Every waterfall flows into a river or the sea. Find the waterfall, and you'll be able to escape this dark, forbidden place." When he turned around, he had a cold expression on his face. "They're on their way. Go. Right now."

I sprinted down the tunnel without even thinking about it. The pounding of my feet echoed over the distant sound of the waterfall. With the impact of the cold, hard ground beneath, the soles of my feet began to burn. Miles had vanished once more, leaving me alone in the cave. I paused every few minutes to listen to the waterfall's rumble. It was becoming more audible, so I knew I was on the right track.

The cave opened up into a large cavern with numerous entrances to other caves. When I looked up, I saw long, sharp spires protruding from the cave's ceiling, inches from my head. In one corner of the cave, a pile of crusty-looking skulls lay, and in the other, a pile of rusty swords and daggers, most likely belonging to the unfortunate souls who had come across Elizabeth. I walked over to the swords and took one that resembled a weapon, tucking it beneath my armpit so I could use it on the guards if they caught up with me before I could try and escape.

I paused once more and closed my eyes, listening to the sound of running water. The sound came from my left and echoed from one of the caves. I took a step closer to see which cave it was coming from.

"We're getting closer! I can hear her heartbeat!" Elizabeth shouted from the tunnel.

I had to make a quick decision because I was running out of time. I pushed my head into both caves, determining which one was the loudest with noise and selecting the one closest to me, hoping that I was correct. Fear was engulfing my mind, making it difficult for me to concentrate, and I didn't realise the cave sloped down with hand-chiseled steps until it was too late.

My legs gave way, and I slipped on the first step, slamming my hip into the side of the wall as I tumbled down each step until my battered and bruised body reached the bottom. The sound of my crumpled body collapsing on the floor was loud enough for the guards and Elizabeth to hear where I was.

I pulled myself up, leaning against the wall for support. My body ached from a searing pain running through my hip, and I couldn't think clearly because of the pounding headache that had submerged itself deep into my consciousness.

"I've got to keep going," I muttered to myself as I moved forward, aided by the wall.

I could clearly hear the waterfall now, and the smell of salt drifted into my nostrils, slightly irritating them. I was close enough that I could feel the tiny droplets of water on my face. The sound of their approaching heavy footsteps pushed me forward as I hobbled through the tunnel, clawing my way through, trying not to slip again.

There it was, an underground waterfall leading to the sea. It erupted from a large hole in the wall, forming a paradise-blue whirlpool. As I got closer, the noise became louder, amplifying the growling and rumbling from within. The silvery flow of water lashed up and foamed around the edges. I knew I needed to jump in, but I didn't want to. I had no idea how far the waterfall would go or how long I'd have to hold my breath.

What if I drowned down there?

No one would find me, and I would forever stay in this hell hole, just like the many others Elizabeth had slain. The water looked anything but inviting, churning and turning in every direction. It would drag me down either way if I jumped in. The sounds of footsteps were nearly upon me, making my heart thump loudly. I started to panic and threw myself in without thinking.

I immediately regretted my decision as the cold water ripped at my body, slicing into my skin like a hundred knives. I barely had time to catch my breath before the water sucked me under, submerging me beneath the rocks and carrying my body with it. My hands were still glowing, casting a silvery light on the water. My eyes wanted to close, but I forced them open to see where I was going, despite the fact that the water was burning them like acid. I didn't bother swimming; instead, I let the current carry me wherever it wanted. If Miles was correct, it should be taking me to the ocean. I hoped he was right. My lungs began to hurt, and I needed air to live. My battered body grew weary, wanting to shut down and rest. It took every ounce of strength that I had left to remain alive and fight my way through.

The cave ahead narrowed into a small hole, large enough for me to fit through if I planned carefully. If I made a mistake, the current would crush me against the rocks. It was difficult to keep my arms and legs as close to my torso as possible, but I knew I needed to do so to avoid being impaled by the rocks. The lack of oxygen was causing my mind to fog up. I needed to act quickly.

I only had a few minutes before my life was sucked from me. The current sucked me into the small, claustrophobic hole, clipping my finger against the entrance. I wasn't even aware of the pain. My lungs were screaming at me to gasp for air. Then I ran into another problem. The current was weakening, and my body began to slow down in the water.

CHAPTER TWENT-FOUR

John's Say

The sun had completely vanished below the horizon, leaving only a sliver of light and the navigation of the stars for the crew to make their way back to the ship. The boats rocked side to side as the crew paddled tirelessly, their arms growing weary from the force of the waves working against them. John clutched the locket in his hand, carefully inspecting it. It was the last invention his dear friend Martin had created before Elizabeth murdered him and used his body for her own evil plans.

He didn't know everything about the locket and what it could do, but he knew enough to make it useful to him and his crew. He knew he had to keep it safe from pirates and greedy shipmen who only cared about one thing: money. If this locket fell into the wrong hands, it could be used to instill fear and destruction upon others. He couldn't let that happen, not just for himself but also for Martin, his friend. Martin would only want it to be put to good use.

"Keep it steady, lads." John ordered.

The moon cast a vibrant glow across the powerful, ethereal waves, giving them a silvery hue. The wind was picking up, coming in from the sea, and rocking the boat even more.

"It appears that we're in for some bad weather, Captain," Bennett said next to him.

When John looked out to sea, he realised Bennett was right. The sea's palpitating pulse moved with the increasing wind, pushing the waves into the dock and rocking its timbers, causing them to creak. He could hear them splashing against the ships docked for the night from where they were. They didn't have long before the storm was right above them, wreaking havoc on the ship's sails. They hadn't had a storm in a long time, which led John to believe that it was Elizabeth's hands causing the storm to prevent them from finding Mary.

The horizon was a thin strip of pure purple that blended in with the dark and ferocious blue waves. The calm before the storm was in the air, beckoning sailors to their deaths, and John could smell it. He could feel the static from the clouds coming their way, the hair on his arms standing on end. The clouds in the distance appeared dark and foreboding. In the incoming tide, a single ship could be seen bobbing up and down. A soft glow from their candles shone out into the night air, and their sails had been lowered in preparation for the impending storm. Every sailor in these waters was aware of what was about to happen, but that didn't stop them from setting sail.

"We have to hurry. The storm's nearly upon us," John warned.

The boat lurched forward abruptly as the exhausted crew used their last ounce of strength to reach the ship. The ship was now visible, floating calmly just off the coast. The torches had been lit to help them find their way home. John smiled to himself as he looked at the ship's fine, strong structure. The ship was now his.

"We can't set sail in this weather, Captain. The wind will be too strong for the sails and may rip them," one of the crew members said as he looked up at the growing clouds coming towards them.

John nodded but remained silent as he gazed up at the rocky hollowness of the looming cliffs. Someone had erected a sign warning onlookers of falling rocks. He wasn't sure why, but the tacky sign written in bright red paint made him laugh. Bennett gave him a sidelong glance and raised an eyebrow.

The sound of the thrashing waves was distorted by the uneven surface of the cliff, making it sound like thunderclaps rather than the normal calm sounds that it should be.

Large rocks protruded from the waves, daring them to approach so they could be claimed by the sea like so many others before them. As they approached the bobbing ship, one of the crew members had thrown down a rope for them to climb aboard.

"Throw down the rigging so we can haul the boats back up. Quickly!" John bellowed.

Bennett was the first to step onboard the ship, followed by John. The crew members were busy preparing the ship to haul up the boats, ignoring the breathless grunts coming from John. He stood there watching them while the rest of the crew climbed on board.

"The boats are ready to be pulled up, Captain," Henry said, appearing beside Bennett.

John acknowledged him and walked away to take the wheel. He wasn't sure if they should set sail in the brewing storm, and he was nervous about screwing up on his first day as captain.

Mary needed him, but was the risk of finding her and losing his crew to the storm worth it?

If they stayed, the storm would undoubtedly blow them into the cliff, destroying his ship and any future voyages. He smoothed his hand over the wheel, thinking long and hard about what to do, when Bennett popped his head up.

"What are our orders, Captain? Should we sail?" he asked.

John rubbed his temple in frustration and then nodded slowly, hoping he had made the right decision. "Get the ship ready."

"Indeed, Captain," Bennett retreated to the main deck to inform the others.

"What should we do with Miles and Tom's bodies, Captain? We can't keep them here any longer," Henry asked as he walked up the steps to the top deck.

John had completely forgotten about them and was staring at Henry, trying to think of an answer. He didn't have one. He knew his captain deserved to be properly buried, but if he waited too long to rescue Mary, she might die before he could reach her if he stopped to bury Miles and Tom.

John spoke softly. "How long until they start rotting?"

"Rigor mortis has already begun to set in. Captain, they must be buried as soon as possible," Henry stated.

"We've got a problem, Henry. If we stopped to bury them, we might end up putting Mary in even more danger. I can't afford to lose her," he confessed.

"I understand that, Captain, but we also have a duty to bury them. I can try and preserve them until we find Mary, but it may not work. Just be prepared to see them become unrecognisable," Henry warned.

"Just try your best, Henry. I promise you that they will have a proper burial. They deserve nothing less," John said.

He turned away from Henry, ending their conversation. He felt guilty, but he knew what he had to do. He had to save Mary. She was his main priority right now, and God knows what Elizabeth was doing to her. She had managed to trick them all by hanging her sister instead of her. Her powers were out of this world, and right now, she could be doing anything to Mary, and he couldn't let that happen.

The love that he felt for Mary was more than just wife material. He wanted to spend every day that he had left on this earth with her. If Miles was still alive, he would have understood the situation. He also had another problem. Now that he was captain, he would need another quartermaster to take his place. He just didn't know who the best fit for it would be.

He peered over the wheel at his crew, busying themselves with getting the ship ready to sail. The boats had been pulled up and placed back in their original spots, covered with white sheets to preserve the wood from the sun. They would all make good quartermasters, but not one of them was right for the position.

The position was a tough job to fill, and it had to be done right. If he died, then the next person would have to be perfect for the captain's post. He then spotted Bennett moving barrels of liquor across the deck, the muscles in his arm bulging from the strain of the weight. He observed Bennett for a while, watching him chat with the other men and laughing while doing his job. A smile played on his lips as he imagined Bennett beside him as a quartermaster. John knew that he was perfect for the position.

He made his way down to the main deck, taking each step carefully and trying to rehearse his conversation with the crew. In his heart, he hoped that he was making the right decision, but he knew that he could trust Bennett. That's all he needed to promote him to quartermaster.

He stopped next to the mast and waved his hands, motioning for the men to stop what they were doing. "Gentlemen, gather around."

The crew placed the stuff that they were carrying down and made their way over to John. There were a few murmurs among the crew, confused by what was going on.

"I only need a few moments of your time, and then you can go back to doing whatever you were doing," John breathed out nervously as he looked around at his crew. "I have chosen the next quartermaster to join me. I have given careful consideration to this choice, and I think it's the right one to make within these circumstances."

Everyone looked at him, eager to know more. The light from the lanterns glinted in their eyes while they waited for John's choice. He knew that some of the crew wouldn't be happy with his decision about Bennett, but as he looked at Bennett standing there with the others, there was something about him that he liked. He exuded a sense of authority. His broad shoulders were chunky and strong, ready to take on anything that came his way. Bennett reminded John of Miles. He had the same dark features and brown, wavy hair. He was a good fit.

John smiled as his eyes rested on Bennett before he looked at the whole of the crew. "I have chosen Bennett to be my quartermaster. From now on, Bennett will also give orders and work alongside me. This is my final decision."

Bennett grinned and stepped forward to stand beside John. He was shaking excitedly, smiling at the crew. He clasped his hands behind his back, and his shoulders broadened, making him appear larger than he was. The rest of the crew glanced around, scanning each other's reactions. There was a mixture of anger and happiness surrounding them.

"That is all. Go back to your positions. We need to set sail as soon as possible," John ordered before returning to the wheel.

Bennett joined him on the top deck, and John could already hear some of the crew making angry remarks. Bennett stood there nervously biting his nails, oblivious to the muttering below them.

"May I ask you a question, Captain?" he asked quietly, not wanting anyone else to hear.

John nodded, waiting for Bennett to talk. He could tell Bennett felt uncomfortable as he stood there, twitching, unable to stop fidgeting. It reminded him of his first day as a quartermaster many years ago. He also felt very nervous as he stood before Martin, his captain. Martin was kind and generous and made him feel safe aboard his ship. His son, Miles, had also been the same, welcoming John with open arms and helping him overcome his grief over the death of his family. John wanted to follow in his captain's footsteps and make Bennett feel at home aboard this ship that was now his.

Bennett spoke quietly with his simple question. "Why pick me?"

John paused for a moment, trying to gather his thoughts, before smiling warmly at Bennett. "Bennett, I believe you are the right person for the position. It will take some time for you to adjust to your new role. It did for me when I first started, but you won't notice any difference after a while. Give yourself some time, and you'll grow into the role."

"Thank you, Captain," Bennett said, his face full of admiration.

John shrugged his shoulders, uneasy with the resemblance to his first day as a quartermaster. All his old emotions returned, bringing back memories of his captain and the many days they spent together tracking down Elizabeth without ever finding her, until that fateful day when she took his captain away from him and never returned.

He became engrossed in his thoughts, not realising that Bennett was standing nearby, waiting for orders. Bennett abruptly cleared his throat, jolting John back to reality.

"Make yourself useful by going to the main deck and ensuring that the ship is ready to sail. The storm is almost upon us." John turned away from Bennett and gazed out to sea.

Dark clouds gathered above their heads, threatening rain. In the distance, flashes of light could be seen, disturbing the waves and causing them to grow larger. John closed his eyes and listened to the sails flapping in the wind. The sound soothed him, quieting his mind and pushing old memories to the back of his thoughts, where they were to stay, never to resurface. Mary's face appeared in his head, causing him to smile. He was prepared to fight again, but only to save her, and then he would take her somewhere safe and forget about his sea life. He wanted to be settled. He didn't want to keep fighting and risk losing everyone he cared about.

"Captain, the ship's ready to sail," Bennett called up the stairs.

"Pull up the anchor and stand ready for my next order," John shouted over the growing winds.

The wind made him shiver as he stood there, staring over the wheel at his men. This was it. There was no turning back now for him. He had to man up and keep everyone safe, and that also included saving Mary from Elizabeth's grip.

CHAPTER TWENT-FIVE

Mary's Life

It was as if time had stopped completely, making every fibre of my being scream for air as the current abruptly stopped, leaving me stranded in the middle of an underground pool of water. This was the most terrified I'd ever felt. I could take on a hundred Elizabeths and still be less scared than I was right now. Terror and fear engulfed me, intertwining with the adrenaline coursing through my veins. My life was being sucked away from me. I was fighting for every breath of air left inside my lungs. The water was like an invisible prison, keeping me incarcerated. My mind was battling with me, trying to open my mouth to let some air in, but all I could see was water. My lungs felt crushed, and my legs grew tired of fighting, leaving me exhausted, weary, and very alone. I was living through my biggest fear.

I took one last look around and knew that this was it. My life was slipping away, taken by the most insignificant of elements. I didn't expect to die this way, but I began to enjoy the chill that crept up my legs and seized control of my body.

Miles appeared in the distance, floating calmly in the water and pointing above his head. "Mary, look up."

I smiled, not paying attention to what he was saying, as my mind began to close off, shutting down with the pressure from the water. It was comforting to see him as my final image before passing away. I stared at him, puzzled as to why he was glaring at me angrily while putting his finger on the roof of the underground pool.

"God damn it, woman, just look up and you'll see!" he snarled.

I looked up hazily at what he was pointing at and realised he was simply trying to save my life. He had his finger
stuck in a pocket of air, trapped inside the small underwater cave. I kicked my legs with the last of my strength to
get to Miles. My legs ached with every movement, but with
Miles cheering me on, I mustered the courage to reach him
and stick my face into the large pocket of air. My eyes widened as I took a deep breath, filling my lungs with air once
more. My lungs embraced it, savouring every last bit. Miles
grinned at me as I inhaled more air, sucking in the last of it.
He then pointed to another pocket of trapped air, and I eagerly swam to it, my lips piercing the water and sucking
even more air in.

As I sucked in more and more air, the fog in my head
began to lift, restoring my sharp mind and allowing me to
think clearly once more. I felt a wave of relief wash over
me, and I realised I might just make it through this nightmare. My attention was drawn back to Miles, who pointed
to a small hole hidden behind a large boulder that could
lead me out of this pit of hell.

"You couldn't see it because you were panicking too
much," he said as he swam towards it. "Take a deep breath,
as you're going to need it."

I nodded and inhaled the last of the air into my lungs. I
swam through the small hole, the sides scraping against my
skin as I went. My worst nightmare was feeling claustrophobic and unable to breathe, and now I was living
through it.

The current began to pick up speed once more, carrying
my body through the small tunnel and into another large
pool of water, but this time it opened up into a small cavern with rocks surrounding the edge. I swam to the surface
of the water, my mouth agape as the air hit my lungs. Even
though the air smelled bad, it was the best damn air I'd ever breathed. My lungs greeted it with open arms, gasping
for more.

I sat up slowly, taking in my surroundings. Spires with

gnarled appearances hung from the ceiling, narrowly missing the large boulders that took up the majority of the cave itself. Moss clung to the rocky, uneven walls of the cave, spreading into a small man-made tunnel large enough to fit someone through.

That was my means of escape. Aside from the small tunnel, there was nowhere else to go. I felt cold and shivery, with water dripping from my clothes as I stood up properly to make my way over, hoping deep down to see Miles again. I didn't want to feel alone, like I was in the dark, freezing water. My throat still burned from holding my breath for too long, and my legs felt like they were on fire. I never wanted to go through that ordeal again, and I needed Miles to keep me from going insane.

"Where do I go from here, Miles?" I asked aloud, hoping he'd show up.

I waited for a few moments, looking around for him, but quickly realised he wasn't coming. This was something I had to do on my own. He was doing this on purpose, so instead of relying on him, I would have to think my way out of there. I took one last look around before entering the small tunnel and leaving my near-death experience with water behind. The glow from my hands illuminated the tunnel, casting my shadow across the uneven surface of the wall. There was nowhere else to go but forward, and if I were discovered now, I wouldn't be able to escape. My heart was beating twice as fast as it should have as I hurried through the small tunnel. The tunnel veered left, opening up into a larger one with cells on either side of the walls. I recognised the location right away. Elizabeth had me held there before the ritual she bestowed upon me.

I knew where I was now, which led me to believe that Miles hadn't shown up because he knew I'd find my way out of there quickly. I only had a few minutes before this nightmare ended, and I was free. I ran the rest of the way with a spring in my step, getting closer and closer to freedom until I could almost taste it.

From the cave's entrance, all I could see was darkness.

There was no light coming in, making it difficult for me to see where I was going and if anyone was lurking in the shadows. I didn't hear any movement, so I went into the next cave, which led to the boats that had been stranded by Elizabeth and her guards. My fingers began to tingle, and a low, beating sound echoed throughout the cave. I paused to listen to the beat, and a nagging feeling started to form in the pit of my stomach. I recognised the sound but couldn't quite place its familiarity. I knew I had heard it somewhere before, but the more I thought about it, the more I was getting agitated. The beating in my ear became louder, and I realised it was coming from within me.

It sounded like a heartbeat, but it wasn't my heartbeat, and if it wasn't mine, whose was it?

"I know you can hear me, Mary. I can hear you," a voice hissed from deep within the shadows.

My heart sank, immediately recognising the voice. It was Elizabeth. I unwillingly stepped out into the open, knowing that I would find Elizabeth standing there. Her eyes looked as wild as her hair. Her sister's dress was ripped down one side, revealing her yellow, rotting legs. She stood there with her arms folded, grinning from ear to ear, with her followers standing behind her.

"That was your heartbeat I heard, but why?" I asked, intrigued.

She smiled. "We are now connected, Mary. You can hear my heartbeat, and I can hear yours."

"I don't want it; I don't want any of this!" I screeched, pushing her away from me.

"It's happened. Deal with it," she snarled, stepping towards me again. "In some ways, you owe me. I've given you powers."

I looked at her, knowing exactly what she was going to try. It made my stomach churn to think that Elizabeth was admitting defeat and attempting to entice me to join her.

"I'm not going to join you if that's what you're asking," I stated.

She was taken aback but quickly covered it up with a sneer. "If you don't join us, you'll never leave this place."

"You're asking me to join you because you know that you can't win against me. You're scared, and I can sense it."

Elizabeth's jaw clenched, and her face contorted with rage. "You've got it all wrong. I was giving you one last chance to survive, Mary."

It was my turn to be terrified, and she sniffed the air, sensing it right away.

Her mouth curled into a smile. "Who's terrified now, eh?"

I forced myself to remain calm and smiled back at her. "I'll let you live if you let me go."

The ancient symbols began to reappear in my mind, eliciting some unsettling feelings and putting me on edge. My tongue began moving on its own, spewing the unknown language. Elizabeth's face changed from aggressive to shocked as she realised what I was about to do. I didn't know what I was saying. It was as if my mouth had a mind of its own, rambling with words that I couldn't understand, no matter how hard I tried. I couldn't control anything, which terrified me.

What if every time I got angry, my mind and mouth moved on their own, hurting the people I care about the most?

What Elizabeth had done to me was worse than murder. I didn't know what was going on in my head anymore. It was filled with symbols and marks that no ordinary person would understand. Elizabeth retreated into her followers, trying to get away from my babbling mouth. She clawed her way through the crowd in an attempt to escape on one of the untethered boats.

Her followers stared at her, puzzled and shocked, not understanding why their leader was abandoning them until they saw themselves rising above the ground, propelled by the power that was emanating from within me. My arms moved by themselves, manipulating the elements sprouting from my fingers. The water inside the cave began to rise, carrying the boats with it while Elizabeth attempted to board one.

She jumped in, smacking her head against the side and cursing aloud. My fists clenched, and a smouldering ball of fire erupted, striking a couple of her followers. As they fell to the ground, the scent of burning flesh filled my nostrils. The rest of them screamed in terror, but they couldn't move as they dwindled in the rising wind, being thrown around by the force of my clenched fists.

"You have to keep it under control, Mary," Miles' voice whispered in my ear. "If you don't stop now, you'll kill everyone, including yourself."

I couldn't say anything because my mouth kept sputtering the ancient language, killing them off one by one. I averted my gaze, not wanting to see the panic in their eyes.

"Mary, if you don't stop now, you'll become her!" Miles yelled, standing inches away from my face. "Think of someone you care about and do it quickly."

Miles was right. I could feel myself transforming into Elizabeth, with her powers coursing through my veins and her deep hatred abusing my body. I didn't want to be like her, but I couldn't seem to stop myself. In my mind, an image of John smiling at me took precedence over the symbols. I shut my eyes and concentrated on his features. As his body embraced mine, his kind eyes stared at me.

Excitement washed over me, and the symbols vanished completely from my mind. A low, gurgling scream erupted from within, quickly overtaking the strange language and silencing it. The waves calmed down and the wind dispersed back into the cave opening, leaving the remaining cult members terrified and shaken. Their screams and wailing pierced my ears as they ran for their lives back through the tunnel from where I came. Elizabeth was nowhere to be found. The boat she was attempting to board had vanished, leaving only one more for me to escape on.

Miles' lips curled into a smile. "I knew you could pull it off."

My exhausted legs collapsed beneath me, dragging the

rest of my body with them. Tears streamed down my cheeks, causing my nose to drip. I was sick and tired, and whatever powers were inside had sapped my will to live. I could still feel it bubbling inside me, taunting me with its venom.

My life was no longer mine, and as I lay there staring up at the uneven surface of the cave, I realised that if I didn't control and contain these powers within, I'd be hung as a witch. I remembered my days on the farm with my parents by my side, not realising how simple they were, not having to worry about anything, and being in the company of my loving parents. Elizabeth had ruined everything good in my life, transforming me into a nasty, shriveled-up prune like her. Maybe this was her plan all along—to make me like her. She had no one to love in her life, and no one loved her. She was relentless and evil. I wouldn't even call her human anymore.

Miles's face appeared, staring down at me as I lay there, reminiscing about my past. "Get up, Mary. You need to leave this place. The ship is almost here."

"I can't have John seeing me like this, Miles. I've become like her," I stuttered, trying my hardest not to cry again.

He held out his hand for me to take and grinned. "You're nothing like her. You couldn't help what you did. You just need to control it."

I took his hand, and he pulled me up gently. "What if I can't control it? I don't want these powers, Miles. It's turning me into her."

"You know how to control them now. By using one emotion that Elizabeth has never been capable of feeling. It's love, Mary. There are ways to reverse what happened to you, but first, you need to find the ship," he explained.

"Can you come with me?" I asked him desperately.

He shook his head. "I'm sorry, Mary, but you need to do this on your own. I can only come to you when you're in danger."

"But I need you, Miles, more than ever."

"That's what you think, but there will come a time when

you really need me. You need to get into that boat and leave before Elizabeth returns. She's conjuring up a plan to destroy you, and once she does, she will hunt you down."

I did as he said and lowered myself into the boat. "If you're not real, then how come I can touch you?"

He laughed loudly, crossing his arms as he watched me untie the boat to escape. "I'm real to you, but not to anyone else. I chose you to see me, Mary. After what I did to you with Felicity, I owe you. I'm here for as long as you need me."

When Miles said Felicity's name, my heart skipped a beat. Even though she was dead and couldn't harm me anymore, hearing Miles say it hurt. He saw me wincing and apologised.

There was a low, rumbling sound coming from outside, and I could see the waves thrashing against the rocks. Flashes of light could be seen from afar, the clouds brightening frequently with their immense glow.

His eyes widened as he looked up in the direction of the sea. "I can feel her returning. Mary, you must leave right now."

CHAPTER TWENT-SIX

John's Way

As the scenery of the island came into view, John's hands hesitated above the wheel. His body shook with fear as he stared ahead at the rocky mountains of green foliage. The sensation in his stomach became denser, and his hands began to sweat. He never wanted to set foot on that island again after what happened the last time, but he knew he had to do whatever it took to find Mary, even if he could feel his impending doom growing stronger within him.

It was dark outside, and he had only the glow of the lanterns to guide him. They were in the eye of the storm, and the wheel shook from the vibration of the thunderclouds above them. Rain poured down, soaking everyone and making it difficult for John to see. He could see the island clearly as lightning flashed, but when it went dark again, all he could see was the outline of the rocky mountains. Dark clouds obscured the moon and stars, making it even more difficult for John to steer the ship away from ominous rocks. As John clutched the wheel and tried to keep it steady, the ship heaved and tossed side to side. His knuckles whitened with pressure as he spun the wheel to the left to avoid a rock thrown up by the water.

Lightning struck the sky once more, illuminating the rocks beneath them. When John noticed that they were heading straight for them, he spun the wheel clockwise, narrowly missing one by a few inches. A gap in the clouds revealed the moon's silvery hue, casting a ghostly glow across the waves that made them appear larger than they were. The ship's timber shuddered and bulged, buckling from the pressure of the ferocious waves. The sails whipped and flapped, splashing the crew with flecks of water, spraying their faces so they couldn't see. A high wave smashed against the side of the ship, flinging everyone to the floor.

"Keep her steady, men!" John bellowed over the storm.

The ship steadied itself once more, giving the men hope that all of this could soon be over. The temperature suddenly dropped, causing a fine mist to form just above the waves. It curled and swirled, entwining with the ocean. No one could tell where the waves ended and the mist began. It kept John on edge as he watched the mist thicken and turn into a fog. The storm had begun to fade by this point, becoming weaker as the fog took over, engulfing everything in its path. John knew what that meant, especially when the fog appeared. Elizabeth was on her way.

"Get yourselves armed, lads! We have company coming!" John ordered. "Bennett, get up here."

Bennett rushed up the steps to his captain's aid. "Yes, Captain?"

John stepped away from the wheel and motioned for Bennett to take over. "Bennett, I need you to keep the ship on course and steady."

Bennett cocked his brow. "What are you going to do?"

"I'm going to get a boat and go look for Mary." Before he descended the stairs to meet his crew he turned to look at Bennett, "You're the second-in-command here. You will remain here and ensure the safety of the ship." He left Bennett on the top deck and gathered his crew around him to take give them orders. "I need to find Mary before it's too late, and I'll need some of you to help me. The rest of you will remain here and keep the cannons ready in case anything comes our way. Who will join me?"

"Something is heading our way, Captain. I believe it's a boat," Bennett shouted.

John's heart skipped a beat, and he dashed back up the stairs, two at a time, hoping to see what Bennett had seen. He hoped it was Mary escaping, as he didn't want to set foot on the island again. He snatched Bennett's spyglass from his grasp and held it up to his face. He could see the dark silhouette of a small boat heading their way in the distance. There was a lone shadow in the boat, paddling quickly over the waves.

Bennett could feel John's shoulders tensing as he scanned the foggy ocean for anything else that might come their way. As far as the eye could see, the waves were shrouded in grey. It appeared surreal, as if the ship were floating on clouds rather than the open sea. The island's mountain peeking through the fog was the only thing keeping John from thinking they'd drifted into the sky. He returned the spyglass to the location where he last saw the boat, but all he could see was the glowing fog that surrounded it.

"It's no longer there," Bennett heard John mutter.

He handed Bennett the spyglass and returned to take the wheel, a sinking feeling in the pit of his stomach that whoever was in that boat didn't want to be seen by anyone.

"I can't see anything, but there was a boat there. Do you think it could be Mary?" Bennett asked as he lowered the spyglass.

John shook his head. "I don't think it was her. Whoever was coming this way didn't want to be seen."

The crew occupied themselves with arming the cannons and aiming them at the island. John had a horrible feeling it was Elizabeth in that boat, and she was heading right for them. The fog around them became denser, making it impossible to see anything in front of them.

"Drop the anchor. It's too dangerous to go any further," John said.

Mark and Henry emerged from below deck. As they approached John and the others, they both appeared disturbed. Something was wrong, but John couldn't put his finger on it. Mark had a bandage wrapped tightly around his head, and he looked exhausted. His skin had a green tint to it, and he clung to Henry for dear life, while Henry struggled to keep him upright, looking as if he had just run a marathon. They were both sweating profusely, with beads of sweat dripping down their brows.

"Is everything alright?" John asked them, a look of concern etched on his face.

Henry and Mark rushed up to him, stopping just inches from his feet and looking down at the ground as if whatever they were about to say would be bad. John stood there, tapping his foot impatiently and staring at them both, waiting for them to respond.

"Captain, we've got a problem," Henry muttered, not wanting the others to overhear.

John took a step back from the crew and drew them both to the side. "What is it?"

Henry fiddled with his fingers nervously, trying to come up with a way to explain to John what they had both seen without sounding insane. "When I was mixing a solution to preserve Miles's body, it moved. We then checked Tom's body, and it was gone."

John's eyes widened in surprise, chewing over Henry's words. None of it made any sense, and he couldn't think of any reason why Miles's body would move by itself unless somehow Elizabeth was involved. He looked them both over, trying to see if they were lying, but by the terrified look on their faces, they were telling the truth. He didn't want to believe any of it. He knew Elizabeth's games and what she was capable of, but this was just too bizarre.

"Secure the ship. We need to investigate what's going on," John ordered.

He grabbed a lantern and made his way over to the stairs that led to the lower deck. But before he went down, he stopped and turned to his men. "Make sure your guns are loaded, gentlemen. Be prepared for anything that comes out of that fog. Mark and Henry, you will show me what happened, and Bennett, you will stay here and be in charge of the crew until I get back."

Mark and Henry nodded and followed John below deck, staying close behind him just in case one of the bodies jumped out at them. Fear rippled through them as they walked to Miles's cabin in silence. John held a shaky hand out, holding his pistol and aiming it in front of him for protection. The air felt dense around them, sending a chill down their spines.

Henry stopped, not wanting to walk any further, and pointed to Miles's cabin door. He was only the ship's medic. He wasn't a hero, nor was he brave. He spent his time reading medical books and bandaging people's wounds. He didn't have the stomach for things like this. He was a middle-aged, balding, and physically unfit man. He wasn't anything like John, and even Mark was stronger and fitter than him.

Henry made a shaky motion with his finger. "He's in there somewhere."

John noticed and stopped. "You're both coming with me."

Henry looked at John with pleading eyes. "I'm just the ship's medic, Captain. I'm no use to you in there. I can't even fight."

"You'll have to learn to stand up for yourself, Henry. It is useless if you are unwilling to learn," John stated as he returned his attention to the door. "Whether you like it or not, sir, you're coming in."

As John dragged Henry along with him, Henry's face screwed up, sulking like a child. Mark remained silent and puffed his way along, attempting to match John's quick steps. Miles' door was open, and a glow of light emanated from the doorway.

Henry looked at Mark, puzzled. "Didn't we shut the door?"

Mark was engulfed in a cold wave, his mouth dry, fear gripping his muscles as he stared at Henry's terrified expression. "I believe so."

John rolled his eyes, looking at them both with pity. "Come on. Let's get this over with."

He continued on without looking around to see if they were following him, and entered Miles' cabin. He was scared as well, but he didn't show it. He didn't want to see his friend walk around as the undead, and he certainly didn't want to fight him. He put on a brave face and took a look around him. The cabin appeared to be normal, but there was an eerie feeling about it that John didn't like. Miles' body had vanished, leaving only a trail of wet footprints leading out of the cabin and away from the top deck. It led to Tom's cabin, where his door was also open.

"Well, you're right about them moving. Miles's body has gone," John called from inside the cabin.

Henry and Mark poked their heads in, scanning the room until their gazes were drawn to John, who stood in the centre of the room, thinking. He ran his fingers through his scruffy hair and deliberated for a long time about what to do next. The fact that Mark and Henry were staring at him from the doorway, expecting a plan, didn't help matters.

"We need to look into Tom's cabin," John said, and without hesitation, he left the room.

He could not shake the feeling of being watched. It clung to him like an icy mist, engraving itself into his veins and freezing them with its touch.

But where were the eyes coming from?

Certainly not within the narrow corridor, as he would have seen them by now. He looked to his left and then to his right, trying to find the source of the feeling.

He shook it off and carried on, taking one step at a time, prolonging the inevitable. He knew that one of them would be in Tom's cabin. He could sense it. His instincts screamed at him to get out, run away.

"Go carefully, Captain," Henry stammered from behind him.

John gulped, his mouth as parched as the desert. He'd been to the desert once before and nearly died from dehydration, but he'd rather go there than face his dead captain any day. He took a deep breath and took his first step into the cabin. He paused for a moment, allowing his eyes to adjust to the darkness of the room. With a knot in his throat, Henry watched him from the corridor. He could feel the dense sensation creeping up his spine. Mark stood beside him, lost in thought, attempting to not watch John walk to his death.

"It's empty," John called from the room.

Henry let out a sigh of relief as he followed Mark into Tom's cabin. It was light enough to see the outline of the furniture, but dark enough that Henry couldn't rely on John's assumption that they weren't there. He retreated into the corridor, not wanting to take any chances.

A crash from inside Tom's cabin made Henry jump. His lips parted in silent terror as the body of Tom came into view, picking John up by the neck and throwing him against the wall. His body became limp and splayed across the floor. Tom's face was ashen, his clothes were torn, and his eyes were a putrid black. His hands twitched spastically, while his knuckles clicked with every movement, making them sound more out of this world than human.

The blood drained from Mark's face, his feet stumbling as he tried to retreat from the room but instead fell on his bum. He let out a yelp and scrambled to Henry, who stood there, his gaze fixed on a rotting-looking Tom. Miles appeared from behind the door with the same complexion as Tom. They both moved rigidly as if the rigor mortis hadn't left their system yet. Their mouths were open, and a black substance started dribbling from their tongues. This was Elizabeth's doing.

John's eyes flickered but remained shut, leaving Mark and Henry to defend themselves and try to save their captain. Mark made the first move by grabbing his loaded pistol and shooting Tom straight in the head. It made a hole in his head, spilling out the contents of his brain, but that didn't faze Tom. He carried on walking towards John, his knees swinging out stiffly.

"We need to get the others." Henry stuttered.

Mark grabbed his shoulders and shook him. "We can't leave our captain here. We have to stand our ground."

"But they can't die!" Henry squealed, his voice growing high-pitched.

"I know. I'll go in and distract them while you drag John's body out to safety. We can then lock them in." Mark stated as he drew his sword.

Henry's body grew tense with panic, but eventually, he nodded, trying to keep his hands from shaking as he moved closer to the cabin door. He stood behind Mark, using his body as a shield, and followed him in slowly. Mark grabbed the closest thing to him and threw it at them with all his strength. It caught them both off guard, throwing them down to the ground in a heap.

"Now, Henry," Mark slurred as he threw another object at them to keep them down.

Henry heard him but couldn't move. His legs froze, and his muscles stiffened to the point of spasming. He could see Mark's mouth moving, but he was unable to hear him. He retreated into his mind, his safe haven, where no one could touch him.

"Move, Henry!" Mark screamed, flailing his arms in an attempt to shake Henry out of his trance.

Mark shoved Henry into the wall and grabbed John by his legs, pulling him out of the cabin and into the corridor. He then went back in and yanked Henry out by his arm, throwing him onto the floor next to John.

Miles' body was the first to rise, followed quickly by Tom's. They both slithered their way towards the door, their beady eyes alight with madness and frothing at the mouth. What had once been glossy hair had become lank, straggly hair that shaped around their gaunt, white-stricken faces. They didn't look like the men Mark had known, but rather like Elizabeth, with her leering eyes and translucent skin.

Mark froze, unable to move, fear engulfing his mind as he stared at them, creeping closer and closer.

CHAPTER TWENT-SEVEN

Reunited

I remained in the shadows, alert and waiting. The tide had pushed the boat away from the island, bringing it closer to the ship's lantern light. Only the small orange glow from the ship could be seen through the thick haze. Miles' assumption was correct, and the ship was just off the coast, lurking in the waters, waiting for me to come to them. I couldn't wait to see John's face again. It was the only thing keeping me going. Without him, I would have given up and let Elizabeth have her way.

The storm had passed, leaving the waves calm and nurturing. Through the fog, I could just make out the stars and the moon, helping the ship navigate its way across the waters. As I watched the white glow filtering through the fog, I couldn't help but smile a little. It was a beautiful sight to see.

I looked down at my pale hands and noticed my knuckles were tightly grasping the oars, ready to row again. I wasn't sure if I could fully control the magical elements that were colliding within me, encircling my heart. I could feel the power surge as if it were a mechanical engine about to take off. Part of me liked the magical power, but the other half was afraid that if I didn't get rid of it quickly, it would completely engulf my body, taking over the last human remnants I had left.

I shook the thoughts from my mind and began rowing toward the ship. The looming presence of rocks protruding from the water scraped against the boat's side, causing the timber to shudder. The lapping waves washed away old seaweed and debris from the sharp, jagged rocks' surfaces. They had a slight green tinge to them, and they glistened in the water like green emeralds waiting to be picked. When I looked closer at the large rock next to the boat, I realised that they were in fact green emeralds clinging to the surface's nooks and crannies.

Not only were there green emeralds, but also red rubies. I wasn't sure if my eyes were deceiving me or if the waters were brimming with glittering gold treasure, enough to make a pirate giddy. I reached down into the water to touch the gleaming coins and diamonds, only to be slapped away by an unexpected hand.

"Don't go near them," Miles' voice hissed from beneath the boat.

When I looked down, I saw his ghostly face emerge from the water, distracting my attention from the ever-increasing piles of gold coming through the waves. He had a look of rage on his face as he pushed the gold away from my sight.

"What's happening?" I asked, confused.

He jumped into the boat, spraying cold droplets of water all over me. "She's trying to distract you, Mary, so it gives her more time to kill everyone on board the ship."

My eyes widened in excitement as my hand neared the water again, wanting to pick up the gold coins. "Are they real?"

In a fit of rage, he slapped my hand away once more. "Stop staring at them, woman. They are real, but touching them will transport you back to the island and into one of the jail cells, which you do not want. This is how she entices people. Ignore the urge and grab an oar instead."

He thrust an oar in my hand and made a rowing motion with his, trying to divert my attention away from the heap of gold that was heading our way. I couldn't think of a way out. The treasure piles just kept emerging from the water, enticing me with their glittery-gold appearance. There was nowhere to go. The water was being replaced with coins, clinging and clanging against each other as more emerged.

"Start rowing, Mary. You have little time left before it

traps you," Miles screamed in my face, shaking my shoulders in an attempt to dislodge the hypnotic treasure that had engulfed my mind.

It worked. My mind became clearer once more, allowing me to leave the island. My hands were clenched around the oars, moving them back and forth over the colossal number of coins. The boat scraped and skidded over them, causing the piles to sink back into the water.

"You're almost there. Keep going," Miles urged, his gaze fixed on the oncoming ship. He smiled as he looked at it with admiration. "She looks stunning in the water."

I had completely forgotten that Miles was no longer alive. I saw his ghostly face looking sadly at his ship, knowing he'd never steer it again. The ship was his pride and joy, and it must have been heartbreaking for him to be unable to board it. I kept rowing, one eye on him and the other on the diminishing piles of treasure as we moved away from the island.

"There's got to be a way to bring you back, Miles," I muttered.

He shifted his gaze away from the ship and gave me a sad smile. "My time was up long before Elizabeth shot me. I was meant to die at that time, but you brought me back to life. I was living on borrowed time. I know that now," he sighed deeply. "Mary, you didn't read all of my father's inventions. If you bring someone back to life, they are living on borrowed time, and sooner or later, their life will be taken away again, this time for good. My father was working on a method to keep a person alive after bringing them back to life, but he died before he could succeed."

With the thought of John on my mind, an anxious feeling began to form within me. I had brought him back to life, unaware that he, too, was on borrowed time. "That means John doesn't have much time."

Miles lightly tapped my hand. "You'll figure out a way to keep him alive. I'm confident you will. After all, you still have me, albeit in spirit form. Mary, I'm still here. I still love you, and the good news is that I will never grow old, but I will get to see you grow old and wrinkled," He burst out laughing.

"Are you planning on staying that long?" I asked.

"You're not going to be able to get rid of me. I'll stay as long as you need me," he smiled, showing off his pearly-white teeth. He then returned his gaze to the ship, his expression becoming dangerous. "Something isn't right. I can sense it. Mary, step on it. We need to hurry."

I obeyed and pushed my muscles to their limits, rowing as fast as I could to reach the ship. When I looked up, I saw the lanterns going out one by one, completely darkening the ship. I couldn't see Miles anymore as the fog thickened, but I knew he was still there.

Miles snatched the ores from my grasp and tossed them into the water, leaving me stunned. "Change of plan. You need to use your power and get yourself into my old room as quickly as you can."

"But I can't control it, Miles," I moaned.

He grabbed both of my hands and squeezed them together. "You have no choice. If you want John to live, I suggest that you muster the courage to use your own power to save him." He stood up and pulled me up with him, turning my body to face the ship. "Close your eyes and imagine you're in my cabin. Imagine as much detail as you can. Feel yourself in there, and you'll begin to sense the magic within you. Don't fight it, just let it happen."

I closed my eyes tightly, nervous about what could happen if I got it wrong. An image of Miles' cabin flashed through my mind, and I clung to it as tightly as I could, trying to remember every detail. A warm, tingling sensation began to develop within my fingers and quickly spread throughout the rest of my body. The power began to erupt through my hands, illuminating them with a gold glow and pointing straight into the cabin window.

I was whisked into Miles' cabin before I knew it, leaving the boat stranded outside. As I stood there, staring wide-eyed at Miles and Tom's dead bodies moving around on their own, the tingling sensation in my fingers faded, along with the golden glow. They both returned my stare, as puzzled as I was to be there.

I watched Miles' gaping wound spew darkened blood, splattering black blotches on his already stained shirt. I could see the remains of his skull poking through his hairline, his yellowy skin peeling away from his flesh as he moved closer to me—close enough for his decaying stench to fill my nostrils. His head was tilted to the side, and his neck was unable to support the weight of his head. I swallowed the hard lump in my throat and turned to Tom, not wanting to see Miles in that state. He would be disgusted if he saw himself now.

This was all Elizabeth's fault. I could feel the magic within them working its way through their muscles, allowing them to move in ways they shouldn't be able to. My stomach clenched, upset by what Elizabeth had done, mixed with anger and disdain. My fingers began to twitch with water energy, conjuring up a spell I couldn't stop. I let my body go with the flow this time, not wanting to fight it.

My fingers began to move independently, pointing at both of them. "Boys, rest in peace," I muttered.

My index finger shot a bolt of blue lightning, zapping both of them in the heart. They immediately fell to the floor, their eyes glazing over and returning to their normal colour. Sadness seeped into my body, causing my eyes to well up with tears for them both. I stood there, numb, quietly staring at their bodies heaped on the floor.

I heard a scuffle behind me and a low voice say, "How did you do that?"

I turned around to see a terrified-looking Mark standing in the doorway. He looked at my hands, puzzled and terrified. I took a step towards him, and he took a step backward, away from me, as if I were Elizabeth. I realised what he saw made me look bad, so I raised my hands in defence.

"Mark, it's me. I will explain everything to you, but for now, please don't say anything. I can't have John know that

I have powers," I begged, my eyes pleading with him.

With scepticism in his eyes, he shifted his gaze away from me and then to the dead bodies on the floor. "How come you have powers? What happened to you?"

"Mark, Elizabeth made me this way. I didn't have much of a choice. Please don't look at me as if I'm evil because I've been through hell and back to get back to you," I marched up to him, pointing angrily at my cheeks. "These are her tooth impressions. She tried to drain my life away, but it backfired, and now I have some of her abilities."

He lifted his finger to my cheek and traced the indents lightly. "They don't look so bad. They will heal in time. I just don't understand why this happened to you."

"I don't either, Mark. But for the time being, could you please keep it a secret?"

He gave me a cautious look before nodding. "Okay, I will, but you must tell John as soon as possible. You're not going to be able to keep that a secret for long."

I kissed his hand, grateful that he understood the situation. "This is greatly appreciated. I'll tell him, just not right now. He won't understand, and I don't want him to see me any differently."

Mark smiled warmly and took my hand in his. "That man will never see you differently, miss. He worships the ground you walk on."

I looked at him, my lips pressed into a thin line, trying to smile but failing miserably. I knew he meant well, but based on the way he had stared at me as if I were Elizabeth, I knew John would do the same. I couldn't let that happen. It would break my heart to see John's face if he did the same. I needed to get rid of the abilities as soon as possible.

A low groan came from the corridor, followed by a grunt. I looked to see where the noise was coming from and found John and Henry on the floor, stirring awake. I raised my brow at Mark, who laughed at me and shrugged his shoulders.

"It's been a long day," he mused.

I kneeled to John's level and shook him until his eyes opened and his arms began swatting at me, convinced that I was one of the dead bodies. I slapped him, knocking his face sideways, to deter him from attacking me. He clenched his jaw in rage until he noticed I was kneeling beside him.

In his excitement, he threw his arms around me, nearly knocking me to the ground. "Mary!"

I laughed, trying to pull him away from my waist as he smothered me with big, sloppy kisses. "That's enough, young man. Pull yourself together. I'm alive and well."

"How did you get here? How did you escape? Are you hurt?" he spoke quickly, attempting but failing miserably, to remain calm.

He bombarded me with questions, never taking a moment to let me respond until I pressed my finger to his lips to silence him. "I escaped to the ship using an old boat of ours that we had left in the cave. I'm not hurt, but I believe Elizabeth is close behind, so we should prepare ourselves."

He leapt to his feet and pulled me up with him. "She's already here. You better not go into Miles's cabin, as it's not a pretty sight in there. She used Tom and Miles to attack us." He turned his attention to Mark. "I'm guessing they've been defeated, Mark?"

Panic rose within me as Mark cast a glance in my direction, unsure what to say. He'd never lied before in his life. He was a genuine man who did not need to lie, but I was hoping that he would tell a white lie just once to keep my secret hidden. I begged him with my eyes, and he stood there, becoming increasingly agitated at being put on the spot. He twitched nervously as John studied him, waiting for an answer.

"I managed to take them both out and bring you and Henry into the corridor to safety," He slurred.

I breathed a small sigh, my body relaxing once more, relieved that Mark didn't rat me out. As I looked at Mark's worried expression, guilt quickly overtook my relief. He didn't want to lie, and I felt bad for him because he had to for my sake. In shame, he turned his head away from his captain's face and bowed his head to the ground. John didn't seem to notice as he took my hand in his and led me toward the main deck.

"Mark, wake Henry up. Make sure he's alright," he called over his shoulder as we jogged up the stairs.

The crew remained silent in their positions as they awaited John's orders. They were ready with their weapons drawn, pointing in every direction in case Elizabeth appeared. Their eyes were wide and alert, waiting to see what would emerge from the fog. The sails had disappeared into the fog as it calmly circled the ship, engulfing everything in its stride. The fog was so thick that I couldn't even see the top deck. With Elizabeth's powers waiting to be unleashed on us and the thick fog that obscured our vision, we were useless. The crew's weapons were nothing compared to what Elizabeth could do, and even though I also had powers, I would not use them and have John think that I was a witch as well.

Miles appeared beside me, taking me by surprise. I yelped loudly, and John looked at me, puzzled as to what I was doing. With a quick glance, he decided to disregard the strange noise that came out of my mouth and instead began barking orders at the others. Miles' ghostly lips smiled as he stood beside me with his arms folded, watching John follow in his footsteps as captain.

"I've taught him well," he smiled. "He's a miniature version of me."

I sighed and rolled my eyes. "If you've come here to annoy me, I recommend you leave."

John stopped what he was doing and looked at me again, this time with a piercing, confused glare, gesturing me to keep quiet. Miles cackled in my ear, making them ring loudly. As John approached me and demanded to know what was wrong, I stood there, trying to remain calm while Miles's laugh pierced through my ears.

"Don't forget that no one can hear me apart from you,"

he smirked, watching John stand impatiently waiting for me to answer him.

"I was just thinking," I said, ignoring Miles's giggling.

"Then go about it quietly. I need to issue orders to my men," he stomped away, but not before looking back at me with a disapproving look.

"Why are you here?" I hissed.

He dropped his smirk and leaned in closely. "I need you to prepare yourself. Elizabeth is coming, and she's not alone."

"Prepare myself?" I asked.

He nodded. "She's done it on purpose to get a rise out of you, so giving her the upper hand would be a mistake. Don't let it get to you."

"What are you on about, Miles?"

He averted his gaze, staring into the mist, listening intently to something I couldn't hear. "It's too late; she's here."

He vanished as quickly as he appeared, leaving no trace and leaving me with a slew of unanswered questions. Even though my encounter with Miles had left me more baffled than ever, I still had a clear head. I sprang into action to warn John that Elizabeth was approaching.

I approached him nervously. The look on his face as he barked orders at the men was very unwelcoming, to say the least. He didn't realise that I was beside him until he turned and smacked straight into me, knocking me backward onto the floor.

"What are you doing, Mary? Why are you sneaking up on me like that?" He looked down at me sprawled across the deck in bewilderment.

He then remembered his manners and held out his hand for me. I gladly took it, and he pulled me back onto my feet. I stood there, slightly embarrassed that John was staring at me with a strange look on his face, wondering why I was acting so strangely. I couldn't tell him about Miles; he just wouldn't understand.

I straightened my shirt and pointed into the fog. "She's

coming, John. Get your men ready to fight."

John put a finger to my lips and looked up into the sky. "Oh, I think I can hear something."

A flapping sound could be heard in the distance, becoming louder as it got closer. It sounded like a drumbeat, and it moved in time with the wind. The only thing we could see was the fog that surrounded the ship. My shoulders tensed as I strained my eyes to see beyond the thick fog that was blinding us from seeing what was coming at us at breakneck speed. John stepped in front of me, his hand guiding me behind him so he could use his body as a shield. Miles' words about John's life being on borrowed time echoed in my head, taunting me. I knew it was a warning of some sort. I needed to protect him, not the other way around.

A squawking fleet of crows appeared through the fog. They swarmed around the mast, nestling in with one another as they rested on the wooden beam. It was as if they were warning us of Elizabeth's return. Each of them let out a horrifying scream, their beady amber eyes fixed on us. More black crows appeared out of nowhere, joining the first group, flapping their wings in a circular motion around the ship, looking for a place to perch. The crew stared at them, puzzled. Their hands rested just above their belts, ready to reach for their weapon.

"What's going on?" Bennett yelled as he cocked his pistol and aimed it at the birds.

"She's here," I muttered, my heart fluttering with the flapping of their wings as the feeling of Elizabeth approaching became stronger.

Bennett began to retreat, with fear in his eyes. "This is such bad luck, Captain. This is not good at all."

"Stand your ground, Bennett," he growled, his gaze fixed on the birds.

As John watched the birds, he kept one hand on my arm and the other on his pistol. His head turned quickly, looking at each of them, becoming increasingly uneasy in their presence. By this point, their little black bodies had taken over the entire ship, gurgling their throats with their coarse squawks and leering down at us from the masts. Their heads moved in unison as they turned to the left to watch what was about to emerge from the fog.

Elizabeth suddenly appeared through the fog, but this time she was a mirror image of Felicity. Instead of a haggard witch, she resembled a majestic version of her sister. Her blonde hair didn't look as dank and wet as it should have in the fog; instead, it shined and gleamed as she turned her head, revealing her beauty to us. Her piercing blue eyes stood out against her snowy-white skin and pale blue dress. She held a knobby-looking staff in one hand and my grandfather's head in the other.

As I looked at her sneering face, my heart leapt into my throat, and anger erupted from deep within me. John tightened his grip on my arm as he sensed my fists clenching. I didn't want to look at Carver, but my eyes wouldn't let me look away from his decomposing head. His eyes remained closed, but his mouth opened, revealing his black teeth beneath his purple tongue. She supported his head with his long, straggly brown hair, which still had beads in it from when he was alive.

Mathew appeared beside her, a smirk on his face as he observed our stunned expressions. Miles' words began to make sense. He knew it was going to happen and that Elizabeth had done it on purpose to get a rise out of me. She knew that if I couldn't control my rage, the magic within me would erupt for all to see. I had to suppress the anger that was boiling within me so Elizabeth wouldn't get her way.

"That's completely unnecessary, Elizabeth," I said through gritted teeth.

Her eyes drew to me, and she smiled sweetly. "I assumed you wanted to see your grandfather again," she scowled. "However, he appears to be a little worse for wear."

Her voice became squeaky, mingling with Felicity's. I

could tell she was trying hard to look like Felicity, but she just didn't have the energy. Her face morphed, her features blended with those of her sisters, and her hair began to turn black again.

My turn to smirk at her had arrived. "Don't you have enough energy to stay like your sister?"

Her eyes narrowed into slits as she glared at me from the other side of the ship. "You've leeched off my energy, Mary."

John cast a glance at me over his shoulder. "What does she mean?"

"Has she not told you yet?" She said, mocking a shocked look.

Except for a few squawks from the crows, the ship fell silent. John looked at her, trying to figure out what she was saying. He eventually shook his head as he watched Elizabeth jump onto the deck with Mathew in tow.

"Mary, you've surprised me. I gave you this incredible gift, and you haven't even shown it to your loved ones? I feel quite hurt about this," She sniggered.

"I think you should stop talking, Elizabeth," I snarled.

Her laughter echoed as she tossed Carver's head into the middle of the deck, landing inches from my feet. My stomach churned violently as a maggot fell from his mouth.

"I demand to know what's going on," John yelled. He yanked me away from Carver's head and looked me dead in the eyes. "This is my ship, Mary, and you are under my command. Tell me what's going on now."

I averted my gaze from him, embarrassed. She knew I wouldn't tell him, so she walked over to him and placed her gnarled hand on his shoulder, smiling innocently.

"Isn't it distressing? Not knowing what she has inside her and her unwillingness to tell you. She possesses something unique. Something incredible, and anyone else would kill for what she has, but her?" she sneered and pointed at me. "She's ashamed of what I've given her."

I could feel his body flinching from her grasp and huddling closer to mine. She noticed and sighed, her hand falling to her side.

"Be quiet, Elizabeth," I exploded.

She ignored me and continued. "I gave her an incredible gift, and now she's mad at me for giving her a piece of myself."

"I told you to shut up, Elizabeth!" I screamed.

She sneered as she retreated from me and my trembling body, waiting for me to erupt. I couldn't keep it together, and she was well aware of it. I could feel the energy coursing through my veins, emitted by my hands as they pointed themselves in her direction. I could feel my teeth chattering and my arm muscles bulking up. Her gaze shifted from John to me as she observed his expression shift from sheer shock to fear.

The expression on John's face imprinted in my mind. Guilt and shame washed over the magic, suffocating it as the glow from my hands faded back into my fingertips. I could see the terror in his eyes as he stepped away from me. Elizabeth folded her arms, grinning from ear to ear, while Mathew clapped his hands, enjoying the drama that was about to take place between myself and John.

"Don't you think it's good, John? Do you approve of what I've done to her?" Her eyes glowed with excitement.

John's eyes pierced mine as he remained silent; keeping a close eye on me in case I turned on him. I could tell he was having a mental argument with himself. Elizabeth began to tap her foot impatiently, becoming dissatisfied with the situation. Bennett's expression was identical to John's. Everyone's face remained stunned as they all backed away from me, fearful that I would attack them.

Finally, John spoke up. His voice trembled, and I could tell his heart was breaking. Within seconds, the look in his eyes shifted from loving to cold as he watched the last traces of magic vanish back inside my heart.

"Who or what are you?"

Elizabeth responded quickly. "She's one of my creations."

"I'm still the same person, John," I said, ignoring Elizabeth's comments.

John shook his head. "You aren't the Mary I know and love. I'll ask you once more. What exactly are you?"

As I pleaded with John through my eyes, it felt like a thousand sharp needles were stabbing at my heart. I felt numb, exhausted, and tired of fighting Elizabeth and having her come back every time I had beaten her. She was like a plague that would never go away. She had turned the man I loved against me. She didn't even have to use her abilities for that. She was well aware that John would behave in this manner, and by the snide look on her face, she was reveling in her plan.

Tears streamed down my cheeks, and I could feel my nose stuffing up. My heart had been ripped out by John's words, and I knew that there was no coming back from this.

"Her spell backfired and for some reason her power had also backfired on me, giving me half of her abilities. I'm still me, John. This isn't my fault."

"Regardless of whether this happened by accident or not, Mary, you are now classed as a witch. I cannot have you on board this ship," John said sternly.

Elizabeth giggled like a child. "I haven't thought of it like that before. Mary, you're a witch like me."

My shoulders trembled with rage as I resisted the urge to punch her in the face. "I'm not a witch. I don't even want these abilities."

"Even if you didn't want these abilities, if anyone discovered them, you'd be hunted down and charged as a witch. I'm afraid I can't protect you here," he averted his gaze, not wanting to see the hurt expression on my face. "Mary, please accept my apologies. I wish I could help you."

Mark appeared next to me. "She's still the same person, Captain. There are ways to turn this around."

"That isn't the point at all, Mark. I have my crew to consider. I can't take the chance," John flatly stated. "If we're found with a witch onboard, then we'll all hang."

I could see the pain on his face as he stepped back away from me as if I were a disease that he could catch. My hand wanted to reach out and touch him, but I knew that he would only slap it away. I could hear Elizabeth giggling next to me, taunting me with her presence. Mathew stood awkwardly to the side, unsure of what to do. I could tell that Mark was as upset with the situation as I was, but he too, took a step back from me, siding with his captain.

Anger, rage, and everything Elizabeth had instilled in me began to rise up inside me like an erupting volcano, ready to explode. My fingertips began to tingle again as the magic within me swirled and rose in time with my breathing. I knew I didn't have much time before the magic engulfed my mind and took over my body.

John watched, his eyes wide with fear, as a beam of light shot from my fingers, striking Elizabeth in the stomach, throwing her backward into Mathew. In a daze, they both collapsed to the ground. Elizabeth's eyes rolled to the back of her head, her body trembling violently from my magic.

"I'm sorry," I whimpered, stepping back away from John, away from the family that I once knew, and edging towards the side of the ship where my boat sat quietly in the water, waiting for my return.

Miles appeared beside me, his face full of concern. "He's angry, Mary, but he doesn't mean any of it. Leave him for a while. He needs to calm down. Come with me," he smiled as he extended his hand. "You'll be safer if you stay away from this ship."

"What about Elizabeth? Won't she kill them all?" I asked.

Everyone stared at me, thinking I'd gone insane, as I spoke to Miles. Except for me, no one else could see him. I could tell what they were thinking, and it didn't help when I looked over at John, who was staring at me with cold eyes. He had returned to the man I first met when I boarded the ship. His masculine energy took over his soft side, encasing the love he had for me, replacing it with his stern attitude.

"You've taken her strength. She has no energy to kill anyone right now. She will be gone soon, but she will return, and you must be prepared. Come with me, Mary. I will help you," he spoke softly.

He wrapped his arm around my shoulders and guided me to the ship's stern. I let him lead the way, snuggling into his cold grasp as we both gazed down into the sea.

"The boat is not far from here. I'll guide you, but you have to jump overboard," he instructed.

"What are you doing, Mary?" John called from behind me.

I glanced over my shoulder at him and gave him a sad smile. "It's been a pleasure knowing you all."

He realised what I was about to do and rushed towards me. "Don't do it! You'll drown."

Miles' grip tightened, and he yanked me overboard into the sea below. My body sailed through the air, hitting the water within seconds. Miles' grip loosened, and I was left to fight the current. My throat filled with water, instantly crushing my chest with the pressure. I gulped for air, but the water submerged my body, pulling me under.

I could see John shouting and throwing over ropes through the water, but it was as if I were looking through a telescope. He was too far away to help me. Only I had the ability to save myself. I pushed and kicked my way through the waves, staying underwater so Elizabeth would think I was dead. The fog helped a lot, obscuring everyone's view and letting me escape to freedom without being seen.

Miles appeared in the water and pointed to a small shadow floating above. It was the boat. The ache in my legs grew as I pushed them to the limit to swim upwards to safety. The disorientation started kicking in, causing my vision to darken. I knew my time was running out. Even though my legs were dead weight, I kicked as hard as I could.

"You have to survive, Mary. Keep going, girl," he repeated over and over, keeping me determined not to drown. He stopped when my head reached the surface.

My lungs gulped in air as my head emerged from the water, and the numbness in my legs began to fade. I was trembling from fear and the icy grip of the water. I grabbed the boat's side and dragged my wet, limp body inside. I lay there, watching the fog move around the boat with the tide, coughing up water and sick. It felt like I was drowning from the inside.

Miles' face emerged, looking down at me. "You did it."

He sat down and grinned, waiting for me to calm down and stop spluttering my guts up. The pressure of attempting to engulf the air too quickly burned my throat. Miles gave me a stern look and told me to take it easy. He drew my head onto his shimmery lap. His grip felt icy cold, reminding me that he was dead.

"Is there a way to bring you back?" I croaked, trying to clear my throat of the salty seawater.

He sighed as he gently stroked my wet hair. "I don't think so, Mary, and even if there was, I wouldn't want to return to a rotting corpse. That would be repulsive. It's a shame, though, because all of my good looks have been squandered," he laughed at his own joke before realising I wasn't laughing with him. His face became solemn, looking into the fog, and ignoring the deathly stare I was giving him.

"This isn't the time to make light of things, Miles. I need you back. You weren't supposed to die," I stated.

"Oh, but I was, remember? I was on borrowed time," he said, still trying to avert his gaze away from me.

I then remembered John was also on borrowed time. "How am I supposed to keep John alive if I'm here and he's on the ship?"

Miles became silent, attempting to make a plan to save his friend. I waited, listening to the sea's gentle drifting of our boat away from the ship.

He spoke slowly, as if unsure of what he was saying.

"We must act quickly. The abilities you possess can aid us, but we must travel with speed if we want to save John's life. I believe there was once a woman who could have helped us, but I'm not sure if she's still alive."

"Who is she?"

"She lives on the outskirts of the bay and was labelled a witch, but the court let her go because she saved one of the judges from smallpox. People seek her out when they are sick, and she heals them. She's a good witch. If she's still around, she might be able to assist us," he explained.

"Then we must act quickly before John's life is taken." I looked at the fog, then at our boat. "We're not going to be able to sail back in this thing."

Miles pointed to my pocket. "You've forgotten about my father's locket. That will be a huge help to us and will cut our time in half."

I pulled out the gleaming locket from my pocket and held it in my hand. I placed it against my ear, listening to the ticking of the mechanical wheels.

"How did your father come up with such a device?" I asked, admiring the gleaming metal with its engraved designs.

He sighed and shrugged his shoulders. "It mystifies me. My father was a very smart man."

I sat up and shifted my weight to face him. "Will you stick by me, Miles?"

"Mary, I'll be there for you every step of the way. I'm not going anywhere," he said.

I took his hand in mine and gripped it tightly. "Then I suppose we should leave as soon as possible."

"It's going to be an adventure to remember!" He scoffed.

I stifled a laugh while holding up the locket, trying to remain serious. "What should I say to it?"

"Mary, you've done it so many times before. and you still need help with it," He exhaled a sigh. "Imagine where you want to go, and it will take you there, but keep hold of my hand."

"I've never been there before, so I'm not sure what to imagine."

He looked at me with a surprised expression on his face. "Oh, yeah. Give it to me. I'll do it."

He put the locket to his lips and began whispering something I couldn't understand. As the locket opened, it began to vibrate and emit a bright glow. It was the same as the last time, and all of my previous emotions flooded back to me. I was a weak, timid woman before meeting Miles and John, but as I sat here next to Miles's spirit, whom only I could see, I realised I had grown wiser and stronger than ever before. I felt prepared for the adventure that lay ahead of me. I knew exactly what I had to do. It was my responsibility to keep John alive and safe, and even if he despised me right now, I would do anything for him.

Love was a strange emotion. It would make a person do weird things for the ones they love. My love for John kept me determined to find a way to save him, no matter where I had to travel. This adventure could be dangerous, but I didn't care. Elizabeth and the others could continue to believe I was dead. That would give me an advantage and prepare me to take her down once and for all.

Miles began to fade into the light, and I stood there watching. His eyes twinkled with mischief as he smiled at me. The pure white light engulfed him, working its way down his arm and across my hand. My arm became submerged in the light as the glow crept across my body. I took one last look at 'The Drifter's' sails as they appeared through the fog before my body disappeared into the light.

"I'll be back, John. I promise."

The End

Coming Soon – Past My Time – Elizabeth's Reign

The third book of the series

Stay tuned for updates on:

www.willowhewettauthor.co.uk

www.facebook.com/storiesthatspook

Past My Time The Witch's Curse – The first of the series

Young Adult Fantasy Romance

Thank you to Canva.com and https://www.vecteezy.com/free-photos/scary-woman for help making the front cover of the book.